The Ghost of Loon Lake

THE SHORES OF LOON LAKE

RACHELLE PAIGE CAMPBELL

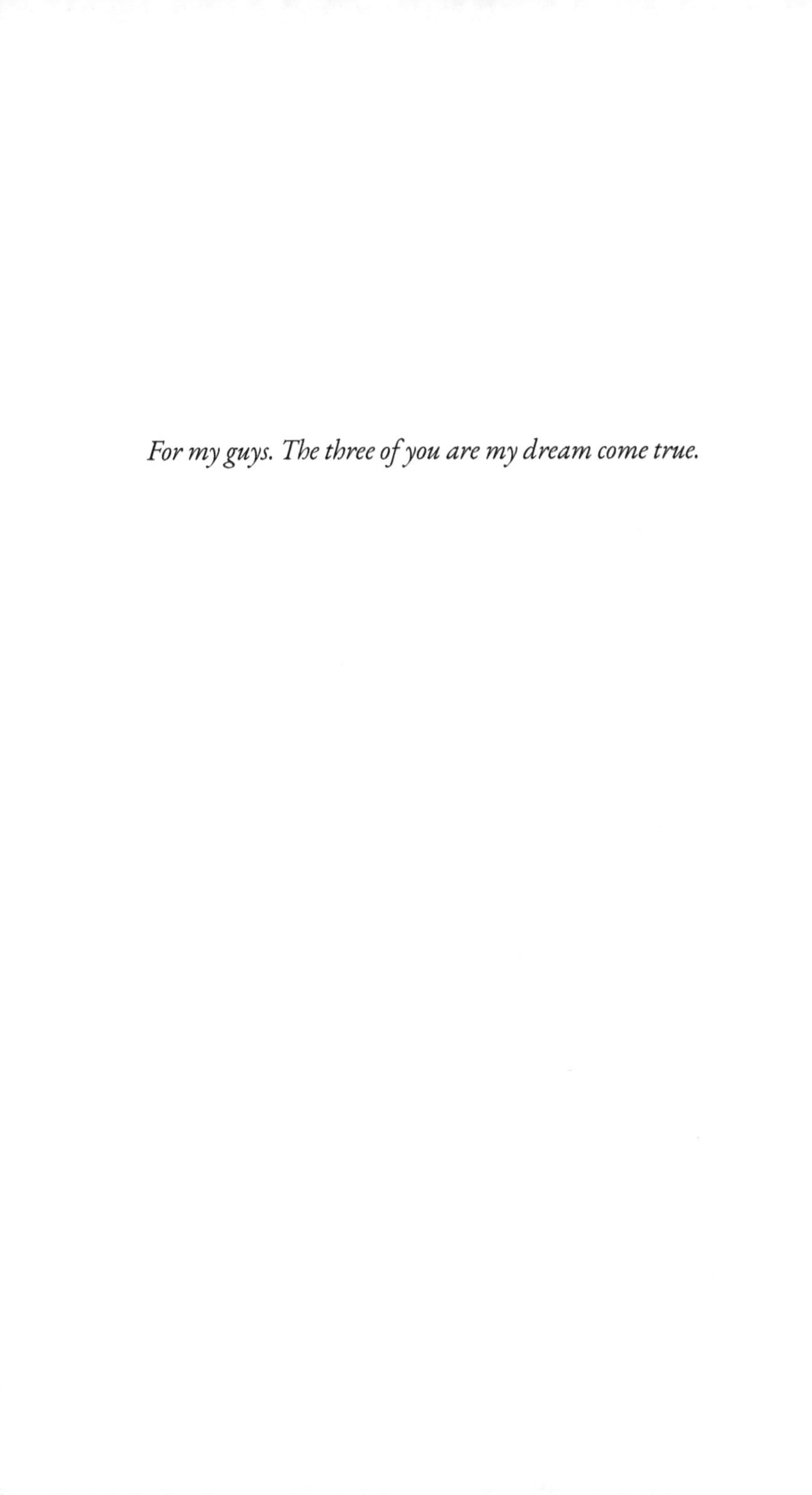
For my guys. The three of you are my dream come true.

Chapter One

Without question, the hardest part about being a fake ghost was crafting the origin story. Ashley Hale—who was very much alive—learned that on the first day of haunting the lighthouse on the little island off the shore of Loon Lake. Jilted Bride felt too trite, and no one could do that narrative better than Dickens. Without the tired cliche, however, she came up empty. Her ideas were too modern for a supposedly early-twentieth-century spirit.

Hauntings didn't just happen. And yet, the trauma of the event should be opaque to the actual phantom. Once the ghost understood their existence on the ephemeral plane, wouldn't said soul fly away? Unless some unfinished business needed to be reconciled first.

Ashley should be able to invent something. After all, she was living through an unresolved problem of her own, and she was looking right at him through the smudged, single-pane window.

Her estranged husband strolled along the perfectly maintained lawn of the historic Queen Anne revival lakeside resort. The white siding gleamed crisp and clean. Green shutters and a cedar shingle roof only added to the pristine appearance. The Inn at Loon Lake was her family legacy.

Her family's. Hers. Not his. Marriage hadn't granted him blood rights. Nevertheless, he strolled along on a sunny June afternoon exchanging pleasantries with the guests as if nary a worry weighed him down.

Christopher's toothy grin remained firmly in place, like a mayoral candidate on the campaign trail. She hated the way his smile curled her toes and electrified her skin. As much as she tried to loathe him over the years, she'd never succeeded. She'd loved him first, and she'd adore him forever. He was her weakness. Ten years ago, she'd learned a hard truth. She'd never be his choice.

The resort wasn't his to claim yet. She had time. Xavier, her father, had waxed poetic about the family legacy for as long as she could remember. But, in the end, he hadn't cared about the typical blood relations' first inheritance. She shouldn't have been surprised.

Dad's backtracking had frustrated her for years. Although Dad had initially railed against her marriage, he had come to consider Christopher his son and his professional right hand. When Ashley wanted to leave after college, Dad promised her a role as an apprentice. Within six months, however, it became clear that Dad wanted to train her husband, not her. Frustrated at not being given a serious role in the organization, she told her husband she wanted to leave.

She didn't have a plan but that never mattered. Her detail-oriented spouse always figured out boring details like food and shelter. Except, he didn't want to go. She figured he would follow if she made good on her departure, and, determined to show Dad what he would lose with her absence, she had struck out. Too quickly, she realized she was on her own.

After his untimely death, Dad had left the property to either Ashley or her husband. The Inn would belong to whoever was the first to stay on the property for thirty consecutive days following her father's death. As the acting innkeeper, her husband had a head start of five days. If she couldn't get him off the property so the clock could start over in her favor, Ashley would lose her only chance at a future. But that wouldn't happen. She'd scare her husband off the grounds in the next twenty-four hours and come out victorious.

As soon as she received word about her father's passing from the family lawyer, she had left her life in Chicago. Growing up, all she'd wanted was to leave. Not too long after she hit the road, she regretted her choice. But the minute she found out her father was gone, she couldn't return home fast enough.

She'd arrived late last night, leaving her car in the municipal parking lot a few miles away. Under the cover of darkness, she had snuck onto the property and into the fake lighthouse, constructed as a folly for tourists in the 1920s.

She had missed the memorial service, arriving after the ceremony and the tossing of his remains somewhere in the murky lake. With her free hand, she rubbed the side of her rib cage against the tight pang close to her heart. Dad had sworn she'd show up and mourn him at his funeral. His parting words traveled with her every stop from Portland, Maine, to Portland, Oregon, and her last known address in the windy city. She had promised him she'd dance on his grave and bitterly regretted those words every day since uttering the careless remark.

Since leaving Loon Lake she'd collected regrets like souvenirs. She swallowed the lump in her throat and narrowed her gaze, focusing all her frustration on her husband on the grassy lawn. After her marriage, her father had demanded the young couple sign a post-nuptial agreement to protect Ashley's assets and the Inn.

Now, she had nothing valuable to safeguard, and the legal document worked against her. She couldn't recoup half of the property in a divorce settlement. Christopher would owe her nothing. He might want to end their relationship officially to be free and clear of her for good. She had never stopped hoping he'd find her so they could reconcile. Had she fooled herself with a childish fantasy?

She sat on a step on the spiral staircase below the window halfway up the tower. Her cheek pressed close to the dusty, spiderweb-covered walls. Arachnophobia had never been her style. Allergies, however, were. Her nose itched. She refused to give in to the sneeze and angled a handheld mirror close to the window sheers, catching the sunlight outside and redirecting it across the water into the corner of Christopher's eye as he sauntered along the shore. He didn't react. He didn't squint or flinch or bat at the annoying spot of light.

Guests relaxed in lawn chairs, played bocce, and enjoyed the on-site restaurant's menu options. From her vantage point, she couldn't spot a single laptop, tablet, or cell phone. It was a scene from another time.

Founded in the nineteenth century, the Inn managed enough activities to distract guests from their devices. Loon Lake was an offshoot from the southern shore of Lake Superior, and a channel connected the two bodies of freshwater. When the Hale family had established their resort, they'd been the subject of scorn from many of the tradespeople in the area. But Randolph Hale, her great-great-great-grandfather, had imagined a time when the lake wouldn't be solely dedicated to commerce. And he'd been absolutely correct.

Another dust mote floated past her. She held her breath, choking on the sneeze. The Inn she'd left had been dingy like the lighthouse. Why hadn't Christopher fixed up this building, too?

Her father had invented a story about cursed treasure to

discourage curious guests after the building had fallen into disrepair. However, the fake legend backfired, luring a few hearty, and gullible, souls to scour the lakeshore with metal detectors. A smart manager would realize an opportunity and use the prime location.

When she was in charge, she'd make the picturesque spot a priority. With a lifetime spent in the hospitality industry, she had only discovered her penchant for marketing after she left. She could use her skills to revamp the Inn for the modern traveler.

She was tempted to grab her cell phone and snap pictures for her carefully crafted social media accounts. *Hey, girlies! Wish you were here? You could be. I'm back at my family's Inn for good. #girlboss.* She'd caption an image of herself in a flowy, white sundress under an overcast sky. She'd give the camera her back. The vibrant greens of the grass and forest would pop. She'd get a ton of likes. In recent months, she hadn't had too many envy-inducing posts. Lately, her accounts had focused on her exploits at her coffee shop job, seeking to reframe her poor barista skills as self-deprecating and relatable.

Nothing about her current circumstance was enviable. She hadn't updated her pages in several days. Curating her life online was much more satisfying than actually living it. In her captions and carefully staged images, she was the heroine of her story. Too often, she felt like the sidekick or the joke. The stories she told herself had changed over the years. Every revisit of her archives was like time traveling. This morning, when she had awoken too early after a night on an air mattress, she relived some highlights. Christmas in Chicago looked aspirational instead of hopelessly lonely as she wandered the Magnificent Mile on the verge of tears.

She gave herself a shake. In every weakness was a strength. She could employ every bit of her recent past, including the current charade, to her benefit. Maybe her backstory as the wayward child wasn't reason enough for a ghost to haunt a building, but it was motivation to reach for her goals and succeed. Everyone loved a second chance, and she couldn't wait for hers to start. Once she was openly staying at the Inn, she'd lean into her passion for storytelling and boost the Inn's profile. She had the shots already arranged.

Much as she would have liked to, she couldn't avoid spotting her father's handiwork all over the perfectly manicured lawn and terrace. From the waiters circulating with glasses of ice water to the staff constantly monitoring the chaises and chairs, pulling down more seats and opening umbrellas as needed, she witnessed the courtesy that had been Dad's hallmark. He had loved to take the utmost care of his guests and badgered her to do the same.

She'd asked him for proper training rather than his occasional anecdotes. He'd laughed then and asked her if she could work longer than half an hour without a break. He was probably still chuckling on the other side now.

Had he wanted her to come and battle for her place? She'd thought leaving would prove he had underestimated her to his own detriment. Was all of this upheaval due to Xavier's desire for her to stake her claim and stay for good? If she wasn't so desperate for the property, her only real chance at making a happy life for herself, she wouldn't give his memory the satisfaction of fighting for it.

"Bocce will begin in twenty minutes." Christopher's calm voice was crisp, and his delivery was short. "Don't miss your chance to be declared the weekend's champion."

She rolled her eyes and tracked her husband as he handed the megaphone to a polo-shirt-clad employee. He turned and shook a guest's hand before patting the man on the back and grinning broadly. *Bocce? Glad-handing? Really?*

The job didn't suit him. Didn't anyone hear the edge in his stilted words? She could, and would, do so much better.

With guests, she was warm and welcoming. Charm was her strength.

Her analytical, logical husband would destroy her dad's legacy. If her father hadn't realized what would happen by changing the terms of his will, she did. She'd known Christopher Lewis her entire life and provided him with every good and bad idea. He wasn't creative or inventive; he left all the brainstorming to her. He'd slowly kill the resort if given total authority.

She pictured the slow unraveling first of the resort and then the nearby community—not to mention her own aimless life—if she didn't take control. She'd been gone long enough to own up to her misdeeds, and she'd lived with the consequences for years.

Losing the chance to make up with Dad would haunt her remaining days. Her shot at redemption required her to take over and successfully run the business. Honoring him with hard work was the only way to exorcise the demons haunting her.

She squinted. Christopher's dazzling smile as he laughed with guests was blinding. His husky, low chortle carried across the water and sent a shiver along her spine. She had loved making him laugh. His genuine amusement was rare. As a child, he'd been serious. During their teenage years, he concealed his emotions like he'd be arrested at any display of feeling. Now he just gave away his smiles for free. *Maybe he has changed.* She harrumphed.

Flashing a light wasn't cutting it. Ashley pocketed the mirror and carefully leaned back on the spiral staircase to avoid making too much noise. Built on a rocky outcropping grandly called an island, the building was little more than a tower with a non-functioning beacon and a widow's walk around the exterior cupola that provided an unobstructed view of the lake.

With no additional rooms or insulation to absorb noise, sounds inside the building echoed outside, carrying over the wooden bridge leading to the resort's shore. If she wanted to grab his attention, she had to get a little loud. She scooted closer to the window, unlatched the sash, and slid it up a few inches. Pressing her face against a wall, she kept her chin even with the ledge but hidden from view.

Too many of her plans relied on a wing and a prayer. Right now, she needed action. She breathed deep, inhaling the smell of fresh water and weeds. Wherever she went, she never forgot that perfume. She couldn't shake a lot of the things that plagued her.

Outside, her husband walked to the edge of the sand, frowning at the water.

Was he trying to gauge the temperature? Cold as ice was her guess. A shudder wracked her body. The water had never been warm enough for her. She expected to catch sight of Steve and Carl Prim on the lake, driving tourists around in their sightseeing boats. She looked forward to it as a diversion from her self-imposed boredom. Without any distractions, welcome or otherwise, she focused all her energy on her husband at the shore. She needed to unnerve him.

Unless he crossed the bridge, he wasn't coming closer. This was her moment to frighten him. She released a breathy sound somewhere between a word and a gasp. "Waaaaa-waaaaa-waaaaafffffles." She teased the word.

He flinched.

She grinned, his jerking motions more rewarding than she'd imagined. This was going to be fun. Scare him off, stay for thirty uninterrupted days, and start the rest of her life. Check, check, check.

* * *

If Christopher Lewis believed in ghosts, which he absolutely did not, he might have had doubts based on recent events that suggested something amiss at the Inn on Loon Lake.

As he strolled along the lawn of the Inn, smiling and nodding at guests enjoying the late morning sun on a day still too chilly for swimming, he heard it.

"Waaaaaaaaaffffflllleeess," a female voice moaned.

He didn't need to look at the lighthouse to know where the sound came from. Only one person thought the property was preyed upon by supernatural forces. Without a doubt, she was the one behind the current ghosting.

A haunting shouldn't be tailor-made for one specific person. Unless she hoped invoking the name of his beloved childhood pet would somehow terrify him. The dog had died of natural causes at the ripe age of sixteen. Waffles wouldn't return to the lighthouse. The terrier hated the place.

Christopher took a full, easy breath for the first time in years. His lungs expanded and contracted, no hitches or hiccups. He'd wanted to call her so many times over the last decade to explain but her father forbade him from telling her what Christopher had learned in his accounting position. He should have told her about her dad's passing. Under the circumstances, however, he had stuck to the tried and true, feigning ignorance of her situation. He had instructed the lawyers to contact her and maintain the façade that he was clueless about her whereabouts.

He'd regretted every second since his wife had left. Ashley was home now. The prodigal had returned with no fanfare or welcome. Instead, she had hatched a plot. He'd congratulate her on her clever attempt to evict him from the property, if she hadn't underestimated his desire to stay.

Scanning the Inn, he was pleased the replacement shingles had finally faded into uniformity with the rest of the roof. Poor flashing around the dormers had caused a leak that cost a bundle to fix. He prided himself on the flawless image of the business but never knew a moment without calculating costs.

Would Ashley understand the relentless passion required for success in this competitive industry? Did she have the drive? She had returned to take over, but they had shielded her from the operation's struggles.

Years ago, he had been culpable in hiding the Inn's dire circumstances from her at her late father's insistence. Carrying on the family's hundred-year-plus legacy, Xavier focused on his business, harming his relationship with his only child because he hadn't wanted her to know the extent of his financial mismanagement. Christopher had had a front-row seat for the pain on both sides.

Xavier had been blind to his daughter's need to be involved and was too proud to admit his faults to her. Once Christopher had shown him the problems, Xavier trusted Christopher to find the solutions. The arrangement had worked well. When Ashley asked Christopher to leave, she had put him in the unbearable position of choosing between his head and his heart.

Christopher's decision to stay had been about preserving her legacy for their shared future. At the time, he hadn't known how to verbalize his feelings without giving away the truth her father had asked him to hide. Every day, Christopher tortured himself by playing what might've happened if he had followed her.

As long as he'd known her, he'd listened to her stories about all the places she'd visit as soon as she left Loon Lake. She'd kept her word, traveling to every one of those and more. He wished he had said something to stop or stall her departure. Ashley had taken the spark of the Inn and the people she loved with her when she left.

She could walk away. Christopher wasn't so lucky. And now, with her return, he definitely couldn't leave. She'd be in over her head. Did she falsely remember the Inn in its current, immaculate state?

He remembered too much. Like every fix over the past ten years and how he'd agonized over triaging the finances to stay afloat. Other flashbacks plagued him, too. In quiet moments, he'd replayed every single moment they had spent together from childhood until the day she left.

"Waaaaaffffffffflllllleeeeesssss," she called again, low and deep.

He turned and spotted a waiter carrying a breakfast tray, the smell of syrup wafting past. His stomach growled. Maybe her moan was more about a craving than scaring him off. But he doubted it. If he knew his wife, he'd expect some sort of elaborate scheme to get him off the property so she could start the thirty-day clock over again in her favor.

He hoped a guest would ask him about the noise so he could loudly proclaim the lighthouse must have an infestation of vermin, but no one seemed to notice. He could imagine her groan at being referred to as a pest. She'd shake the lighthouse to its foundation. Sure, he'd been foolish enough as a child to find her fictional ghost stories scary, but adult life was far too terrifying to worry about anything else.

Would he have known it was her if he hadn't been expecting her every minute of the last week? Her father's sudden death took everyone by surprise. Xavier Hale had been inimitable and, at times, more institution than human.

With a nod to another guest, Christopher strode back the way he came, dodging and weaving through the servers and bussers as he entered the Inn through the restaurant.

Linen-topped tables filled the walnut-paneled room. Overhead, the chandeliers sparkled. The setting was both intimate and grand, the thick carpet absorbing sounds and creating a hushed environment.

"Monsieur Lewis," a heavily accented male voice called.

Christopher lifted his gaze, spotting the maître d'.

Dressed in a tux with slicked-back hair and a tiny mustache, Pierre Leduc was straight from central casting for a French maître d'. Holding a stack of menus, he tipped his head toward the kitchen.

A problem already? It's barely eleven. Christopher shook off the thought. Whatever crisis arose, he could solve it. He always did. Now his wife was back, and he could make amends with the biggest outstanding issue in his life—his marriage.

He strode to the swinging door, restraining himself from whistling. He didn't want to startle the employees with a cheery tune and good mood. Instead, he schooled his features into a calm mask and followed his longtime employee into the bustling kitchen. Chopping knives, rushing water, and time calls bounced off the walls from every direction. Add in the melting butter, frying eggs, and baking bread, and Christopher's stomach growled again, this time louder than the other-worldly moans echoing over the water.

Pierre stopped inside the door and thrust the menus forward. "Have you looked at these?"

Christopher shook his head and then frowned at himself. "I haven't inspected the box, no. I verified the order before we sent it to the printer." He grabbed the stack.

Typically, he didn't miss a single detail. The delivery had arrived in the chaos of the funeral, and he'd forgotten to check the boxes. He opened the first leather portfolio. His heart dropped. The new menus were printed off-center. He could kick himself. He'd lost a couple days of fixing a problem because his focus wavered.

"As you can see, Monsieur, the product is unacceptable," Pierre said, sniffing.

It wasn't the worst oversight. Most guests wouldn't notice. But the spacing would bug Christopher. He'd know and remember every time he passed the restaurant. For the perfectionist maître d', the menus would not pass muster, either.

Christopher had taken the resort's business to a family-run print shop in town for years. The company, Print Your Way, was under the son's management after the tragic loss of the father due to a short illness a year earlier. Clearly, Christopher had to keep a better watch as the printer worked through growing pains, not a totally unexpected occurrence as yet another generational hand off occurred. Add in the new boss's side projects, drumming up interest in a lake monster and a burgeoning motivational sticker business, and it wasn't surprising that errors happened.

Christopher nodded. "Apologies."

Pierre tipped his head, mollified. The Frenchman took any error as a personal slight.

Christopher would fix the problem like he always did. He was a walking fire extinguisher and a compass all in one, putting out flames and guiding the lost in the right direction. His skills weren't always appreciated, but he carried on, undeterred by the lack of enthusiasm or gratitude. "I'll take care of this right now," Christopher said, meeting the gaze of the maître d'. "Thank you for bringing it to my attention."

"Of course." Pierre nodded. "I'll have your order of oatmeal delivered to your office."

"Actually, can you get me the waffle special?" Christopher licked his lips. He could almost taste the syrup.

Pierre turned and snapped at a server. "Waffles for the boss."

Christopher backed out of the busy kitchen and continued to the employee-only hallway with the spiral staircase in the corner. He jogged up the steps to the top of the building, smiling to himself once he was out of view. While he had missed something during an understandably tense few days, how much would she miss? Ashley wasn't known for her attention to detail.

Did she intend to kick him out and take over the resort?

She was kidding herself if she thought running the Inn was easy. He'd be curious to watch her try.

With his steps ringing on every metal riser, he opened a door and let himself into his top-floor office space. He had converted the attics into more guest accommodation and created an office and apartment for himself. Striding past the large partner's desk, he dropped the stack of menus onto the inset leather top. He'd call the printer and have the situation handled in minutes. His years of experience were invaluable and made the work look simple. Every single day, he handled problems of various sizes. Amid the chaos of hospitality, he remained unflappable.

He crossed the room toward the seating area near the window overlooking the lake and the lighthouse. He probably had binoculars somewhere. Not that he'd be able to spot her inside the building.

Her official return was five days too late to claim the resort, unless he abandoned the Inn. Regardless of the details, he had no intention of leaving. He'd worked too hard for too long, sacrificing a lot along the way. But now, maybe, they could both find a different path forward. They could find a resolution to their strained situation. They could let go of each other and move on for good.

He sank into one of the leather club chairs, slumping against the back. He'd hoped she'd have arrived in time for the funeral. His mind had tricked him into thinking she had.

Xavier hadn't left specific instructions regarding his burial but general guidelines. He detested the idea of rotting in a coffin in the ground. Instead, he had asked to be tossed in the lake with no religious rites. Christopher didn't dump a body into the icy waters like Xavier had suggested off-hand at one point. Instead, Christopher had the man cremated and welcomed the townsfolk to the shore, giving everyone the chance to say their goodbyes without any doctrinal ceremony.

As he had stood at the front, the breeze had blown off the lake, carrying a hint of his wife's perfume past his nose. But when he had turned, he hadn't spotted any secret mourners grieving behind the trees.

Leaning forward, he dug his elbows into his thighs. The change in posture didn't improve his view of the lighthouse. Short of knocking on the door and letting himself inside, he wouldn't get visual confirmation of his suspicions.

Not that he needed to do so. He was one hundred percent certain.

He knew she was here.

Her social media went dark two days ago. That was the biggest clue she was on her way north. It must be killing her not share everything she was doing and seeing with her eager followers. And eating. Ashley loved a hot meal.

He based his convictions on more than surfing the web. In his very bones, he was aware of her presence. He couldn't help it or turn off his awareness. She pulled him towards her like a magnet, recalibrating his polarity and world.

If he waited her out, would he see smoke rising from the lighthouse in the evening as she cooked? He was going to enjoy this. With warning and time, he'd figure out the best path for both of them. Hadn't she accused and praised him for being cool and collected?

First, he'd hold a movie under the stars tonight. He'd play her favorite but angle the screen out of view. And then he'd have the kitchen to prepare fresh popcorn. Culinary torture was going to be fun.

Without her, he hadn't much to enjoy. His world had gone from bright to drab the second she left. She could forgive him for his behavior. He'd do the same for her. All she had to do was meet him face to face.

A knock sounded at the door.

With a heavy breath, he stood and pushed aside his plans

under a veneer of professionalism. She couldn't help but cloud his thoughts. Her attempt at haunting threw him for a loop. But he'd right himself.

The door shook again, the knock insistent.

"Come in," he called as he sat in his chair. He was the boss. He'd let no one forget it.

Chapter Two

Ashley's second, and perhaps most important, lesson about haunting came on the fifth day. A fake apparition couldn't survive on sandwiches alone. When the breeze wafted the smells of the resort's kitchen into the lighthouse through the open windows, she found her resolve to remain inside the building wavering. One excursion wouldn't cost her anything. What were the odds the website advertised her favorites as the daily specials? BLT with scrambled egg, mushroom risotto, and chicken enchiladas verde had nothing in common. Except her.

Christopher must suspect she was back. Why else would the Inn screen *Failure to Launch* and *The Cutting Edge* over the past week? Attendance for both movies had seemed poor, as far as she could tell from the dirty windows.

She hadn't been able to watch the action on the screen. The projector was angled out of her view. If he had done so on purpose, however, he had once again underestimated her. She'd watched both films enough to have the visuals memorized and enjoyed her favorite movies like radio plays.

Perhaps her husband was spurred by nostalgia. She

preferred that perspective. Wistful, estranged husbands were easier to frighten than those who were too aware of their wives' movements.

She'd waited for dusk before placing her order and sneaking out of the crumbling tower. She had changed out of her Victorian nightgown and into a black T-shirt and jogger sweatpants. Pants had been a relief. The billowing nightgown had been a pain inside the lighthouse, catching on the stairs and restricting her movement. Now she needed speed. With each step, she strained for any noise above her own labored breathing and pounding heartbeat. She wasn't cut out for subterfuge.

Crossing the wooden bridge in a few hurried steps, she leaped to the lawn and dashed to the tree line that marked the property boundary, with unkempt woods behind a neat row of shrubs. The cool night air held the scent of pine and fresh-cut grass. She raced along the edge of the forest towards the Inn's kitchen, past the restaurant and employee door.

She'd grown up at the resort and eaten almost every meal in the kitchen. Over the past decade, she had never learned how to cook for herself. Surviving off takeout and microwave meals, she hadn't been put to the test. However, she'd finally reached her breaking point after nearly a week of peanut butter and jelly. She'd learn to cook a few basic things as soon as she was out of the lighthouse and into her home. Could she kick her husband out of the cottage?

A branch cracked under her foot, and she froze, taking in her surroundings. Night had descended around her. The sky melted from soft blue to inky navy. If anyone spotted her, she probably resembled a startled deer caught by headlights. In the north woods, darkness didn't bring silence. The buzz of bugs rivaled traffic noise, in her opinion. A frog croaked in the distance. More importantly, she didn't hear any human sounds.

She focused on her feet, picking her way through the forest. She neared the kitchen side door, and the wafting smells tickled her nose again. Once she had a hot meal, she'd reclaim her rightful place as owner and operator. She stepped into the thick row of tall boxwoods. Sharp branches dug into the exposed skin on her neck and arms. Physical pain was fleeting and only solidified her resolve. She was not pinning her future on the whims of chance. Her plan was solid.

For the time being, however, she hid in the bushes outside the kitchen's back door, waiting for her food and replaying her tactics to date. Her mysterious sounds and lights hadn't drawn any notice. She had to make the lighthouse impossible for Christopher to ignore so he'd abandon the Inn. Christopher wasn't known for giving up. For years, she had enjoyed the full benefit of his loyalty. Ultimately, however, he chose to stay and proved his ties were stronger with her father than her. She'd had no choice but to leave.

At some point, she became the Wickham to his Darcy. And she hated that. Why was she the dissolute child of the respectable parent? Why couldn't she be the steadfast, stable one?

She blamed his lack of imagination. As a kid, she was forced to come up with every ingenious plan to entertain them. And, of course, she'd taken all the blame when things went haywire.

It didn't matter. She couldn't change the past. Her future remained open with possibilities, starting with the Inn. Christopher wasn't easy to scare, and he swore he didn't believe in the paranormal. But she remembered the fear in his eyes as she told ghost stories by flashlight. She'd terrify him, and then she could reclaim what rightfully belonged to her.

He was hardly a Mr. Darcy. In truth, he was nothing more than a peacocking Mr. Collins. The entail was void. The rightful heir would claim her legacy.

Her stomach growled.

She pressed her hands against her belly, hoping to dull the sound. She'd been explicit in her instructions. The delivery driver was to leave the paper bag next to the large pine tree closest to the building's side entrance.

From her position, crouched in the trimmed boxwoods that created a neat wall of greenery on the eastern edge of the property, blocking the wild, unmanicured forest, she'd be no more than thirty feet from her meal when it finally arrived. She'd duck out of her hiding spot, grab the bag, and hightail it back to the lighthouse before anyone was the wiser.

She wanted to take over a successful business, not terrify her customers and assume control of a ghost town. Hanging back allowed her to marvel at the beautiful structure up close. The expansive building was modeled after the great Gilded Age cottages on the East Coast. The roof boasted gables and two towers on either end. Luckily, the covered porch didn't wrap around this side of the building but skirted the western edge, inviting guests to stroll and admire the sunset.

The building was immaculate and better than her childhood memories. When she left, she'd known where to step to avoid every rotting floorboard from the porch to the staircase to the top floor. *Christopher's handiwork? Or Dad's?* Had she been such a burden that the pair and property were better off without her?

She'd wanted her absence to frustrate Dad. She doubted he'd laugh or flash a genuine smile without her around. He'd called her his joy, but she wanted to be his pride, too. He'd never taken her seriously enough to give her a chance to prove herself. And, in a moment of anger, she made a drastic decision, overwhelming herself with regrets.

A rolling lawn behind the Inn sloped towards the lake. From its perch, the Inn looked down on all its neighbors, including the old sawmill jutting out near the channel and the boardwalk on the south shore of Loon Lake. Owned by the Inn and the unofficial downtown, the boardwalk shops were just as mired in history and tradition. Leases passed from one generation to the next, so a Jenkins would always serve ice cream, a Phillips would run the arcade, and a Treacle would pull taffy.

She'd fought hard against history, hating the ties that didn't just bind but suffocated. She'd had a partner in crime for childhood and then married him on a whim. But when she'd needed him most, he picked the better option, and she'd found the door on her own.

Headlights flashed.

Blinking, she shielded her gaze and spotted the car driving towards her on the road in front of the building.

The red sedan stopped on the driveway where the pavement circled back towards the main road.

A man hopped out of the driver's side and strode to the main entrance.

The car engine ran, filling the air with exhaust. Carry-out orders waited at the host stand inside the restaurant's front entrance. The man might be gone for as long as ten minutes.

She swallowed, fighting the cough building in her lungs. If she wasn't so desperate for her favorite meal, the one she'd helped develop back in high school, she'd call the front desk about the idling engine outside. The earth wasn't going to be saved by one car turning off. But every little bit helped.

As her vision adjusted to the car's bright lights, she realized her hiding spot was no longer concealed. She knelt, branches scratching her as she repositioned herself on the ground. At least with the chill in the evenings in early June, she remembered to pack joggers, or she'd be covered in even more marks.

Footsteps echoed off the pavement.

In her back pocket, her phone vibrated.

She didn't need to check the cell. She watched the delivery

driver tap his phone and carefully set the bag in the designated spot. Her mouth watered. She could taste the smoky, thick-cut bacon with the rich eggs and crunch of the lettuce. Choosing between her favorites had been hard. She chose the easiest to eat in her cramped quarters.

"Please leave a good review," the man yelled. "Thank you for the tip."

She flinched. *Had he seen her? Had anyone heard him?* She couldn't glimpse his face.

Heavy footsteps retreated. A car door opened and slammed shut. The sedan sped off, tires squealing on the asphalt.

Air whooshed from her lungs in a heavy exhale, her shoulders rounding forward. Pulling her phone from her pocket, she confirmed the delivery and left five stars. She shimmied out of the bushes, snapping the delicate branches and scrapping her exposed cheeks and arms with each twist. She probably left a human-sized dent of destruction in the poor plants. Mr. Willie, the groundskeeper, would demand an explanation and a budget increase to fix the problem.

When she was in charge, she'd gladly give him both. Darting out of the shrubs, she tripped over her feet on the way toward her dinner. Twisted ankles weren't part of her plan. Righting herself, she grabbed the paper bag from its resting spot against the tree trunk and raced at full speed around the corner of the building. She leaped into the shrubs.

Cracks and snaps accompanied her, every movement as loud as fireworks over the lake. Her hands took the brunt of the assault. She sucked in a sharp breath, but she couldn't slow down and assess the damage. She pushed on, past the bushes and into the forest, until she was sure her presence was undetectable.

She didn't need an employee taking out the trash to spot her and call for help. She needed to reach the lighthouse on the little island several yards from the beach. Luckily, the cloudy night provided cover. Under a full moon, someone would spot her for sure.

She didn't stop until she reached the fake lighthouse, racing over the wooden bridge and into the building. She dropped onto her air mattress, taking up much of the floor space in the large room, and dug in. She'd figure out her next step. When a person had nothing to lose and everything to gain, they were unstoppable. She snorted. That summed up her situation.

* * *

Christopher had heard he didn't have feelings more times than he could count. Now, he started to believe public opinion. Operating with cool efficiency made the resort a success. He didn't need friends. The closest he'd ever had ended up high-tailing it out of Loon Lake the second she could and hadn't been back in ten years.

Except, of course, she'd returned and now crouched in one of the bushes at the front of the property. Standing on the front porch, he was half hidden by a potted topiary. Coming outside after twilight was one of his favorite traditions, almost like meditation. He'd breathe the fresh air, inhaling a unique perfume based on the season. In late summer, the air hung heavy with honeysuckle; in the fall, dirt and leaves took precedence; in the winter, woodsmoke. But with spring finally giving way to summer, he smelled fading lilacs and hyacinths. No matter what happened during his day, he paused outside, to appreciate the beautiful place where he lived and worked.

Long ago, he'd vowed to give the business his all. What started as duty morphed into pride. When his commitment faltered, and his heart wanted him to track Ashley down, he found an inner strength and kept going. With the lines blurred between his professional and personal lives, he couldn't stop one without impacting the other. Of course, she wouldn't realize that he stayed for her sake. If he'd left, she wouldn't have had any financial support.

He had resigned himself to accepting she could never appreciate the tough position he was in. Her father had given him a chance to prove himself but ended up relying on Christopher completely. Xavier had insisted on keeping her out of the mess his poor financial management and sidelined her. She'd been frustrated. Christopher hadn't been able to explain then and doubted she'd agree with his characterization of his devotion now.

She had wanted grand—if somewhat reckless—gestures and over-the-top speeches. He had believed in actions. Although she couldn't know the depth of his loyalty to her and her father without breaking her heart, she would learn Christopher's true fortitude now in a fight for their respective futures.

As he took his evening stroll, he'd been intrigued by the sedan pulling in front of his hotel. The faded red car parked at the end of the building, near the pine tree planted fifty years earlier that had grown so large they needed a crane to string the lights for the annual Christmas festival. He did a double take when the car's headlights beamed onto her.

He knew she was back. Her presence changed the atmosphere. Seeing her was startling, nonetheless.

She hadn't aged a day in ten years. She was perhaps a bit at a disadvantage, hiding in the shrubs. Dressed in black, her flawless skin glowed like a phantom.

He was surprised she'd lasted five *whole days* in the lighthouse.

Last night, a worried guest had approached him, asking if a hurt animal was trapped inside the stone structure accessible via a rickety bridge. With a rope strung across the bridge, the little island and building were off-limits to anyone with sense. Not that Ashley had ever concerned herself with logic.

This scheme was classic Ashley behavior. He used to find her plans fun. She livened up his days and made him look at the world from an absolutely bonkers perspective.

But that was before he'd needed to step up and take over the resort. At the time—and to the present day, if he'd done his task correctly—she had had no clue how dire the finances were. She was protected in that way, insulated from life's reality. Her father limited her exposure to the inner workings despite bringing her on board as his apprentice. Christopher had been complicit in keeping the knowledge of the Inn's poor finances from her. Now she wanted to push him out? After he'd not only saved the resort but reinvented and expanded it, drawing more clientele than even in its heyday? No chance.

All he had to do was wait her out. Easy. He'd been doing that since the dawn of time. While she might be brash and bold, she wasn't particularly insightful or observant. She'd claim she suffered from harsh discipline. Never seeing the twitch in her father's stoic smile. The man couldn't stay mad at her and had rarely enforced her punishments.

Christopher had had a hard time with it, too. She'd had to be the one to walk away. He never could.

He'd foolishly wanted to see her at the will reading and settle everything then. For a man who prided himself on dealing with clear-cut absolutes, he'd let her twist and turn him upside down. But she hadn't been informed of her father's death at that time. Christopher had instructed the lawyer to find her, and then he'd waited for her return.

This morning, he'd had enough stalling. He requested a change to the day's specials. Then he updated the website himself. And last, he opened the windows in the dining room facing the lake and turned on every fan in the kitchen. His lame excuse of proper ventilation fooled no one. But, luckily, none of the staff questioned his odd behavior or why he was in the kitchen. He used the excuse of discussing the latest menu printing concerns as a cover.

Narrowing his gaze, he refocused on the boxwoods. The neat wall of shrubs created the last vestige of civilized order before the forest full of chaotically arranged pines and aspens. Christopher couldn't spot her.

The driver exited the hotel, passing Christopher on his way. He strode to the old pine at the end of the shrubbery row, set the bag on the ground, shouted something, and hopped into his car. Tires squealed as the car peeled out of the Inn's driveway.

Christopher caught his breath, holding it until his lungs burned. He wanted a clearer glimpse of the one who got away. For as long as he'd drawn breath, he'd loved Ashley Hale. While he wasn't her enemy at the moment, he wasn't classified as her friend either. He wanted to settle the business between them so that they both won. He just hadn't figured out how. For someone who always had a sensible solution, he really hated the current predicament.

Once again, he'd been trapped between a rock and a hard place, aka his wife and his father-in-law.

She burst out of the shrubs, branches snapping and interrupting the insects' nightly serenade.

He winced. Her sudden movement was startling.

If her skin wasn't a bleeding mess from scratches at risk of infection from dirt, it would be a miracle. The groundskeeper, Liam Willie, would be livid with the human-shaped broken branches. He'd sneer at every small child he spotted in the morning. Christopher would have to redirect the groundskeeper to work on the other side of the property tomorrow.

She grabbed the bag at a run and tore off around the side

of the massive inn. Dressed like a thief, she raced away like she'd been caught red-handed. The clothes hugged her figure, reminding him of the feel of her in his arms.

He clenched and unclenched his hands into fists at his sides, fighting the muscle memory. He would not risk his composure in his workplace for something he could never have. Once, he'd been a fool to think he could hold her. He wouldn't make the same mistake twice. The wounds from her departure still ached.

He strode back into the hotel, taking the shortcut through the lobby and out the doors to the patio. She raced over the rickety bridge, flying like a raven. For a second, he was lighter than air. More than happiness, he liked being right. Or so his actions of the last decade would proclaim on his behalf. Years ago, he'd been victorious, and for his prize, he had claimed a cold, lonely bed in a marital home that felt like a mausoleum without her nonstop singing and chattering to fill the high-ceilinged rooms.

With a shake, he focused on the present.

He'd known food would lure her out and asked the chef to add her old favorites to the menu, feigning a memory of some important guest's preferences. He risked too much because he wanted to see her.

He strode back inside the building, nodding and smiling at the guests he passed on his way to the spiral stairwell near the kitchens. With each step, he climbed to his office in the attic and refocused on his goal. He'd taken the section in the turret for himself, liking the ability to glance north, south, or west with ease from his desk. And, because he couldn't stay in their marital home by himself. The decision had been his biggest gamble and most successful payout.

It had been that chance that solidified Christopher's heir apparent status. Xavier Hale knew Christopher would manage. When the time came, however, Christopher hadn't felt prepared. Losing his father-in-law and mentor, knowing the full depths of the emotional damage that had never been reconciled between Ashley and Xavier, Christopher had ached to do the right thing. For the first time in years, however, he didn't know what that was.

Xavier must have sensed the unease within Christopher at the prospect of taking over the Inn from Ashley and had, no doubt, included the odd stipulation to comfort Christopher in accepting what he had rightfully earned. The Inn at Loon Lake was as well-known for the gregarious and outgoing personalities of the Hale family as it was for exceptional customer service.

Christopher wanted a compromise. He could give her fifty percent of the profits, and she could start over wherever she wanted. Or she could stay and work for him. But, knowing his wife's stubborn personality, she would balk at reporting to anyone and especially him.

Whether he liked it or not, he was trapped in a winner take all scenario.

He crossed the room to his private office, closed the door, and settled behind the large partner's desk. With summer starting, he had enough work to remain chained here around the clock. From the corner of his eye, he saw the lighthouse in shadow. Hopefully, she remembered to ask for utensils. As a rule, they didn't pack disposable forks with every order and gave up on plastic straws years ago. He chuckled, imagining her using the crusts of her bread to spoon every bite of scrambled egg.

She was creative and inventive. She'd find a way. Because she always did. And he couldn't help but cheer her on, even when it was against his best interests. He'd always been a fool for her, and he couldn't seem to change his ways.

Chapter Three

S ince when did a to-go order not include a fork? Ashley used the remaining sourdough crust as a utensil, shoveling every last morsel of creamy, perfectly scrambled eggs into her mouth. Cross-legged on an air mattress with only the ambient light of her cell phone screen, she devoured her food. After every bite, she fought off a moan. She supposed giving into the sound would only add to the otherworldly atmosphere she created. Not that she'd had much success in scaring off Christopher.

With a snort, she wiped her hands on a napkin, assessing the angry, red scratches on her hands. Nothing oozed. In a few days, she'd heal. If she had access to an antibiotic cream, she'd improve faster. The unglamorous start to her return only solidified her resolve.

Without Dad to block her, she could finally take on a real role in the business. Even if it was a little late. A decade was a long absence. She had felt every second of it, her heart hanging back on her home shores. But she wasn't leaving again. A warm meal convinced her she had the wherewithal to claim it all. Now. She finished eating, changed into her nightgown, and turned off her phone. She grabbed her pocket flashlight, holding the pink cylinder in her mouth as she worked.

She powered on LED battery votive candles in three glass lanterns and hooked each to a rope, climbing the spiral staircase to adjust each lantern and double-check the line's strength. During the day, she'd set up a pulley system. Her plan was simple. Create a ghostly light show with just enough lanterns to grab attention but not too many to make it seem suspicious. She couldn't have planned the weather better. With the thick cloud cover, the lights would pop against the dark night.

She had owned the props long before she came up with her current scheme, ordering the accessories for staging photos at her previous address. Her roommates hadn't put up any fuss about her leaving. She'd found a subletter among the other coffee shop employees to cover the last three months of the lease. If anything, her roommates liked the new roomie better than her. They definitely had more in common with the younger woman.

Ashley had been something of an elder stateswoman at age thirty-three, seven years older than the college best friends who put an ad in the paper that she accepted. Or, perhaps more accurately, she was a living, breathing cautionary tale. She proved every parental fear justified. From the comparative literature degree she'd earned but never quite adapted to a real-world job, to her failed young marriage; if a parent advised against a rash choice, Ashley proved why the choice was doomed. For the first time in years, she'd made the right choice. Now she needed to keep that positive momentum going.

Buttoning up her high collar, she adjusted the sleeves of the gown. She'd owned one like this in her childhood when she'd been obsessed with *Anne of Green Gables*. That was the same age she'd been when she first started daydreaming about a ghost haunting the property. She wasn't scared of the idea but electrified by it. A chance to continue her life's pursuit from beyond the grave? Yes, please.

She had spent a whole summer sneaking into the attic to set ghost traps of her own invention. Long before the town had reliable internet, she dug up what information she could find about disappearances or deaths on the property at the local library. Surprisingly, she found nothing. Given the history of the Inn, she expected at least one tragedy or accident on the grounds.

But she remained undeterred and switched her focus to fiction. She read gothic romances and gleaned the importance of the attic to any phantom regardless of the place of their death. With her research, she developed a flawless plan. She could see when the surface was disrupted if she covered the floor with either paint or flour. With candles set around the room, she'd have both a talisman against any bad spirits and a way to monitor any disturbances in the air. Images of flickering flames stoked her imagination.

Her scientific study would have given definitive proof. Her questions would have been answered. Christopher was the unexpected hitch in her otherworldly experiment. Instead of helping her carry six boxes of votive candles and three ten-pound bags of flour, he watched with a scowl. He sat cross-legged on the floor at the base of the rickety, pull-down stairs to the attic. She counted to ten when she finished her last trip to the supply closet to acquire her necessary supplies. From the corner of her eye, she spotted him as he entered the attic. He must have followed her to snoop.

She set the last candle in its place and realized she hadn't grabbed a matchbook. The second her feet hit the carpet below, her dad grabbed her from behind. Her father yelled like he never had before. Christopher hid in the corner, like she wouldn't know he was there, and had ratted her out to her dad. Afterward, she spent the rest of the day cleaning the attic from top to bottom. She hadn't had to suffer alone. Her tattle-tale had offered his assistance then. She had given him the silent treatment, ignoring his protests that he had acted out of concern.

When she reached the easternmost turret, near the window overlooking the lake and the lighthouse, however, she experienced an odd sensation. Her skin suddenly chilled, and the quiet in the attic became oppressive. Maybe she could pause her anger for a moment.

"If I were a ghost, I'd hide there." With half an hour of quiet, her voice squeaked from disuse.

Had he heard her?

She glanced over her shoulder.

He straightened, dumping a full dustpan of flour and dust into the garbage they'd lugged up the steps.

"Right over there, you know?" She pointed to the light-house. She knew the lighthouse was fake. But why couldn't a ghost choose that spot? It had a superb view and a cozy setting on its own little island.

He rolled his eyes. "Stop pretending. Ghosts aren't real."

"Why do you keep insisting they aren't? You're smart, but you don't know everything. Plenty of stuff can't be explained."

"No one has ever reported seeing a ghost on the property. Ever. Ghosts don't just happen."

She shrugged. "Maybe sometimes they do."

"No. They need a purpose."

She crossed her arms and stuck out her bottom lip.

"I'm serious, Ashley. Stop it. Drop it."

And roll? Usually, her pouting worked its charm on him, convincing him to see her side of things. But that day, Christo-pher held firm, and she didn't push him too far. That might have been the only time she didn't keep up her side of an argument until he surrendered. And it stuck with her. He didn't always agree. If only she'd known then that his love had limits, she would have saved herself a lot of pain by not falling so completely head over heels.

Over the years, she had floated the idea of a ghost on the property a few times. Christopher had never taken the bait. She hadn't been able to shake off the experience or her belief. While she had eventually conceded that her imagination impeded the true scientific method, she wasn't eager to repeat the experience for research. A person could live the rest of their life fearing a mysterious entity.

Although, now she supposed she was becoming the mysterious first wife figure she'd long feared.

"Okay. Here it goes," she told no one.

A cold feeling settled over her shoulders. *Dread? Fear? Something else?* When it came to fear, she was her own worst enemy, part of the downside of her enthusiastic creativity.

She grabbed one end of the cord she'd looped through the staircase. She had tied knots to secure the lanterns on either side of the hooks. Her plan was simple. Pull the cord back and forth, lifting and shaking the three lights.

Besides not getting attention, her only real concern was broken glass cutting her air mattress. Sleeping on the ground wasn't ideal. She tugged on the cord, the votives dancing. At the same moment, an icy breeze howled past the lighthouse.

For a moment, the wind had a deep, raspy voice. Good, maybe someone would shut a window against the sound or the chill. She didn't care as long as she got attention from the the Inn's occupants. She pulled harder and faster, desperation fueling her. If her haunting was going to get noticed, she couldn't waste the prime opportunity provided by nature.

"Mmmiiiinnne now. Mmmiiiinnne now." She sang the words low, the hum coursing through her whole body.

A chill snaked through her veins.

"Mmmmiiiiinnnnnee," she chanted the word, letting the reverberations warm her from the inside out. "Mmmiiii-innnneee."

She shook the lanterns harder, a tremor wracking her and her chin trembling. Outside the lighthouse, the night was quiet. The wind stopped. She was the only noisemaker around. The silence covered her like a heavy blanket. She had experienced the same oppression once before in the attic with Christopher. Had she predicted her doom that day? Was THIS her ghost origin story?

She wasn't sure how long she kept up the work. Lost in her old fears and new worries, she entered an almost meditative state. When the lanterns smashed, and the fire sparked, she was unsure how to explain the events. Could an LED get hot enough for a blaze? Had she witnessed a dangerous, deadly miracle?

The flames caught on the sheer window treatments at the top of the lighthouse.

She had triple-checked everything. While she was, admittedly, a bit unreliable in the long run, she was meticulous and detail-oriented in the short term. Schemes demanded her full attention. But it didn't matter. She refused to go up in smoke. Haunting the fake lighthouse for eternity? No, thank you. She'd be too out of sight, out of mind for any meaningful encounters.

She grabbed her phone off the mattress and raced to the door. Smoke filled the tower now. She coughed, choking on the acrid air, grabbed the handle, and rushed outside.

She raced forward, unseeing. Her steps were loud and heavy as she ran barefoot over the wooden bridge.

Barreling ahead, she didn't look up. The second she slammed into a solid chest, muscular arms wrapping around her, she collapsed. She didn't need to see to know. She was in his arms, and she was home.

* * *

The rescue was a fluke.

Christopher gripped her upper arms. She clung to him like she would drown in the lake if she didn't. If he clutched any tighter, he'd bruise her. He couldn't bring himself to let go.

Christopher shouldn't have spotted the flames. Well past his usual quitting time, he stayed in his office, facing the lake and finishing a few emails. From the corner of his eye, a spark of light had flashed. Turning toward the windows, he hadn't seen anything else. And then a burst of orange flame.

He had raced out of the attic down the tight staircase to the employee exit on the main floor. He grabbed the fire extinguisher off the mount near the door, one of many he had set up around the Inn. Fire terrified him. Since watching a well-meaning but harshly delivered cartoon PSA about not getting trapped inside a burning building, he only gave one element the power to scare him.

As he had pounded the grass under his feet, all he could think was, what if he'd gone to bed? In his studio apartment, the window facing the lake was up high in his bathroom. He'd have slept soundly. What would have happened to her?

He reached the bridge, his heartbeat picking up pace until he thought his boiling blood would poison him. He couldn't lose her for real. Whether by the hand of fate or a human accident, the reason he jumped to action didn't matter. Whatever the cause, he was on his way to the rescue. *Because she matters more than anyone else in my life.*

A world without Ashley Hale in it was sad and gray. He knew from first-hand experience. But if he thought she was gone for good? He'd never recover.

The door to the lighthouse had opened, slamming against the side of the building.

He had frozen in place. As if time slowed, he stood, waiting.

Her nightgown billowed behind her, like an angel. As she came closer, her blue eyes widened, looking hot and wild with fear, he never pictured her terrified. This wasn't a dream come true.

He held open his arms, and she crashed into him.

She had thrown her arms around his neck, sagging against his chest as if it was the most natural thing to do.

He wanted to wrap her tight in a hug. He needed to squeeze her and hold her and never let her go. She belonged in his arms. She'd hurtled back into him, and he wasn't letting her slip away again.

But he couldn't. His clammy palms slipped down her arms. He couldn't grip her. A fire raged behind her. He had to stop trying to embrace her and save the lighthouse. He dropped his heavy arms to his sides.

"Stay here," he murmured into her ear, catching the smell of her lavender shampoo. The scent haunted him for years. He could never find the exact bottle and brand. Or maybe she was the secret ingredient.

She stepped away.

The chill snaked his skin at the sudden loss of her warmth. He'd think about that later. Right now, he focused. He jogged over the bridge and stopped several feet from the open doorway. Flames licked the wooden frame. The burst of oxygen from the open door fueled the blaze. He'd be too late to save the building if he didn't stop the fire now. He pulled the pin from the fire extinguisher and depressed the handle, spraying the foaming detergent in a wide arc. Was he making enough progress? Time lost meaning as he focused on the current situation, his famous myopia activating.

The white foam coated everything, but still, he saw sparks in the back. Coughing, he moved forward and into the doorway. The still smoky air hung heavy, irritating his lungs. He sprayed inside the tower. Miraculously, he extinguished the last spark as he emptied the canister.

One problem tackled.

He scanned the interior. It remained as sparsely decorated as ever. It hadn't been in use for decades. He'd meant to look into renovating the property as a specialty suite. He spotted an air mattress, a duffle bag, and backpack. His heart sank. Her whole life packed in a couple pieces of luggage.

In his worst moments, he hadn't wanted her to be miserable. Mired in sadness enough for the both of them, he took no joy in her pain. He dropped the empty metal can on the ground.

Footfall echoed off the wooden bridge. He turned.

She entered the foam-filled mess. "Thanks for your help," she said. Her voice sounded fraught and far-off.

He studied her.

She nibbled her lip, wrinkling her nose in that adorable fashion she'd had since childhood. It was the admitting-guilt face that always betrayed her protests of innocence during a crime.

"Do you think we should call the fire department?" she asked. "I can't believe no one called the emergency number already. Doesn't anyone care about their neighbors anymore?"

The woman, squatting on private property, was upset she hadn't been noticed? She hadn't lost her nerve. Or she correctly called his bluff. He wouldn't have called the police to escort her off the premises, and he doubted anyone would have taken his side in an argument about her unlawful trespassing. Then he remembered who he was dealing with. She was Miss Center of the Universe. He'd forgotten that unfortunate side of her personality in favor of the good things. Like her eternal optimism. Although, positive thoughts hadn't helped her much.

She sank to the ground, pulled out the plug on the partially melted air mattress, and stuffed her belongings into a duffle. "Guess you're surprised to see me."

He almost snorted. Instead, he joined her on the floor, kneeling on the air mattress to speed up the deflation process. "I'm shocked you set fire to the lighthouse. I thought you liked this building."

"I did. I do," she squeaked. She finished packing her belongings and zipped the bag. With a huff, she straightened. "This was an accident that I am not responsible for! I have committed no crime."

He folded the mattress and frowned at his handiwork. Better to make faces at plastic than his wife. "This mattress is a lost cause." He dropped it to the ground and straightened.

She sniffed her backpack and coughed. "I might need all the detergent in the Inn to get the smoky smell out of my clothes."

He dusted his palms together and studied her billowing nightgown. The color was dull and dingy, probably from the smoke. "I can wash your clothes. You should have planned better. Pyrotechnics are hardly for amateurs."

"You can't really think this was me. If I would have deliberately set a fire to create a big scene, it would have involved something much showier, like fireworks."

He shook his head. She backed away from outrage to self-deprecation fast. Very few things in her life received careful consideration and seriousness. They had filled their days with hijinks and hilarity. He'd enjoyed very little of either in the years since she'd been gone. Without her, he had no reason to laugh or tease. He had no one to share his life with.

"Come on, I have a vacant suite upstairs you can stay in."

She nodded, slipping the backpack on her shoulders. "Sorry about the fire."

He bent and grabbed the duffle, surveying the surroundings. It wasn't particularly late. But the unusually frosty night kept the guests from promenading on the back porch. Good. An idea was forming, but he needed her not to be noticed. Invisibility was a laborious task. "It's fine. Follow me."

He strode across the lawn, and, for perhaps the first time on record, she didn't talk. At the employee entrance by the turret, he held open the door and pointed to the spiral staircase.

She shuddered.

He stopped himself from rolling his eyes. She'd gone from one of her imagined haunted places to another, trading the lighthouse for the attic. Well, at least he vanquished those ghosts for good.

She climbed the stairs, her footsteps almost silent.

Following behind, he realized she didn't have any shoes on. She was lucky she hadn't gotten seriously injured.

At the top of the stairs, she pushed through the door and into his office.

He followed, setting down the bag to retrieve a key to the available suite.

"Oh." The word was a gasp, a breath, and a reverential statement.

She noticed the renovation. He couldn't help but smile. "See, no ghosts up here. Like I told you."

"This is your office?" She spun in a slow circle.

She'd be analyzing the room with her typical critical eye for detail. He doubted she'd find fault with the comfortable, elegant room. Besides his giant partner's desk, he'd furnished the rest of the large space with traditional pieces. A large, faded, antique Shiraz covered the pine floor in the center of the room. Smaller Persian rugs anchored the different seating areas on either side. He had a large walnut table and chairs for a conference set on the north side of the room, overlooking the front of the Inn. At the south, overlooking the lake, he had a pair of leather club chairs sharing an oversized, tufted ottoman and a pair of floor lamps. He did his best thinking there.

"You're at the top of the world up here," she said.

Her voice shook. Was she giving a compliment or dishing a condemnation?

"It's a little cold, though." She rubbed her hands.

"I run warm."

She turned toward him. "That's not what I meant."

He wasn't sure how to read her expression. That stung. He didn't need her approval. Too bad he couldn't seem to stop seeking it. He walked across the room to the door leading to the hallway. Twisting the knob, he pulled the panel open, his gestures stiff. "Through here, please." He kept his voice low, not wanting to disturb any guests, or so he'd tell himself.

He adjusted his grip and remembered the duffle bag in his hand. "Actually." He cleared his throat and set the bag on the ground. "Leave your bag here, please. I'll wash your things tonight."

"But..." She nibbled her lip.

"What's wrong?"

"I won't have anything to wear tomorrow."

"If I don't wash your things, you will give yourself away as an arsonist."

She tucked her chin against her chest.

He hadn't intended the words as a reprimand. But he wasn't exactly sure what he meant about anything. Despite five days' warning, he hadn't prepared for the moment of speaking to her again. She'd always been his blind spot.

He grabbed the duffle off the ground, shut the door to his office, and opened the first door on the right leading to his studio apartment. He didn't want her entering his personal space. The four walls had been his sanctuary from thinking about her. She forced his hand.

He waved her inside, flipping the light switch. "Stay here." He pointed to the other side of the door.

"Okay," she murmured.

As the adrenaline faded, he took stock of his body. His muscles ached from exertion, and his throat was scratchy from smoke inhalation. The pungent aroma of soot rolled off her and seeped out of her duffle bag. He could tackle the smell first and walked through the entryway to the bathroom. He'd forgone a tub for a stackable washer and dryer, favoring practical appliances over simple luxuries.

He set the duffle on the ground and opened the dryer, which was always full of laundry he never had the time to fold. He grabbed a T-shirt and returned to the entry. "Here. You can wear this tonight and leave the nightgown in the trash. I'll do my best with your laundry."

She accepted the cotton shirt and raised it to her nose, sniffing. "Thanks."

The gesture was so ordinary but touched him. Memories crashed into him. She had done the same every time she borrowed one of his sweatshirts. He needed space. The sooner she was in her own room, the better. "This way." He motioned to the hall.

She stepped past him.

He closed the entrance to his studio, continuing down the hall. At the next door, he pulled the old-fashioned iron key from his pocket and slipped it into the plate. The bolt unlocked with a click, and he held open the door for her to precede him.

She oohed and ahhed as she toured the room.

The attic rooms held an entryway with a door leading to a generous bathroom with separate shower and tub areas and another door opening onto the studio-style suite. A half wall separated the well-appointed living room area with a mini kitchen from the bedroom. His studio apartment eliminated the spaciousness of the bathroom, taking away the tub to create a larger kitchenette. Otherwise, his living quarters mirrored this space, separated by one wall.

When guests had stayed next door, he had never noticed noise. With her, however, he worried about hearing every flutter of her eyelashes and the hum of her snores. He needed to think up the details of a plan. She'd never been an early riser. He had time.

In the living room, he left the heavy key on the coffee table. "You should be all set. If you have any problems, I'm just in the room next door."

"Why not go home?" She turned toward him, arching a brow. "Are you worried I'll burn down the resort?"

"Not exactly."

Her nostrils flared. If she hadn't given away her frustration, she provided the perfect cover for his truth.

"I converted the space into my studio apartment," he said.

"You live here? What happened to the cottage?"

"I rent it out to guests. It's become popular with long-term tenants. We've seen a robust growth in work-from-home employees eager for a change of scenery."

"But... it was our home. You let strangers stay there." Her voice was flat.

I had to move on. Every part of that little corner of the former stables, lovingly referred to as the cottage, symbolized another time, a happy life he never expected to end. He'd known she'd be upset. She'd carefully chosen every item in the cottage, handcrafting many pieces and personalizing others to give the cottage a cheerful warmth that was hard to replicate. And that same joy taunted him in her absence. Without her, he needed cold and impersonal. He wanted factory standards. He didn't want to feel. But how could he explain any of that without looking like a lovesick fool? Or that he only trusted a select handful of guests in the quarters. People he'd known for years. "I converted the rest of the building, too."

"Is this why he added the stipulation about living onsite? Because you already do?"

He shrugged. Glad she'd moved on and offered him another answer. He'd forgotten the benefits inherent in her jumping to conclusions. She never looked too hard at reality. She never saw what he felt. "Have a good night. We'll talk in the morning."

She saluted him.

He turned and let himself out of the room, moving with quiet efficiency. He didn't want to disturb the other guests. On wooden legs, he strode toward his apartment and shut the door.

Only a wall separated them. The distance was negligible to most. In his opinion, the space between them was vast. How could he be sure she was okay if he didn't watch her?

His heartbeat thundered in his ears, and his arms hung limp and useless at his sides. He'd almost lost her forever in an accident. She was back and playing a dangerous game.

He had once again underestimated her. The only advantage he had left was the level to which she had never understood him. And the sleepless night that awaited him to figure out how to keep her safe.

Good thing he had laundry to tackle.

Chapter Four

Ashley stretched her arms overhead. Every inch of her body pressed into soft bedding. From her calves tangled up in a crisp duvet to her lower back arching against a pillow-topped mattress, she was either in a dream or in heaven. At the moment, she didn't care which.

With a sigh, she opened her eyelids and stared at the ceiling. In the dark room, she couldn't determine the color. But she was certain it would be the particular shade of off-white radiating with a dull yellow undertone used everywhere. She'd hated the color her whole life. The ceiling and trim in every room of the Inn used the same shade. In the hallways with chair rail molding, she couldn't breathe. The overuse of the paint suffocated her, pushing down on her chest and collapsing her ability to make sense of depth. She had tripped through the corridors for years, racing too fast in search of blue sky and fresh air.

Now I can change it.

She smiled, shaking off the weight of childhood frustrations. A lot sucked about being an adult. But not the ability to make decisions and execute change. Or her husband's caring nature. He'd lent her a shirt to sleep in. One of his stretched-out undershirts, paper thin from years of service, the V-neck was almost scandalously low.

Had he really done her laundry? She hoped so. After three rounds of shampoo, she hadn't quite washed the stink of the fire out of her hair. If she wanted to leave the room without embarrassing herself and flashing too much skin, she needed her clothes.

Turning onto her side, she glanced at the alarm clock on the bedside table in surprise. Seven A.M.? She didn't voluntarily rise before eleven if she didn't have a morning shift at the coffee shop.

She hadn't slept so well in years. She must have actually achieved REM and enjoyed a restorative night. Which, all things considered, she probably didn't deserve. She swung her legs out of the bed, leaving her crisp sheet cocoon and tiptoeing across the room.

At the window, she pushed back heavy drapes and wispy sheers. In the soft morning light, the sun burned off the morning dew on the grass, and steam rose from the lake. On its small island, the lighthouse was a fantastical fairytale-type setting, surrounded by a hazy fog.

From inside the Inn, she could hardly see the windows. Her great idea hadn't been so well thought out. How on earth had he seen the lanterns and flames? Probably a miracle or...

She shivered, remembering the cold, clammy feeling on her skin. She hadn't been entirely alone in the building. Christopher would accuse her of an overactive imagination if she told him. She would admit that had terrified herself with stories entirely devised in her imagination before. Last night was different.

The air had changed, becoming thick and still like gelatin.

Ashley slowly suffocated under the awareness that she wasn't alone. She'd only escaped when the flames snapped her out of her daze. She would have suffered serious smoke inhalation if she remained too much longer and would have frozen in the elements if the ghost hadn't fetched help. Or had her rescue only been a fluke?

What would she have done if Christopher hadn't come down? Anonymous call to the front desk as she walked the three miles in the dark to her car parked in the town lot near the boardwalk? Then slept in her car and shown up on the Inn's doorstep a bedraggled, smoke-scented mess?

That would have been even worse and unavoidable. She had nowhere else to go.

From the safety of the room, the lighthouse looked the same as always. Guests would never realize last night had been so dramatic. She was sure she'd get an invoice if she'd done irreparable harm.

She might want to roll her eyes, but she couldn't be mad. If the roles were reversed, she'd charge him for any damages incurred through unlawful habitation. On the positive side, the lighthouse remained intact and primed for renovation. It would be a perfect selfie spot, a hashtag haven. As long as the old haunts abandoned the spot...

Shutting the curtains, she retreated to the bed, pulling the duvet to her chin. She wasn't sure her visceral response was fear. She worried her body was reacting to something she'd never quite shake.

Was she wrong to have been so relieved when Christopher came to her rescue? He'd been like a dashing hero from the pages of a romance novel, gallantly turning up in her moment of great distress. She'd launched herself into his arms.

His hug? Her skin tingled. She nestled deeper into the bedding, wrapping herself up tight, almost like he held her again. His warm embrace had reactivated all the memories locked in her muscles. How he had always treated her like a treasure to be admired with tenderness. The way he had created a protective cocoon, demanding nothing of her in return, had made her knees buckle until she had gone limp in his arms.

Tears stung her eyes, blurring her vision. Had she really lost him to her hurt pride? Why had she let anything, specifically anyone, rile her enough for such rash nonsense? *Because I've only been part of what he wanted, I've never been enough on my own.*

She couldn't argue with herself over that topic. Luckily, last night, he hadn't noticed how she melted in his embrace. If their situation was lopsided, she'd rather he didn't realize it played in his favor.

He had been too absorbed in the disaster unfolding on his property. Or rather hers. He'd doused the flames, and she had recollected herself and her purpose. She didn't need him. Not anymore. He'd made his choice, and she was no longer hurt. She knew where she stood with him. She was the bonus but not the prize. And now she would reclaim her hotel and push him out. He'd lose it all. Maybe then he'd regret not choosing her.

With a good night's sleep, she was clear-headed but remained unsure how to remove him from the property. She needed him gone for one night to restart the clock. Finding a reason for him to leave couldn't be too difficult. She shuddered, hating the underhandedness after he saved her.

He wasn't hers anymore. She had to claim her inheritance, or she had nothing. Now that she was back, he'd undoubtedly hand her divorce papers before she took off again, and then she'd really not belong.

Her phone buzzed on the bedside table. She crossed the room and grabbed it.

The hubs: let me know when you're awake. I have an idea.

Seeing his official title flash on her screen sent a shiver down her spine and pierced her heart. She forgot she hadn't changed his identification on her phone. She should have deleted the number. Not that she could have erased it from her memory.

She stared at the phone. Her curiosity overrode any thoughts of stalling. She was the schemer and would offer help in improving whatever plan he formed. He was a novice at creative thinking. Or, he had been when she left.

She texted back. **I'm up now.**

A knock pounded the entry door, loud enough to carry through the foyer and into the studio suite.

"Coming." She stared down at herself and her bare legs. The bright light of day bouncing off them encouraged her to cover herself and add a little dignity to this meeting.

She grabbed a robe from the closet, slipping her arms into the plush sleeves. She purred at the touch of soft velour, rubbing her cheeks into the collar. She tied the belt at her waist and ran her palms over the front.

Had this been one of Dad's choices or Christopher's? The luxurious in-room extra seemed like Dad, but Christopher also cared about details. She glanced at the messy bed and half-heartedly tugged the duvet over the top. She hated making a bed, but it was one of those chores he insisted on.

The knock came again.

She strode out of the room and into the foyer, pulling open the door and glaring at him.

With his fist raised, he was poised to knock again. Was he intent on waking all of his guests? She scanned him, hair neatly combed and dressed in a two-piece suit with a tie. Well, at least she'd grabbed the robe.

She stepped to the side, shielding herself behind the door. She wasn't sure why she made the effort. Staff wouldn't be upstairs yet. If a maid or bellhop saw her, so what? Showing up in her family's hotel was hardly remarkable. And many of the employees would have no idea who she was. Her stomach dropped. No one would recognize her. *A stranger in my family's home.*

"Good morning." He tipped his head and shut the door.

He sounded a little wooden and moved stiff and jerky. She remained in place. Without the door, she was fully in view. She didn't shy away from him.

Any conversation between them would have to be short, if not terribly sweet. She didn't need to offer him hospitality or make him comfortable. Which was wrong, considering he had given her exactly that. But now that she was out of the lighthouse, she'd lost the upper hand and the element of surprise. And he seemed determined to capitalize on the security of his home turf.

He cleared his throat. "Mind if we sit down?"

She arched an eyebrow. Direct and no-nonsense, he wasn't the people-pleaser she'd left. The man who asked but never demanded. Otherwise, he'd barely aged in the past decade. There were no obvious fine lines or wrinkles or gray streaks near his temples. Her fingers itched to cover the roots she needed to touch up. Her skincare regime helped her maintain a rosy glow.

"Please?" he asked. "No more games."

"What do you mean?" She kept her tone light.

He stared at her hard. "You arrived at ten-twenty on Monday morning but waited until dusk to move into the lighthouse. You thought you wouldn't be seen? I have eyes all over the property and town."

She blew out a heavy sigh. Either he had extensive

surveillance on the property or a gut feeling about her return. She liked the second option but also feared his ability to predict her next step. He liked to say he knew her better than she knew herself. For a while, the statement was true. Until she left.

"I have a plan that'll help both of us. You can trust me."

She lifted her gaze to his. She could. She'd always put her faith in him.

Another knock sounded on the outside door.

"Go inside and sit down. I'll get this," he said.

She nodded and stepped inside her suite, shutting the door, pressing her cheek against the panel, and straining for any sound outside.

A few muffled words accompanied the opening of the main entry. Then the outer door shut.

A thud shook the panel.

She bounced back. Had he realized she was eavesdropping?

"Can you open this please?" he asked.

She pulled open the door and stood back.

In his arms, he carried a massive tray with a coffee carafe, two mugs and saucers, and two large, covered dinner plates stacked one on top of the other. He set the spread on the coffee table.

Her mouth watered. Her stomach rumbled. But she didn't move an inch.

He sat on the couch, poured two black coffees, and turned toward her. "Aren't you hungry?"

She stood straight and still. Christopher always knew what she needed before she did. She wanted to hate that about him, but once again, she could only be grateful. Her plan fell apart, and she'd been foolish to imagine having the upper hand. He knew her too well. Still.

He lifted the cover off plates on the tray.

In an instant, the buttery, cinnamon-y, sugary smell of French toast filled the room.

She leaped across the room. Settling cross-legged on the ground, she dove into her food with a knife and fork, spearing a huge bite and raising it to her mouth. She moaned. The chef hadn't changed the recipe, using Hawaiian-style bread cut into thick slices. Then, she reached for the coffee, gulping the rich flavor. She hadn't had decent coffee in several days. Her attempt at instant hot beverages had been pathetic and stomach-churning. The best she managed was room temperature, and the instant granules mostly mixed in. She returned to her French toast, her second favorite dish.

As she savored her bites, she couldn't stop her brain from whirring. All her favorites lived here. Another reason to never leave. She included him in the list, not that he'd ever believe her apology, and she wasn't sure how she would start. She had never changed her phone or email. He could have reached out to her. She didn't hide. He always waxed on and on about her stubbornness. He had some too. He wasn't always Mr. Nice Guy. But this was pretty good of him.

"Okay. Let's talk," he said.

She gulped down her bite and slurped her coffee. She had nothing to lose. And perhaps she could gain everything. She nodded and topped up her coffee.

* * *

Christopher sipped his coffee, willing himself to slow. He'd lose his tenuous grip on the higher ledge if he moved too fast. Or she'd pull him down. Both had happened before.

From the corner of his eye, he studied her.

She inhaled the French toast, eating as ravenously as if she'd been starved. He'd asked for the powdered sugar to be lightly dusted on the edges and the syrup to be thoroughly warmed for a smoother pour. He'd overseen the sprinkling of cinnamon into the pot of her coffee.

She devoured her meal just like he'd known she would. He forced the smirk off his face, aiming for a neutral expression. Knowing his wife so well had tricked him into a false sense of security before. He'd imagined he understood her responses before she even formulated a reply. Doing so, he forgot her love of a shocking twist.

When she'd announced her departure, she left him speechless and unable to form an argument to convince her to stay until long after she'd gone.

However hard-won the battle, he couldn't rest. And he knew better than to assume he was ready. His victory this morning wasn't without a cost last night.

He was more tired than he'd been in years. After the adrenaline rush had diminished following the fire and confronting her, he'd returned to his office. He had known sleep would elude him, so he hadn't bothered to go into his apartment and stare at the wall separating them. He'd only imagine her snoring if he had. A bone-deep weariness persisted; keeping his eyes open was an arduous task. And yet, he had never been more energized.

From following her social media accounts over the years, he knew that she had never really settled in any place for too long. Her reappearance solidified her intent to come home for good. He had hope. He wouldn't need to be vulnerable if he kept her at arm's length. She would do what she wanted when she wanted without thinking about him or anyone else. This time, he was smarter. He wouldn't take the unintentional pain personally.

Besides, she couldn't shatter his heart again. It was already irreparable. "Is it good? Do you need more syrup?"

She shook her head.

He leaned forward, setting the coffee mug on its saucer on the low table and resting his forearms on his thighs. "I'm sure we can resolve the estate peacefully. It might take the lawyers some time, but we will reach a satisfactory resolution." *Although, we'll have to give up a lot of money to do so.* He could make more money. With her, he'd have one chance not to become a sworn enemy. He had lived without her. He knew he could do that again. But he didn't want to be dead to her. That fate was his worst-case scenario. "In the meantime, we need to talk."

"We do." She licked her bottom.

Her pink tongue darted across her full lower lip, clearing the sheen of powdered sugar and missing the dollop of syrup in the corner. He rose from the couch and, catching himself before he made a move, dropped back against the cushion, making a big show of buttoning and tugging his jacket into place. If he touched her, he was doomed.

She covered her mouth with a hand, unconcerned by his behavior. "I want to setup some ground rules, though. You said the word *plan*. That implies we are working together." She said through her last bite of food, setting a world record for eating most doctors would find reprehensible. She reached for her coffee and took a long sip. "I did not agree to be your teammate."

According to the law, you did. He wouldn't share the snarky tidbit. But in the light of day, pretending not to know she wanted him out was ridiculous and beneath them both. Forewarned was forearmed. He needed more information. "What do you want? What is your intention? Have you come to take over the Inn and kick me out?"

She sipped her coffee, arching both eyebrows.

A rock settled low in his gut. At least the confirmation fully quieted the raging, lusty beast inside that demanded he make a move. She really thought so little of him and what he'd accomplished. She was here to sweep in and take over without a care.

He couldn't be surprised. He'd worked for years to conceal the actual state of the finances at the Inn, apprenticing her father before taking the reins for himself following her departure. He was complicit in her ignorance while he labored hard to turn the business around and reach record-setting heights.

The hospitality industry wasn't for the weak of heart. He imagined his skin was thick and tough after so long in the business. Her opinion and underestimating his abilities shouldn't hurt. But it did. "Seriously? You think you can run this business without me?"

She shrugged.

Her nonchalant gesture rankled him. He might have growled. The casual response, making light of his life's work, showed a thoughtlessness he'd forgotten. She was fun and easy. Her inability to take anything seriously, however, sparked her cutting remarks. Nothing mattered because she never toiled to earn anything. In those scattered moments, he remembered she'd grown up with privilege, and he'd had to work for his place at her feet.

Not anymore. He was no one's loyal dog. He was the boss. He swallowed. Better to silence himself than regret his response. He'd deal with her false self-confidence later.

"You're the one who brought up an idea. Let's hear it," she said. "Split the property fifty-fifty?"

"We could. Or the legal system might take over and divide the estate for us. During divorce proceedings, the lawyers and the judge could throw out the post-nuptial agreement and claim we signed it under distress."

"Your distress, at that time," she muttered.

"We'd be tethered to each other. Or the contract would be upheld, and we'd be free and clear of one another." *What did she want?* He scanned her face, searching for the answer.

She finished her coffee and pushed herself off the ground. Pacing the carpet in front of the bed, she couldn't hide her twitching lips as she muttered to herself.

But she was just far enough away that he couldn't hear. Probably for the best. "Listen, we have to set that aside for the time being. Last night, you claimed you didn't set the fire."

She whirled around, facing him with a wild look in her blue eyes. "I didn't."

"I believe you. But if you didn't start the fire, someone did, and it was probably to get you out of the lighthouse to get the treasure."

She snorted. "The treasure again? No one believes that. It was a made-up promotion during a slow summer."

His beliefs as a skeptic weren't important. He'd learned how many people wanted a little magic in their lives and would jump on any prospect of the supernatural, including a supposed cursed treasure that wasn't discussed until the 1990s. "Fine. You tell me what happened. How do you explain the blaze?"

"A ghost."

He could feel the long-suffering sigh building deep in his chest. It was a familiar friend. Often, he had to arrest a sense of logic and order to go along with her flights of fancy. This was too much. "You can't pretend to be a spirit in a fake light-house and then claim there is a real ghost there. What's the supposed origin story?"

She stiffened, drawing her shoulders up to her ears. "I don't know. But people have reported odd occurrences since the eighties."

"Yes, on and off, mostly by the Prims, and every encounter was explained rationally. If someone is trying to undermine the business, it is in our best interests that we figure it out before actual damage happens."

"Why can't you investigate?"

He slipped a finger under his collar. He'd tied his Windsor knot too tight. His pain was all physical and external, nothing to do with the chasm slowly eroding the trust between him and the townsfolk. "I'm not well-loved in town. I've had to make tough choices for the greater good."

"I don't need to wait you out?" She widened her gaze. "I can have the townsfolk run you off the premises?" Crossing her arms over her chest, she exuded triumph.

Her borrowed robe and comped suite didn't detract from the victory. She took to both as if they were hers.

"Don't look too pleased," he said, hating the frown in his words.

"I'm not unhappy about this news."

He rolled his eyes. "I have my defenders, too. And you might like to know I can count on the entire Inn staff as my allies. Don't drum up support for a coup."

"I guess we'll just have to see how popular you really are. Now that I'm back, your staff has a choice in leadership. They didn't before my return."

Do they have a choice? Again, he fought to keep a curt response to himself. She might think she had the upper hand, but she stood on shifting sand. She didn't understand the work involved. He could appreciate her side. She considered the property her birthright. But he'd poured everything he had into the business. He wasn't mad that the resort wasn't left to him outright. Xavier would want to maintain appearances. But Christopher's labor made the business successful. Without him, the Inn would crumble. He didn't want to come in later and rebuild. He intended to stay and continue on the upward trajectory.

"Fine," she said. "Let's get back to right now. What is your plan? You must need something from me, or you wouldn't have reached out this morning. I figured you'd leave me to languish in here until I got desperate and gave in to letting you have the Inn."

Tempting. "For the time being, we both need each other, and what I propose is two parts. A public display and a private investigation. You need to arrive in an over-the-top way. Let everyone know you are back and are determined to make your mark. Be openly hostile to me."

"That part is easy." She folded her arms over her chest.

"Then I'll make a show of involving you in the business, and you can interrogate the townsfolk on my behalf. I have no doubt you'll find the truth about who started the fire." He wasn't certain she'd learn the why. "I have an idea I'd like your help with for the Inn. Help me turn the lighthouse into a private suite."

"I could be interested in part of that offer." She tapped a finger to her chin. "But what do we do about the inheritance?"

"If we don't solve this problem first, we will have nothing to fight over. You believe someone committed arson."

"I already know who started the fire and why."

He drew his brows together. Was Ashley in communication with someone from town? Was it Zach?

"It's a ghost. Believe me."

"No. We are not going down this path again. There has never been a ghost on the property. No one has ever died of mysterious causes." *Except for your father.* Xavier's death was untimely, but with his unhealthy diet and stress-filled life, his demise wasn't totally out of the realm of possibility. Ghosts needed to be the victims of a grisly murder or other tragedy. Why would a spirit hang around if not to avenge themselves?

He curled his fingers inward until his nails bit into his palms. Less than twelve hours into their reunion, he was following her flights of fancy again.

"I had an encounter that cannot be explained away," she said, her voice firm.

He drew in a deep breath and counted to ten. Reasoning with her was futile. He knew from plenty of experience. She sidestepped logic at every turn with her quick wit and sassy comebacks.

"Okay," he said slowly, placating, "while we attempt to contact the other side, can we also eliminate those alive right now? I don't want to involve law enforcement if we don't have to. I'm not anxious to have the sheriff interviewing guests on their vacations. That won't be good for business."

She nodded. "Fine, but I know what happened. My ribs were squeezed." She placed her hands on either side of her waist and gripped, her knuckles turning white.

He studied her, fighting the desire building as she tightened the velour fabric over her figure. The v created by the robe's collar deepened, flashing a little lower. Was she wearing anything underneath? *Not helpful.*

He slipped a hand into his too-tight shirt collar, pulling the fabric off his Adam's apple. "What happened was a fire. A very destructive accident that could have been tragic." He stood and strode toward her, extending a hand. "We have to find the culprit before they can destroy anything else. Can we take care of the Inn before declaring a winner?"

She frowned, looking at his hand.

He had the urge to stretch his limb even further into her personal space. But he didn't. That was growth and maturity.

"Agreed." She accepted his hand and shook it.

A tremor shot through him from her slender fingers rippling down to his toes. The zing was still there. His head would win the day this time. "Great. Let's sneak your bags out, and you can make your grand, notable entrance. Meet me in my office when you're ready. I'll leave the door unlocked."

"Can you bring me my clothes?"

His mouth went dry, and his skin burned. He'd spent too much time handling her garments, imagining why she'd need such pretty dresses and dainty undergarments. "Fine. Sure. I'll drop them off."

"Thank you." She offered him a placid smile.

He tipped his head to her and let himself out of her temporary quarters, heading the short distance down the hall to his kingdom. Back to the old patterns of her putting on the show while he dealt with the repercussions. At least he was well-rehearsed.

Chapter Five

Driving her sedan the long way from the parking lot to the highway via backroads and then exiting from the ramps, might have been a poor choice. Ashley didn't really need more time to think about her actions or, more accurately, inactions. Her chosen path provided sixty uninterrupted minutes of consideration.

When Christopher had told her his idea, he had been so cute and calm. She remembered everything she loved about him. From the way his eyebrows drew into a solid line to the firm set of his chin, he was his most adorable on a mission. Maybe to others he was intimidating, but not to her.

He had hardly aged, his slim and trim figure still taut in his tailored suit. All those years of sitting behind a desk all day had not affected him physically. He must have maintained his running routine.

She watched enough rom-com movies to picture bumping into him under the guise of following her own exercise regimen. She'd wear something cute, tight, and short and strike up a conversation. Anything for a repeat of the way he looked at her.

When he had stared at her mouth, his eyes held a simmering heat, like melted gold. *Good.* She wasn't the only one all too aware of the other. Using their attraction for her purposes would only burn them both. She'd let her mind wander and forgot the important thing: he stood in her way.

For the moment, she didn't have any other option besides following his lead. While she never lacked an idea, she wasn't ever sure of the response and effectiveness of a plan before she moved on to the next. She had never trivialized her time by considering outside perspectives.

To secure her future, however, she needed a different approach. She needed to listen and learn first. If the town really didn't like Christopher, maybe her comment about waiting him out wasn't so far off base. Besides, she had enjoyed a hot meal, a soft bed, and standing under a warm shower. She wasn't eager to leave the comfort of the Inn.

And he wasn't half bad at laundry. She'd be tempted to give him the Victorian nightgown for a cleaning if she hadn't tossed it already. A shudder shook her from her head to her toes. When she had picked out the garment, she had no idea she'd nearly die in it. She wasn't wearing nightgowns ever again.

He might suspect foul play among their neighbors, but she knew better. The lighthouse was most definitely haunted. After packing her bags, she dressed, reapplied her makeup, and strolled to his office.

If she'd been worried her pink, seersucker sundress, espadrilles, and wavy hair tied with a thick, satin ribbon had been too much, she reveled in the appreciative glint in his eye. The slow rake of his gaze over her figure was like a caress. As long as she could throw him off track, she had a chance. The power dynamics between them might be more evenly distributed than she realized. Or they reached a new level of personality in their estrangement.

He had recollected himself, created a momentary diversion, and whisked her off the property in his car, dropping her at the parking lot. She had almost convinced herself he intended to throw her into the bushes like an unwelcome guest on a 90s sitcom. His frown upon taking in the state of her vehicle almost had her questioning her nerve for the whole endeavor. She couldn't keep sweating through her clothes whenever she needed to fetch the vehicle. She'd have to deal with his opinion with a solid dollop of her own instinctual snobbery. Old money wasn't flashy.

She tightened her grip on the steering wheel of her little sedan. The same vehicle she'd left Loon Lake in. It was a little beat up after parallel parking in various urban locations for the past decade. But she still loved it. Her loyalty was unimpeachable. If he didn't understand that, then more fool him.

She signaled and turned onto the drive leading to the front of the Inn. She hadn't asked him what he'd been up to for the past decade. Work was the obvious answer. The likelihood he'd found another woman in their tiny town to replace her was slim. Ten years was a long time. *Should I worry? Had he strayed from our vows?*

Surely, the vague, faceless female wouldn't want to live in a studio apartment in *Ashley's* family business. Wouldn't she be worried about the ghosts? Or, at the very least, aware she'd be subject to constant comparison?

Only if I have any loyal friends left at the Inn.

Ashley slowed the car and parked in the circular drive, leaving the engine humming as a valet approached. From her quick tour through the office and apartment last night, she had spotted no stray hair ties or discarded garments strewn around the place. Not that another woman would be so blatant about her presence, per se, but she'd have to know she was a mistress and want to leave some sort of evidence of her existence behind, right? Like marking her territory with a lacy bra or pair of high heels? Were all mistresses inherently as sexy as the women on soap operas?

Unless it's Elise McKenna.

If Ashley hadn't parked, she would have rolled the car into a tree. Her heavy limbs stopped working. A shudder wracked her body. The town's ice queen, and the only potential rival for her husband's affection, wouldn't waste her time being messy. Oh no, Elise was cool perfection.

Ashley had never been a fan of the other woman's staid demeanor and vice versa. Thrown together often because of their age and the limited number of females, the pair had never warmed to each other. No amount of cajoling and sleepovers had worked. To her father's chagrin, Ashley had preferred to spend her time wreaking havoc with her sidekick, Christopher.

Christopher had often tried to include Elise in their schemes and games. He brought her up in their childhood conversations often. He'd always had a soft spot for the practical, serious Elise.

Ashley had no idea what might have happened during her absence. Perhaps, with his pushy wife gone, he had finally found the right moment to pursue something with Elise. No. Ashley gritted her teeth and willed her imagination to stop. She had her own twisty road to destiny, and it started now. The other woman would find herself out of luck.

The valet opened the door.

The young-ish-looking man in a crisp white shirt, black tie, black vest, and black pants waited patiently outside as she swung her legs out of the vehicle.

He extended his hand.

She didn't recognize him.

"Are you a guest, ma'am?"

Ma'am? She glanced in the rearview mirror. Hadn't she done a decent enough job with her makeup to hide the fine lines around her mouth and the bags under her eyes? Her concealer was a little cakey. Her shimmer eyeshadow was thick.

She pressed together her lips, refreshing the color and her resolve. "I am the owner. Mrs. Hale-Lewis. Please have a bellhop grab my bags from the trunk." She lifted her chin and accepted his help out of her car.

The youth widened his amber eyes but bowed and extended her a claim for the sedan. He gestured for a bellhop and popped the trunk. "Very good, Mrs. Hale-Lewis."

She almost smiled. To irritate her father, she'd taken Christopher's last name. Online, and soon enough in real life too, she'd be Ms. Hale again. He was probably drafting divorce papers as he waited for her grand entrance. She liked hearing her married last name while she could.

She stepped onto the curb behind the bellhop, who was pushing a cart with her bag. She scanned the entrance of the Inn, emotion catching in her throat. Too much of her life, identity, and soul were wrapped up in the bright, white building. Hiding in the shadows, she hadn't had a genuine opportunity to process the monumental shift in her life. This was hers now. And the future had never been more wide open or terrifying.

Without her father to supplement her life with a monthly allowance, she was truly on her own. The poor-little-rich-girl status would not win her any supporters. Despite that, for the first time ever, she was in control of her choices and her fate.

She strolled inside the automatic doors to the lobby and breathed deep the scent of cut lilacs and hyacinths, releasing a delicate perfume. The large, open space held the reception and concierge desks to one wall, a large seating area opening to the porch in the back, and at the side, the entrance to the restaurant.

The bellhop had stopped at the reception desk. Chatting with the woman behind the high counter, he tipped his head toward Ashley. The woman met her gaze and offered a tense smile.

Ashley didn't recognize her either. Never mind, she plastered on her biggest smile and approached the stranger at the concierge desk. Fake it till you make it propelled her through her hardest challenges. This moment didn't even crack the top ten.

"Good morning," she greeted the man in the suit, standing before his desk. "I am Ashley Hale-Lewis, owner of the Inn. See that the Gardenia Suite is prepared for me and my bags brought upstairs." She tipped her head. "Thank you."

She strolled across the marble tiles, her espadrilles silent as she floated to the dining room. She tried her best to channel every rom-com heroine she'd grown up watching. Too bad she didn't have on a great hat, her arms laden with shopping bags to inform everyone of their huge mistake.

As she stepped over the threshold, from tile to patterned carpet, she dropped her shoulders and enjoyed her first actual smile in a long time.

Standing at the host stand, his mustache as neatly combed as his hair, Pierre Leduc checked through a ledger. He lifted his head. And did a double-take.

"Good afternoon, Pierre," she said. Finally, one familiar face. The tight coil in her tummy released. She hadn't anticipated how much would change at the Inn. The business always experienced turnover, but she hadn't understood the extent.

The building was cool and efficient, just like Christopher. From the outside, she hadn't seen the transformation. Growing up, the Inn had reflected her father's often cheeky demeanor. Since her husband assumed control, however, the operation permeated with logic. She missed the playfulness of the past.

"Madam Ashley," Pierre stammered. He stepped out from behind the stand. "How may I help?"

"Right now, I'd love a good table."

"But of course." He turned and snapped at a few servers, pointing toward the window. "Please, right this way."

She smiled and lifted her chin higher. She couldn't lose her nerve or drop the false bravado. As much as she wanted to retreat upstairs and hide in the comfortable bed again, she couldn't be defeated. She'd have to show no weakness in front of the staff. No doubt the spies had already run upstairs to inform him of what was happening.

As she passed tables full of diners, she nodded and took the seat selected for her overlooking the lawn. She'd order and then make a big show of asking the guests about their stays. When he came down, he'd witness that she'd followed his plan with her own deviations.

If all was fair in love and war, she'd fire the first shot.

* * *

What did it mean that Ashley drove the same car? Clinging to the past?

Christopher wished he didn't care. Safely back in his office after escorting her off the property before anyone realized she was here, he had turned the question over in his mind on a terrible loop. He wanted to turn off his brain and stop analyzing every piece of information.

His subconscious had other ideas, working overtime to fill in the gaps about her life. Her semi-frequent social media updates and occasional blog posts presented a rosy picture. He'd fooled himself into thinking he had the full scope of her world through her updates. He heard her voice in every description.

She'd had roommates over the years and kept the Inn as her reference for every job. He'd intercepted most of those phone calls, providing a good recommendation. With every call, he'd wanted to reach out and ask her to come back. But her father hadn't relented on his stubborn stance that she'd beg to return. And Christopher knew his equally willful wife would expect a tearful plea to come home before she entertained the idea.

But Christopher had often feared her pride would ruin her. How much had she depended on the allowance he sent her for her basic expenses? Slowly, he realized how much he didn't know about her despite trying to stay informed.

Another thought chilled him. Was the car not a choice but a necessity? If she had funds, would she have bought a newer vehicle? *What if I hadn't wired money to her account?* Xavier had been explicit that money would not follow her off the property. But Christopher couldn't help himself. Good thing, too. He didn't want to think about her being destitute. How was that even a possibility? She was clever and quick-witted. She could charm her way out of any situation. As a kid, he'd been annoyed. As a teen and adult, he'd leaned into her skillset.

Why had she returned? She always waxed poetic about a fresh start. As far as he could tell, she'd enjoyed about fifteen. He didn't want to think her coming here was truly her last option.

Because she simply couldn't stay. He'd survived because of the distance. With her close, she threatened the equilibrium of his carefully ordered life. Quitting her had taken him years. And he'd fall into his addiction all over again at the first flutter of her eyelashes. He wasn't leaving. He'd never dreamt of a better life somewhere new. As far as he was concerned, he liked history. Everyone knew him and vice versa. For better or worse, he never fought at the constraints of their small town.

Even when some of the townsfolk would gladly push him out with a little help from his wife.

He wouldn't think about that now. They would find a way towards a better future for both of them. It wouldn't be together. Because now that she was back, they could resolve their business and officially move on. Legally. All the ties cut forever. Had she moved on already? Had there been others in the past ten years? She was fun and flirty without ever realizing how intoxicating those qualities were.

And now she'd be free to pursue whatever her next path was. He would too, although he didn't see any change from the past decade. He wanted a family, but he couldn't imagine one that didn't include her. She came back looking for a fight, not friendship. He couldn't let himself get confused.

The phone rang on his desk.

He stopped in front of the window overlooking the lake and crossed the room. He picked up on the third ring. "Hello, Christopher Lewis speaking."

"Mr. Lewis, there is a woman downstairs claiming to own the Inn and requesting the Gardenia Suite."

Christopher smiled. He appreciated the tone of outrage in the concierge, Mr. Brixen's, voice and could picture Ashley waltzing in through the door, making quite the entrance. She'd done exactly as he asked. So why did he have a strange tingle along his spine like he wouldn't approve of the result? *Because she's never really followed any of my plans without her own spin.* He cleared his throat. "Where did she go?"

"She walked straight to the restaurant, sir. Should I have someone run after her and kick her out?"

A knock pounded on the door.

"No, thank you, Mr. Brixen. Please see that the room is ready for her, and I will take care of the situation." He hung up the phone and sat behind his desk. He interlaced his hands on the desktop, assuming a position of cool confidence and intractable power. "Enter."

Pierre Leduc strolled into the room, leaving the door ajar behind him.

"Pierre? Is everything all right?" Christopher asked. It was unlike the man to leave his post. Ever.

"She's back." Pierre sputtered and took several steps into the room, twisting his hands together. "She's sitting in the restaurant."

"It's really her?" Christopher tried to instill his voice with as much wonder and surprise as he thought others expected. The truth was, he didn't overly concern himself with outside opinions. He felt like the husband on a crime show being interrogated by the police. They would analyze his reaction for guilt or innocence ad nauseam for the entire sixty-minute program. He owed everyone a show.

Pierre nodded.

At least Christopher convinced one person. Besides himself. He wouldn't give her the satisfaction of his heartbeat skipping. "Very well," he said. He pulled open a drawer and found the folder he'd spent last night compiling. He pushed away from his desk, and gripping the portfolio in his hands, strode toward the center of his office and waved to the door. "Please lead the way, Pierre."

The maître d' turned and looked slightly more confident than he had upon arrival.

Besides a few cleaning staff, Pierre was one of the last people who remembered Ashley. Everyone had heard of the epic fights between Xavier and his only child. Only a few employees remained who had witnessed the rows.

If Pierre expected a big, elaborate show of force from Christopher, the maître d' would be disappointed. He would officially start the way he meant to go on. Giving her a chance, for show, while working behind the scenes to ensure a settlement everyone could live with.

He knew she wouldn't be happy with it. But neither would he if he was honest. He never wanted to be in a situation where one of them won at the other's expense. But Xavier took that choice away from them.

He followed the maître d' down the guest stairs and corridors.

Pierre turned toward him at the base of the stairs in the lobby. "Do you think she'll really attempt a takeover?"

Christopher smiled, adjusting his grip on the documents he prepared for her job. "Doubtful."

He nodded at the staff and strode through the lobby and into the restaurant. Her light laugh danced in the air, bouncing off the crystals in the chandeliers and mixing with the clinking of utensils in a symphony of pleasure. He hung along the walnut paneled walls, skirting the perimeter of the room.

Everyone else hung on her words.

She'd amassed quite the gathering in the center of the room.

Servers and guests turned toward her or stood nearby.

With broad hand gestures and energetic facial expressions, she told some sort of lively story. She was charming. It was hard to turn away from her under normal circumstances. When she was on her best behavior, she was the most captivating person in the room. He ground together his molars.

He forgot about that. If he'd expected her to be off her game after he rescued her, he'd underestimated who he was dealing with. He worked hard to develop his go-to small talk starters, filling a notebook in his desk with ideas. Greeting guests didn't come naturally, but he attempted to improve his people skills and practiced for hours. She started on top. With a sincerity to her cleverness, she was witty and warm, never condescending or off-putting. How? He'd analyzed her for years and never learned her secrets.

"Sir?" Pierre whispered at his side.

"Not here. Let her know her suite will be ready, and I'll stop by later. Please tell Mr. Brixen?"

Pierre nodded and backed away.

Christopher gave himself one last look at her in her element. And then he continued along the perimeter until he reached the glass door leading to the porch and saw himself out. He made his way to inspect the lighthouse and look for clues. He'd almost welcome a ghost today. Rather an apparition to confront than the ghosts plaguing him from inside his head.

He didn't get to simper and smile and order room service. He had a business to run. Unlike his wife, he had control. And he wouldn't forget it.

Chapter Six

Ashley had received the note, or as she saw it, the summons along with her decaf coffee. She'd been relieved. Her big, bold show took more energy than she had anticipated. If Dad had been able to entertain the guests with stories, she had reasoned it couldn't be that hard. Under normal circumstances, finding her inner charisma wasn't challenging. But her subterfuge added a layer to the endeavor that drained her. She refused to give her father a win, even after his death.

She sipped her drink and studied the neat cursive on the crisp folded sheet of letterhead. Her own handwriting was messy and illegible. Her thoughts came too fast to worry about penmanship. Christopher took time in everything.

Swallowing a sigh, she set the mug on the saucer, lifted her chin, and met the gaze of the maître d'. "Of course. Thank you. Please charge the meal to my room."

"Very good, ma'am." Pierre bowed and held out her chair.

With her head held high, she walked through the restaurant at a leisurely pace. She tipped her head, nodding and waving at a few friendly faces. She'd been glad he caught at least a hint of her show. She'd felt his eyes on her, the awareness of him as comforting as a favorite sweatshirt. While she often found herself in the spotlight, she only cared if he was watching. She still craved his attention. Otherwise, why was she performing at all?

In the lobby, she held her shoulders back and continued at her own speed. Resting her hand lightly on the polished railing, she floated up the stairs to the top floor. She didn't let her mask slip until she reached the attic hallway. Then she braced her hands on either side of her waist and dragged deep breaths into her burning lungs.

She hated to appear winded, even if it was the truth. Smoothing her hands over the skirt of her dress, she continued down the corridor to the closed door. She knocked, her fist rapping against the wood in her three-knock-two-knock pattern.

"Enter." Christopher's deep voice carried through the solid panel.

She twisted the doorknob and let herself into the room, shutting the door behind her. Last night and earlier this morning, he had rushed her through the space without giving her a chance to study his office. If he wanted to put on a show of demanding her presence, he'd have to allow her to do so at her own pleasure.

In the early afternoon, the sunlight filled the room with a golden glow. With windows on three sides, it was almost like being in the tree house she'd always wanted and never received. Christopher created a sanctuary for himself. While the room was very one-note and seemed to be the result of an online shopping spree, incorporating no refurbished pieces or hints of his personality, he did a better job than she would have imagined.

The leather armchairs and ottoman were almost the same color as the massive desk. He didn't have any blankets or pillows. The lamps were all the same boring stick shape. Only the sizes differentiated them. He'd done well with the colorful antique rugs.

"Care to revise your opinion about my decorating in the light of day? Does my office meet with your approval?" he asked.

Heat crept up her neck, burning her ears. She glanced at him, seated behind his desk. She shrugged her shoulders and pulled out one of the wooden spindle back chairs opposite him. "It's not particularly cozy."

He snorted.

"But it's not bad. You did a decent job. I wouldn't hire you as a decorator based on the continued use of that awful cream paint everywhere."

He frowned, furrowing his brow. "What's offensive about a neutral color? Isn't it the standard, acceptable beige?"

"Exactly. It's predictable and boring. Shouldn't the Inn be a little bolder? More adventurous?"

"With paint?"

"With everything. The paint is a good start."

He scrubbed his hands over his face.

She hated it when he did that. The mannerism was dismissive. She wasn't here for his amusement or derision. She was here for her destiny. "You did a nice job in this room."

He dropped his hands to the desk and met her gaze. A soft smile tugged the corner of his mouth. "I had help."

Like Elise? Ashley's upper lip trembled, cracking the façade of her brittle smile. She couldn't let him see that she cared. Or, maybe she should start implying she had a far more interesting life. Like she left something, or someone, behind to grace everyone with her presence. If only she believed that, she wouldn't be groveling. "I've answered your call. What's next?"

"Working."

She waved her hand dismissively. "I am. You need my valuable input."

"I'm serious, and I need more than a few comments on my interior design skills." He slid a folder across the desk and tapped a finger against the smooth cover. "I've compiled everything you should know if you really intend to take over the resort."

She reached for the folder, careful to tug the free end. No accidental touches or innocent hand brushing. Unless she could somehow manage her expectations and only leave him wanting more. Opening the folder, she stared at the stapled sheets filling each pocket almost to bursting.

She leafed through one side. Numbers. She frowned at the collection of dates and times followed by spreadsheets with dollar amounts. On the other, she discovered pages of bullet points. He hadn't given up his micromanaging ways.

Maybe she'd have more support from the hotel staff than she first assumed. And she'd been foolish enough to go along with his plan this morning and act like a snob. How many people had she turned off with the act? It wasn't too late to correct her course and show more of herself. She could be charming. Far more than him. "I don't understand how this is part of the plan? Aren't I supposed to be investigating?"

"In due course," he said. "If you want to take over, you need to know what is involved in running the place."

"I can do this." She shut the folder and returned it to the tabletop. "I can run the resort. It's in my blood."

He rolled his eyes.

"I'm serious. It's my blood, not yours."

He didn't correct her. Their marriage had been against Dad's advice. Within a few months, she had regretted the whole situation. As she fell more in love with her husband, he seemed intent on ingratiating himself with her father more than ever. She found herself the odd woman out. Everything always worked out in Dad's favor. Even now, he continued to pull the strings and make them dance to his tune. "If this is a discussion of nature versus nurture, I have the advantage of both."

"Genetics notwithstanding, you need a general grasp of all the layers of the business. I have firsthand experience at every level. I can appreciate how my decisions reverberate through the ranks."

"How I run the Inn won't follow some strict set of arbitrary guidelines. It'll be more..." she studied his face. She knew the perfect word to set his teeth on edge. "Collaborative."

He flinched.

She was probably petty for how much she enjoyed his squirms. No doubt, he was imagining sharing circles and teambuilding therapy. The victory was short-lived.

"Making money isn't running a democracy," he intoned.

"As Dad told me plenty of times." If he were around, she'd ask him why. Dad could have written her out if he'd wanted to give Christopher the business. Why include her at all?

"What's your experience in the hospitality industry?"

The matter-of-fact question deflated her. He hadn't been following her brief stints in food service? She'd hoped he checked in on her social media accounts. She shifted on the seat. "I've dabbled in the service sector over the past few years. I'm more of a big-picture thinker."

He nodded. "Which is great, and I don't doubt your sincerity. But you need a practical understanding of the Inn. You have to get your hands dirty."

"Is that really necessary? Do I have to learn? Or am I proving something to you?"

"If running this place is so easy, why don't you show me?" He leaned forward, his hot breath tickling her cheek. "Unless you're scared, you can't..."

Her shiver had nothing to do with fear. She straightened

her shoulders. "Fine. Great. I'll be the hotel manager." She'd been the assistant for a short while during the summer before she graduated college. However, she remained fuzzy on the details. She had skipped the tutorial about the booking software in favor of sneaking to the beach as he lifeguarded. With her eyes closed, she could remember how the sun had glistened off his lean muscles. She had failed the swim test miserably and been put to better use indoors at Dad's insistence. She was sure she'd be more than capable as an adult.

"Oh no." Christopher waggled a finger in her face. "You'll work your way up. Just like I did."

She hoped he wasn't speaking literally. He'd started on the ground crew in middle school before moving on to bussing and then lifeguarding in high school. When he graduated college, he assumed a management role.

If she followed his path, she'd spend the day weeding the flower beds at the front entrance of the Inn, inhaling exhaust from idling vehicles waiting for the valet. She studied her chipped manicure. At least she hadn't fixed her nail polish yet. Within hours, her palms would be callused from manual labor.

With a placating smile, she studied him. How could she get out of it? Play into his concern about appearance? "Isn't that sort of vindictive? Do you really want your employees to think poorly of you? And give the townsfolk even more fodder?"

He steepled his fingers together and rested his elbows on the desk. "Exactly. I need you to make a show of doing whatever it takes to get the Inn. You'll look like the wronged heroine of the whole situation. You'll earn everyone's sympathy."

He had a point. She needed more. She wanted his support. "What will you do while I'm otherwise engaged? Ghost hunting?" She wanted him to find the answers. But she hoped he wouldn't poke around and disturb the ghost. Whoever haunted the abandoned building didn't want company.

The more she considered her experience with the lighthouse phantom, the more she questioned why her late father hadn't used that angle to keep guests from poking around the building. His treasure myth had stoked interest.

"Not quite." Christopher sighed. "I need photos and documentation. If it's foul play, I'll need to file a police report."

Reasonable and rational, as always. She wasn't surprised but concerned. Ghosts could still hurt non-believers. "You really think it's sabotage?"

"I don't know." He dropped his arms to the table. "An accident still seems the most reasonable explanation."

"When will you inspect the lighthouse?"

He stared at her, holding her gaze until his left eye twitched. Then he looked away. And she almost cheered.

"I'll have a look tomorrow. I don't want to make an insurance claim. The rates would spike, and I intend to renovate, anyway." He stared at her hard. "You're welcome, by the way."

She frowned. What could she owe him gratitude for?

"If I wanted reimbursement for the property, I'd have to involve the police." He steepled his hands together, pressing the fingertips against his chin. "You'd be in trouble for trespassing and held liable for the fire."

She hoped he was only thinking out loud. A legal issue was the last thing she needed. "I didn't start it," she said.

He pushed back his chair. "Whenever you want to tell me what happened, you don't need to worry about repercussions. I wouldn't be upset about an accident. I wanted a blank canvas. An intentional blaze, however, would change things." He strode around the table to lean against it, standing close and staring down his nose at her.

"I love the lighthouse. You know that." Her voice and

words were weak. She loved many things but had proved capable of blowing those up with the right motivation.

"Regardless of the lighthouse, you have to get going for your first job."

"I do?" She frowned.

He nodded. "The first sheet on the left pocket is a schedule for you of various jobs I've assigned you. You'll need to get started. You might want to change into jeans."

She opened the folder and scanned the page he mentioned, fighting the urge to roll her eyes. Concessions at the afternoon movie? She'd swap her heels for flats, her only compromise. She could do everything he did but better. She'd show everyone.

Shutting the folder, she interlaced her fingers on her lap. "Not today. Whatever you've assigned can start later. I have somewhere I'd like to go right now." *Start the way you intend to finish.* Dad's old advice rang through her mind.

"Already giving up?"

She snorted. "Hardly. If I'm back in time, I'll stop by the matinee and help." She stood and, with one quick nod, spun towards the door and left.

She was the one to exit first. Every time.

* * *

Christopher gritted his teeth as the door shut.

She was careful not to slam it behind her as she flounced away.

Giving up? Already? He'd barely given her a checklist, and she hightailed it out of the room. Rolling his neck, he rubbed the base of his skull just above his spine. He wasn't being fair. He hadn't asked for details. Now that she was officially back, she probably had places to go and people to see.

Who? He wasn't a jealous type. If she'd moved on during

the past ten years, could he really be that surprised? Out of sight, out of mind?

He powered up his laptop and glanced at his inbox. A message from a friend he'd met at a hotelier conference a few years ago popped up on the top of the to-be-read queue. The subject declared, *Don't say no immediately.*

Tom Lavande ran a resort on the Big Island of Hawaii. Roughly the same size as the Inn at Loon Lake, Hotel Lavande catered to high-end clientele with Tom's trademark French hospitality. Closer in age to Xavier than Christopher, Tom had hit it off with both men and jokingly tried to steal Christopher away from the Inn. While Christopher had never had the chance to visit, he'd felt a twinge of envy at the beautiful images of sun-soaked lanais off every room, an open-air lobby that led to the beach beyond, and a truly spectacular restaurant for viewing the sun dip below the ocean at dusk.

He clicked on the email.

I have sent you information and have a room ready. I would very much like to discuss selling Hotel Lavande to you. Sincerely, Tom Lavande.

Christopher stared at the screen. Tom offered paradise on a platter. Only a fool would turn down the offer, especially with the uncertain ownership of the Inn. Moving to one of the most remote islands in the world promised the ultimate escape. Christopher would have to take out a loan to make a purchase but would earn the money back in no time. He could start over somewhere new. He could leave everything behind.

He pushed away from his desk. Leaning against the windowsill, he angled toward the sunlight. If that happened to be the same direction as the main entrance, who cared? She'd have to be racing out of the Inn to make it through the lobby in the next few minutes. He still had plenty of time to observe where she was supposedly heading on her important errand.

Just don't date Zach Jenkins. If she moved back and settled here, she'd live her life in full view. He couldn't handle watching her move on with his enemy. Loon Lake didn't have many eligible bachelors. With slim pickings, Zach probably rose in any woman's estimation. Steve Prim might even be a candidate. Hadn't he had a crush on her years ago in high school? Sending her flowers on Valentine's Day before Christopher made his feelings known?

Christopher hadn't glanced at anyone else. Ever. To even consider dating again was ludicrous. Besides the fact that there were fewer eligible bachelorettes than bachelors in town, the very idea was ridiculous. How could he look at another woman? He'd held a diamond. He wasn't going back to rhinestones or sequins.

She drew every eye with her friendly, flirtatious personality. She was charming and endearing. She never met a stranger and seemed taken aback whenever she received a compliment or a phone number. She was a rare jewel.

Where could she head off to on some sort of all-important rendezvous that didn't involve another man? *If I consider Tom's offer, I wouldn't have to watch.*

He scrubbed a hand over his face, tension building in his temples. Leaving Loon Lake had never been a possibility. The community knew him from birth. Starting over was a shocking consideration.

However, he couldn't write off the idea. He had to consider everyone's best interest. Packing up and moving on would simplify everything. He didn't have generational ties to Loon Lake. Unlike Ashley.

Being curious about her had led him into repeated trouble. This time, he couldn't and wouldn't chase after her. He had his own problems and work to attend to. If he assumed the role of villain in her life to protect her from the truth, he would deal with the fallout. He couldn't unburden himself with honesty without inflicting pain.

For years, he'd been treading water in the icy lake. He had to stop. He'd reach the moment of either taking a full stroke toward the shore or letting go and sinking to the bottom. He couldn't stay in place any longer.

Back at the desk, he dialed the phone number he'd accidentally memorized over the past few weeks. Tapping a pen rapidly against the desktop didn't soothe him. Ashley returned, and a sudden tidal wave of emotions hit him.

"Boyd Printing," Seth answered. "How may I assist you today?"

"Seth, hi. It's Christopher Lewis at the Inn."

"Oh, good morning. How are you?"

Christopher smiled. Seth was a remarkably cheerful person. He was an optimist gliding from one day to the next. If he ever got upset, he never showed it. He rolled with the punches with his trademark good humor. "I'm well. Listen. The menus aren't quite right."

"Really?"

"Looks like the margins are off by an inch. We're nearly there. Can you rerun them?"

"I sure am sorry. I thought I nailed it this time."

"Me, too," Christopher said. After all the back and forth, he would usually be out of patience. But not with Seth. Getting angry with him was like raging at a dog. It served no purpose other than to show him he needed empathy. "Do you think you can run them this week? I want to get the new menus out as soon as possible."

"Absolutely. I'm finishing up another round of stickers today and plotting Soupy sightings on a map. But I'll add this to the list."

Pointing out that his side hustles barely broke even while the contract with his major customer kept his business afloat was also an exercise in futility. Seth operated on his own schedule. Christopher knew better than to explain his side of things again. Seth was one of his few allies in town, and alienating him wasn't an option. Instead of looking for problems, Christopher focused on the positive of Seth's passion project, a lake monster legend for the community. "How is Soupy? Any new sightings?"

"None lately." Seth sighed. "But the Prims haven't been out on the lake too much this year. I expect we'll be hearing about him soon. Zach is going to bring up the legend with his customers. I think once the idea spreads, it'll take off from there."

Christopher frowned. Should he do the same? Most of the Inn's tourists returned year after year. They'd notice something amiss on the water. But he was never sure how to explain. Soupy was Seth's very own Loch Ness monster. While Christopher couldn't understand how the creature existed, he appreciated the creative and industrious spirit that dreamt up the idea.

His world was black and white. This or that. Rational. Logical. He had always been drawn to imaginative, romantic types who understood the world on a completely different level.

He'd missed the wild fantasies of one particular mind in person. For too long, Seth had been the only visionary in town. Christopher supported anyone with a big plan. "Keep me posted."

"About the menus?" Seth asked.

Christopher smiled to himself. "And Soupy."

"Okay. Have a great day," Seth said.

"Bye, Seth." Christopher hung up the receiver, refraining from any sort of breathy exclamations until the call ended. At least he could count out Seth as a potential love interest for his wife.

He cradled his heavy head in his hands, digging his elbows into the desktop. His wife. Had he missed her? If he ran to the window now, could he catch a glimpse?

He couldn't. She came back to claim his hard work. She'd run the Inn out of business with her whims. He hadn't given everything he had to let her ruin the town. Enough with feeling sorry for himself.

He grabbed his tablet, flipped back the cover, and unlocked the screen. In a few swipes, he brought up Zach Jenkins' blog. While the website was almost solely dedicated to slandering Christopher, he couldn't stop himself from checking every day, several times. He probably had an excellent case for a libel suit. But he wasn't into censorship, especially when silencing his enemies would only embolden them to work in secret.

He'd rather see someone's ugly behavior so he could act accordingly, rather than think he had friends.

The blog had been updated in the last hour and was its usual diatribe about the community's ruin because of the Inn. Christopher's heartbeat slowed. No mention of his wife.

Wherever she went, she hadn't run off into Zach's arms. Good. That was something, at least. If he racked his brain, he didn't remember the few years older Zach ever paying Ashley any attention and vice versa. But only a few appropriately aged suitors lurked in Loon Lake. And he felt confident she wouldn't be interested in Seth. Only one dreamer per relationship seemed a solid rule for success.

It had never been him. He wasn't creative or witty. Not like her. She shined so brightly. Her leaving was inevitable.

He stayed. His strength was his character. He was steadfast. Years ago, she might not have said the words, but she delivered an ultimatum by leaving.

While he wasn't the cleverest, he wasn't a fool. As a rule, he learned to listen and consider. Then he'd plan and execute.

When Xavier had come to Christopher for help, he'd had to assist. He'd shielded her from the truth and couldn't tell her now—justifying his actions—without causing more pain.

He made his choice and would gain nothing by trying to rewrite the past. He could only go forward. And hope she moved on with someone he could stand.

Chapter Seven

As Ashley climbed to the top of the hill, she stumbled. Righting herself, she braced her hands on either side of her waist. Huffing and puffing told her more about her physical fitness than she cared to know. Of course, struggling in a nice outfit only added to the drama.

She was glad she'd put on sneakers before setting off from the Inn to her destination. The highest point in town was roughly a quarter of a mile east of the resort, overlooking the lake, and belonged to her family's property. The Hales had claimed a large portion of Loon Lake, selling parcels over the century but maintaining this secluded patch and the boardwalk as the farthest reaches of the empire.

Her dress clung to her back. Sweat beaded on her brow. She should have changed clothes. Once he had suggested the same, however, she refused. The dynamic between them had shifted. He'd always obeyed her orders. As the unquestioned boss, he expected her to listen to his demands. She bristled.

Conventional wisdom told her she should have swallowed her pride. But she hated that phrase. She wasn't opposed to benefitting from the intellect of others. She appreciated learning from those who had gone before and avoided repeating obvious mistakes.

What bugged her was the word *conventional*. It implied following along blindly to someone else's standards. She preferred to travel in her own direction and walked away.

She might have wiped that smug look off his face if she'd told him she wanted to head to the cemetery to pay her respects. But she didn't need to justify her actions. She wouldn't explain or complain. Relearning how to interact with him would be more complicated than she'd first thought.

The breeze picked up, tickling her cheeks. She gazed at the lake. The light danced on the dark water, making it sparkle despite its murky depths. The brightly painted boardwalk shops added cheer and pop against the otherwise green surroundings. The old sawmill gave her pause.

Alone on its own dock with massive concrete pylons, the building prioritized function over form. The business hadn't been operational in decades, however, thus finding fault in the argument with its current state. Only the giant wheel was visible from the original structure. The rest of the historic building had been clad in vinyl siding, erasing any character or interest.

In contrast, the lighthouse's exterior was fully intact and perfect. It had been off-limits for years. No one would glance at it twice. She shuddered. What if she'd been asleep during the fire last night? Smoke inhalation could have killed her, or she might have been trapped if the door caught the flames. She hadn't considered the danger of occupying the barely habitable space with no emergency alert system before her actions. Not that she was known for her circumspection, but as an adult, she should take more care.

"Mrs. Lewis?" A deep, familiar voice called.

She turned and squinted, raising a hand to shield her gaze as she blinked into the sun.

A large, shaded figure stood in the Hale Family Cemetery.

The hint of stale cigarettes danced on the breeze. Although, surprisingly, she'd never seen the person in question smoke. Groundskeeper Willie was more myth than man.

He stepped into the sun, his silver hair and beard almost blinding.

She rubbed her eyes, smiling as she neared. But he had already turned away, giving her his back as he worked.

At least Mr. Willie remained the same. Ashley found comfort in his typical, quick dismissal.

A wrought-iron fence enclosed the small cemetery plot set aside for the Hale generations' eternal rest. A rather extraordinarily grand vision of the legacy they'd leave, given all the challenges that arose in the years since and the decades of only children to boot.

"Mr. Willie? Now, you're using my married name?" Ashley inflected her voice with every bit of teasing she could manage. No one called her Mrs. Lewis. Ever. Not even when she had wanted them to use the moniker. Why did her heart skip a beat at hearing it now?

He stopped at the entrance, widened his stance, and crossed his arms over his chest.

That was probably the best response she'd expect from the often-irked man. She walked toward the entrance, swinging open the gate.

Rusty hinges squealed.

He flinched and pulled out a cell phone. He held the device to his mouth. "Oil hinges," he said, dropping the cell back into his pocket. Next to a plastic yard waste bin, a pair of pruning shears rested on the ground.

"Cleaning?"

He nodded. "Always. I wondered when I'd see you."

"I'm a little shocked you're still here," she said. And she was.

Mr. Willie had a reputation for working around the clock. Constantly on the prowl, no one knew the Inn's property better. *But he hadn't spotted me in the lighthouse?* She was glad he hadn't, but something about the oversight struck her as odd.

Christopher gave no indication he learned about her presence from any of the staff, including Mr. Willie. Mr. Willie had been neither her enemy nor her ally. Allowing her to squat in a derelict building was out of character. *Unless, he was responsible for the fire? Unless, he wanted me out of Christopher's way?* She swallowed, forcing down the lump choking her.

In his fifties, Mr. Willie was one of the people in the generation between her and Dad. Mr. Willie, as he requested she address him, had joined the staff in her early teens. While he knew her, he never had the best opinion. She'd been too old to leave the impression of a charming child. She'd been nothing but trouble from his first day, creating extra work for him after her escapades with Christopher.

Mr. Willie's job must be easier without her around.

"Are you back for good, then?" he asked, barely above a murmur. "It's been...different without you."

A sudden flash of sentimentality at his soft delivery took her by surprise. "Did I really leave?" Her voice wavered. From suspecting Mr. Willie of wanting her gone to almost asking if he wanted her here, her emotions swung too widely. She clasped her hands behind her back and strode forward, making a show of studying the graves, even as she gazed unseeing.

"Things changed while you were gone."

Like my husband. She wouldn't lead with that. She wasn't here because of Christopher. She'd come to pay her belated respects to her dad. The ending would be her lasting regret. Xavier had done the impossible, making her question herself. She should have been around for a proper goodbye. Not that anyone could have known. He went to bed and never woke up. His passing was peaceful and almost enviable, according to the lawyer, if someone could feel jealousy at the inevitable.

She smoothed her clammy palms on her pants. "Are you laying a headstone?" She stopped next to the grave of the mother she'd never met. The carved stone was weathered and beaten by time. But she knew it by heart, able to pull up the image whenever she needed comfort or to feel grounded.

In her opinion and imagination, the cemetery held no ghosts. She was hounded by her past and regrets far more in familiar places than the graveyard on the hill.

"No. Your father didn't want the ceremony or stress of a carved rock. He didn't want anything," Mr. Willie said gruffly.

She nodded. Xavier hated the idea of being buried. She agreed with him on that one point. Why waste the earth with her rotting remains? "Seems a shame not to have a place to go to think about him."

"Mr. Lewis was thinking of adding a bench."

She lifted her chin. "Really? Where?"

Mr. Willie pointed to a tree outside the confines of the cemetery.

She left the hallowed grounds and strode toward the spot. A few yards away from the gloom of the tombstones and iron fence, it was a nice location. The picturesque location made her mind whirr with potential posts. *Miss me, girlies? I've been offline. Can you blame me? Check out this gorgeous view.* If she wanted Dad to haunt her, she couldn't do more to disturb his restful slumber than overshare. She swallowed the dry laugh bubbling inside.

The longer she stayed off her social media accounts, the less she considered her faceless followers. She didn't crave their attention and validation. She was almost free from the need to please other people. Once she claimed her hotel, she'd chart her future to please herself first and foremost.

The breeze rushed through the Aspens, shaking each leaf. She turned toward the lake and the Inn below. From her vantage point, she could survey all that her family held so dear. *A good place to say goodbye.* She swiped at her misty eyes.

Out of the way of most hotel guests, the location wouldn't become a social media outpost as long as she didn't share the latitude and longitude with her followers. She'd transition her social media into a public relations vehicle to drive business. She turned back, retracing her steps to the enclosure.

On his knees, Mr. Willie tugged at weeds poking up around the granite markers of her ancestors.

"I don't suppose you could take me to the cottage?"

He leaned back, wiping a hand over his brow. "I can't."

Her heart dropped. She wanted to peek in on her old home.

He slipped a hand into his pocket and retrieved a keychain. He examined the tag and tossed the keys to her.

With a start, she reached forward and caught the keys.

"It's vacant today. Housekeeping might be cleaning before the next crowd. Lock up when you leave."

"Thank you." She pressed the keys between her palms. Turning, she strode down the hill and continued toward the cottage.

The former stables had been abandoned her entire life and her father's before her. She'd spent years daydreaming about it, utilizing it as a clubhouse and stage in childhood before the idea of moving out of the Inn and into the ramshackle stone walls. At first, she had set up an air mattress inside a tent in the open room with the sloped, brick floor. After a battle of wills, her father had given in and set her up with a budget and help.

She approached the building and slowed her steps, taking in every change. Calling it the cottage was a misnomer to make it seem quaint. The building was large enough to house carriages and horses. At nearly nine thousand square feet, she hadn't had plans of taking over the entire space. She'd happily claimed one-third of the building.

The stables had been further divided, an idea Xavier had shot down when she'd broached it. Christopher must have taken the lead. Her father would not have pushed ahead with more renovation. Christopher would have championed the expansion after the success of the cottage.

Her idea had sparked change. She would use every ounce of her creativity in running the Inn.

Outside the painted green door of her former home, she slipped the key into the deadbolt. The lock twisted open. And she stopped.

Her heart leaped into her throat. A dull ache settled in her cold, heavy limbs. From the outside, Loon Lake hadn't experienced any significant transformations. The little adaptations she learned about, from how the business had expanded to her father's final resting place, added up to one irrefutable fact.

She had been gone, and life had continued without her. She wasn't selfish enough to pretend the community had been held in stasis while she was absent. But this was one instance where she didn't want to know how time marched on. She didn't want to see what had changed on the other side of the door of her beloved home.

Maybe he had kept her paint colors and the cobbled-together kitchen, assembled from various reclaimed cabinets found on the property and at the town dump. Maybe he had upgraded the bathroom and installed the clawfoot tub she'd always talked about. Maybe he had left the building as a time capsule to their early days.

But probably he hadn't.

As a businessman, he would have swept in with his cool efficiency and erased everything nostalgic. She wasn't ready to accept how much the world moved forward while she was trapped in the past.

Instead of facing the situation head on, she locked the door, pocketed the key, and turned away. What were the odds that she'd come here to frighten her husband off the property and really only succeeded in finding all her old ghosts?

Striding out the front door and down the covered porch toward the gravel path, Christopher wasn't looking for his wife. Stalking her was too much. While he'd admit his curiosity peaked earlier, tangling up with an unexpected surge of jealousy, he had calmed down over the past hour. Rationality surged, subduing the excess of emotions, and he reasoned he could give her a little leeway. She hadn't rejected the schedule outright. She had merely said she had business to attend. He understood the value of seeing commitments through to completion.

As long as it's not romance. He gritted his teeth. He might have growled.

"Oh, hello," she said.

He lifted his head and spotted her.

She walked towards him from the direction of the cottage.

His heart caught in his throat. He shouldn't read into her visiting their former love nest. But she told him she had a big, important errand. Perhaps a sudden longing for the good old days prompted her.

He was disappointed by how the idea heartened him. She could have been curious about the updates. Then he'd have to be worried about what she'd think. She never wasted a chance to offer an opinion.

When he had renovated the other two spaces in the stables, he'd planned to update the worn-out features of their home for guests. He hadn't let the crew do much more than slap fresh paint on the walls and remove their belongings. Without their things, the cottage lost its coziness and intimacy. He had no qualms about renting the space to guests with the heart of their home long gone.

He cleared his throat. "Hello. Are you heading to the movie? You still have time to make it."

"Yes, I'll head over there now."

She sounded a little strained. Did she stop herself from rolling her eyes? He wasn't a nag and had never micromanaged her. But he had found a skill in being the one in charge.

"What are you doing? Looking for me?" She arched a brow, and the tilt of her mouth gave her lopsided expression a coy hint.

It did something to him. He hadn't had a visceral response in years. With her, he felt the overwhelming urge to kiss her until she had an entirely different reason to smile. If she could think straight. If he could remember why he grabbed her.

She stared at him pointedly.

He coughed. "Not quite. I was taking a walk to clear my head and get out of the building. I try to get fresh air every day, or it feels like I'm trapped under glass."

She rubbed her hands together, her gaze darting side to side. "Are you sure you want people to see us together?"

He shrugged. "It's sort of inevitable, isn't it? We're still married."

She had no response.

If she was worried about being spotted together, she shouldn't have introduced herself to the staff as Mrs. Hale-Lewis. His employees reported their initial meeting as soon as it happened. Distancing herself now didn't make sense. It was foolish to think they could pretend nothing shifted, or they hadn't evolved. She'd hurt him, and he'd hurt her. They had to deal with it and move forward the best they could. Something inside couldn't help but issue a challenge, though. "Want to run the gauntlet?"

She pulled a face and grabbed her waist, her skin turning green. "My stomach hurts just thinking about it."

He laughed. "You can't run to the boardwalk, drink three milkshakes, and run back anymore?"

"Can you?"

He shook his head. He hadn't been successful in their youth. "I haven't tried. I don't think I'd be welcome at the ice cream parlor anymore."

"Maybe we could just do the running and leave the dairy portion out of it. I wouldn't mind some exercise. I can't handle sugar anymore."

He wasn't sure he'd be welcomed or served inside Scoops, There It Is. He stuck out his hand. "Deal." He fought the urge to grip her delicate fingers tight and pull her close. A surge of warmth swept through him from the handshake. Letting go was never his choice.

She slipped her hand free and turned toward the front entrance.

He followed in silence. Being with her had always been enough. While she was exuberant and entertaining, she drained herself with her schemes. He liked the quiet times, too. Her company was enough.

A valet held open the front door for Ashley.

Christopher stepped back to let her pass first. As soon as he entered his lobby, he lost his grip on his new-found peace.

Steve Prim prowled near the base of the staircase.

Never a good sign. Steve Prim was a kind, if not very deep, person. The one-time high school sports star had become his father's stooge. Carl Prim was a known bully. Christopher feared Steve would go from victim to abuser. Ashley needed no part in that, whatever happened in their marriage.

Hopefully, she hadn't noticed the newcomer. Christopher reached for her elbow, lightly grazing it with his fingertips. Any more would be torture. She wasn't back to reconcile. She was here to destroy his whole world. He couldn't hand her the keys and walk away.

She turned toward him.

"The movie starts soon," he said. "I'll meet you there."

She shook her head. "Let me join you."

She recognized Steve and knew he'd only come for business. Christopher gritted his back molars. "Can you be a silent partner?"

"Hardly." She chuckled. "But I won't deliberately step in your way. I'm curious. If I take over, I'll need to work with the Prims."

At least she was honest. Christopher didn't want or need a complication in the surprise meeting with a vendor. But perhaps a glimpse of his reality would wake her up. Maybe she'd walk away. Again. "Alright."

Crossing the entryway together, he extended a hand as he approached the younger Mr. Prim. "Steve, hello, I didn't know we had plans to meet today."

Steve widened his eyes. "Ashley?"

"Hi, Steve, it's been a while. Nice to see you." She tucked a strand of hair behind her ear.

Judging by the man's shock, he wasn't a candidate for the secret romance she may or may not be conducting. Steve had never hidden his feelings. If he was still in love with Christopher's wife, Steve could get to the back of the line. Christopher mentally kicked himself. He had to focus. Business. Nothing personal. He crossed his arms over his chest. "Steve?"

"Right. I wanted to discuss the summer schedule. My apologies for the delay in launching the tours. The weather has not been cooperative," Steve said.

Christopher ground his molars. He hated excuses in general and saved special scorn for those easily proved false. Today's beautiful weather labeled Steve a liar or an idiot. *Why must I choose?*

"I would like to add to the tentative plan I've given you," Steve said.

This was good news. Maybe he'd misjudged Steve. It wouldn't be the first time one of his opinions had to be amended. But it had been a while. "More trips?"

"Actually, dinner cruises."

Christopher gaped. "Our guests love the tours. They are expecting a fun day on the water."

"Why not expand and let them dine under the stars?" Steve asked.

"Because that isn't what they are interested in," Christopher said. "Because it is a big undertaking. Because the restaurant business is hard, and most new ventures fail within the first year." Christopher said the words with slow deliberation. His main argument against the idea was that it could, potentially, undermine the Inn. At the moment, Christopher's business provided the only real fancy dining around, keeping a lot of the tourist dollars under his roof for the durations of their stays. He hadn't heard any complaints. The Inn's offerings were enough to convince guests to return year after year.

"What a lovely idea," Ashley exclaimed. "Are you launching this summer?"

"Yes, we have a chef and staff." Steve bobbed his head and grinned broadly, basking in Ashley's glowing encouragement. "We were hoping to send updated material soon. Seth's a little backed up on print jobs at the moment."

Christopher side-eyed Steve at the last statement, disliking the cheap slight aimed at Seth. Christopher hated hearing about a fully formed plan like it was merely an idea.

Steve hired staff and a chef. Christopher hadn't heard any rumors or read any *now hiring* posts on the town's website. Christopher questioned the whole endeavor.

The Prims were the only business outside of Christopher's purview. He had consolidated power to never be caught unaware. No one could blindside him like she had. Yet, somehow, someone found a way. He pressed his lips together. He had nothing to say that wouldn't leave him with regret.

"Do you have anything you can leave? A mock menu or a list of price points on scratch paper?" she asked.

Steve reached into his back pocket and handed over a folded sheet of paper. "It's a rough draft of the brochure. Seth is going to print them for me as soon as he finishes the menus."

Don't hold your breath. Christopher kept his gaze fixed on Steve to stop his eyes from rolling. Instead, a vein throbbed in Christopher's temple for the exertion of restraint. He couldn't let Steve walk away thinking he had the upper hand. "You have a good set-up here. You sell out most of your tours. Get your boats back on the water. Leave this idea to another time."

"Review the materials. We can talk again. Great to see you again, Ashley," Steve said. With a slight bow, he strode away.

Ashley opened the sheet and narrowed her gaze at the wrinkled paper. After a few seconds, she looked over his shoulder and sighed. "He left. Why weren't you more encouraging?"

"Because... this is a... change." The words sounded flimsy the second he said them. He had doubts about Steve and Carl. But Christopher wasn't sure Ashley would listen and commiserate as his spouse or roll her eyes at his concerns.

She shot him her incredulous, withering stare. "Life is change."

"Not always for the better. We don't have to force transformation. Let it evolve naturally. Slowly." *Like us.* The thought tickled his Adam's apple. Their failed marriage was hardly the proof he wanted. Yes, they'd gone from childhood friends to madly in love. And the breakdown of their marriage —one fight he hadn't realized was the end, when she asked him to choose between the Inn and her and he froze—only signaled they had been wrong to ever try for something more. Not that he'd regret a single day he held her in his arms. He only mourned for the loss.

"The glaciers made more progress during the Ice Age." She crossed her arms over her chest. "Give me the real answer."

He scrubbed his hands over his face. Whatever role she assumed, she wouldn't be his subordinate. Acting like he was the sole decision-maker wouldn't work. He'd try a different tactic. Honesty. "Okay, it's competition. Part of our success was keeping guests on our property. These cruises will steal from the restaurant."

She nodded.

He felt a little lighter. Her agreement eased his inner critic more than was good. Her insistence on the plain truth revealed something he'd hidden. He'd spent years running away from confrontation by avoiding frank discussions like this. He operated as the boss and never an equal. Only Xavier had given him orders. But she challenged him in the best way. "Great. You're on board."

"I understand your perspective," Ashley said. "But I disagree."

Those three words popped him like a balloon.

"It's an entirely new branch for the Prims," she said. "It might not last a month, let alone forever. Why not encourage them? At the very least, you're expanding the Inn's offerings. Maybe it's something different enough to encourage families to return; they feel like they haven't had a chance to see everything here."

"Have you?"

The corner of her mouth quirked. "I hope I never learn all the Inn's secrets. I love a mystery."

"I don't."

She rolled her eyes. "Oh, I know. You're very black and white. Case in point, the Prims' expansion. You can't control everything, and you shouldn't want to. Let guests create their own narratives. Give them the freedom to choose you."

He opened his mouth and stopped. He'd totally forgotten her capability. Part and parcel of her unwavering self-confidence was her ability to jump into any situation and navigate to success. She'd drawn him in with her bravado, and he had tried, unsuccessfully, to emulate it. She always had answers. Letting her call all the shots again was more tempting than she could realize.

The concierge, Mr. Brixen, approached. "The movie is starting. Are you helping us, Mrs. Hale-Lewis?"

A funny look passed over her, clouding her blue eyes for a second. She nodded. "I guess that's my cue?"

He didn't reply, watching her leave and letting the moment sink in. Shouldn't his loyalty to her family and the legacy be worth something? She remained charming as always. He'd been more susceptible to her charm than anyone else. He could see himself slipping under her spell all over again. It would be easy to let her take charge and not look too far into the future.

He couldn't. He had to resist. Everything was different now. Especially him.

Chapter Eight

In the chilly, pre-dawn air, Ashley tucked her hands into the cuffs of her sweatshirt, seeking warmth for her icy fingers, and continued around the perimeter of the Inn. She was up early with a purpose, find Mr. Willie and return his keys. Her simple mission encountered one set back after another.

The front desk clerk spotted Mr. Willie headed to the back lawn ten minutes earlier. By the time she cut through the building, she found only a couple of employees arranging the chairs on the patio. They pointed her toward the front entrance. Once again, she arrived too late. The valet saw Mr. Willie on his way to the coach house. She tired of chasing him but refused defeat.

She turned toward the cemetery, thinking one step ahead. Hopefully. Or perhaps she needed more physical exertion and the calm that hung in the air at a higher elevation. She'd been suffering from an excess of feelings for the past week, and she wasn't sure what to make of it.

Yesterday, she had started to think of herself as capable. She had answers and a clear head when Steve Prim appeared.

She could offer something of value and another perspective to the Inn. When her husband had been flabbergasted, she had found her strength. It was too bad her ego had burst like one of the balloons she'd overinflated at the movie matinee only minutes later. Balloon animals required skills she hadn't mastered.

At the children's request, and after a few tears from popped animals, she had shifted to snack duty. She couldn't stop thinking about the Prims, her husband, the Inn, and her father. Her distraction led to burned popcorn in the kettle. The smell had dissipated somewhat but hung like a phantom in the lobby as she exited.

With a shake, she focused on the slippery grass as she climbed the last bit of the hill. Huffing and puffing, she hadn't managed to shift from her issues to the pain in her aching muscles. She found a spot and sank onto the damp ground, drawing her knees to her chest and slipping her legs into the oversized sweatshirt for warmth.

"Dad? You out there?" she whispered. She hadn't said that name out loud in a long time. It scratched her throat. "What did you want to happen? Why weren't you more explicit with your will? It's not like you."

A weight slipped off her shoulders. The tickle in her nose disappeared. "You know what bugs me the most? We left so much unspoken. Neither of us wanted to share what we were actually going through. I don't want that anymore. I want everyone to know everything I'm feeling and thinking. I want to be understood."

Or maybe just one person. She gazed toward the Inn, willing him to appear. He didn't. Christopher was busy somewhere with something more important than her whims.

"It would be so easy for Christopher and I to slip back into our old patterns. We can't. He's different. So am I, although I'm not sure how much of my transformation has been positive." She untucked her legs and reached for a weed, ripping the leaf along its central vein. "You might have liked how I've been humbled. I wish I could get to know Christopher. You set him up to be my enemy. Or maybe you thought he'd be an ally? Why didn't you just tell us who deserved to take over the resort and why. Then I wouldn't have to decide..."

She couldn't say the next part. She could barely think it. Tugging the sweatshirt lower, she searched for every ounce of warmth and protection from the chill in the morning air.

"Why is Christopher so discouraging to Steve Prim? Why not encourage him? The expansion has nothing to do with Christopher's money. Why should he care?"

Because he knows what happens when you run out of money. She shivered. She remembered the hard days in middle school. Christopher's parents worked hard and provided him a normal, middle-class life. Until his dad got injured on a construction job when Christopher was eleven and a string of surgeries created a mountain of medical bills. It was almost impossible for the Lewis family to ever get out of debt. Christopher became a zealot about saving for a rainy day. As a kid, he had taken every odd job he could find.

She didn't have a healthy relationship with money either. She wouldn't have survived without Dad's continued financial support. What happened now that Dad was gone? What was her next step?

"Hey, stop ripping up my grass," a deep voice called.

Startled, she scrambled to her feet, wiping her hands over dew-soaked pants and pulling the sweatshirt low. "Mr. Willie?"

"None other." He lifted the latch on the gate and let himself inside the cemetery, hinges squealing. From a tool bag on the ground, he pulled out a canister and sprayed indiscriminately.

He wasn't silent, making noise as he worked, and, the

smell that clung to him—stale cigarettes—permeated the air. Her senses should have alerted her to his presence earlier. Lost in her thoughts, she was too easily startled.

Or was he capable of stealth?

She'd never been a kid detective, and she wasn't a paranoid person. Days later, she couldn't shake the awareness during the last night at the lighthouse. She hadn't been entirely alone inside the building.

Christopher ignored her ghost claim and insisted a human was responsible. She didn't think anyone in town could have crossed the bridge without alerting her. But Mr. Willie snuck up on her a minute ago. *Had Mr. Willie started the fire?*

She feared that answer more than any other. She preferred a ghost.

"Stop messing with the grass," he barked. "Don't rip it. Don't kick it. Just leave it."

She froze with the toe of her shoe digging into the ground. Being called out like a child didn't feel good. But she was relieved. Mr. Willie couldn't be the ghost. He would have berated her for trespassing and disturbing the sanctity of the lighthouse. He couldn't stay silent about any of the property under his purview. "Mr. Willie, did you track me down?"

The pinched expression he shot her as he looked over the gate chilled her. She delivered the question as tease. She'd been hunting him. His reaction was too serious.

"Can you blame me if I did?"

She reddened. No, she could not. As much as she might wish to erase some of her more spirited escapades from the community's collective memory, she couldn't. Part of coming home was accepting that everyone had a firm opinion of her.

The best she could do was prove she'd matured through her actions, not her words. But, right now, she needed a little clarification. "Are you acting on your own accord? Or going along with someone's orders?"

He chuckled. "I'd forgotten how your mind fills in the blanks. You're always so darn entertaining."

Like a clown? She smiled weakly. He'd evaded her with skill, a worthy verbal sparring partner. She'd keep that in mind for future encounters.

He turned away. "No one told me to follow you. I saw you on my rounds and thought you might have my keys."

She approached the fence, the top railing only reaching her waist. "I was looking for you all morning. You're tough to stalk." She tossed the keys.

He caught them with one hand. "Good. I'd hate to be predictable. How did you find the cottage?"

"The same." *More or less.* She wasn't sure telling him she'd been too chicken to go inside reflected well on her.

Mr. Willie attached the keys to his belt via a retractable clip. "I've fixed a few leaky pipes and patched the roof over there. Not much else."

Good. The ramshackle décor had been thrown together out of necessity. Christopher had money now and could easily fix up the place. He could rip out the mismatched cabinets and tear out the broken tiles, leveling the floor. But she hated to think anything had changed. The cottage remained a perfectly intact love nest, waiting for their reconciliation. "What are you doing now?"

"Oiling the hinges and scraping off the flaky paint." He flicked his fingers to the fence. "Touch up with a coat of spray paint for the time being. Until I can get more time." He dropped the canister into his bag and faced her. "Why are you back?"

"Why not?" She shrugged.

"Weren't you off having adventures? Nothing adventurous around here. Same old, same old." He shook his head.

"Mr. Willie, do I hear regret?" She was intrigued. He wasn't a person to her as much as a living, breathing symbol of authority. He was his role. But even Mr. Willie had hopes and dreams.

"Lass, I'm not one for wishing my life away." He shook his head. "Why come back if not to take over? What are you going to change?"

"Why do you think I intend to shake things up?"

He chuckled. "Isn't that your MO?"

She would have blushed. But a surprisingly cheeky grin hadn't accompanied his rhetorical question and softened the delivery. "Well, I can assure you. I have nothing planned. Not a thing," she said. *Except everything to do with my dad's plan.* Perhaps that was unfair. Just because she was haunted by ghosts didn't mean anyone else was. She couldn't toss out everything that worked to satisfy her need for exorcism. And, more than likely, it was impossible. "Any suggestions?"

"Ha. Right there." He waggled a beefy finger. "Do you see? You've got a clear advantage. The difference between you two. What's lacking now? Since you left, it's been one vision, and that's it. Either we fall in line, or we leave. You are open to ideas. You'll go a long way."

It was also part of why she left. She'd grown tired of trying to get her father's approval and be welcomed into the fold of upper management. Once Dad had taken her husband under his wing, she had had to work for Christopher as well. Had she been missed? She'd ponder the idea later.

"As long as you don't focus on anything too trendy," Mr. Willie said. "Of course."

"What do you mean?"

"Your photos and posts. You seem very involved on those websites. Life is about a lot more than a pretty picture. I'd rather not chase guests out of restricted areas because they are snapping selfies."

Her skin burned. While she happily asked for details about her husband, she couldn't forget she was also under close observation. Her movements were open for public dissection. She'd done that. If Mr. Willie followed her exploits online, everyone in town must do the same. She'd left her profiles public, hoping to reach her husband as he scrolled online, spurring him into missing her.

She had thousands of followers and interacted with many of them. But she didn't know the commenters on a personal level. Performing for a faceless crowd was easy. Sharing her hopes and fears with the people she knew best was terrifying. She aimed for vague wording so no one saw through perfection to the loneliness.

She knew she was a lot. She had a history of doubling down on her mistakes. She wasn't sure if she wanted redemption or a second chance. Both worked.

"I better get started on my list."

"No more popcorn?" He winced.

She rolled her eyes. "Goodbye, Mr. Willie."

* * *

The morning never quite dawned. With a frown, Christopher blew across the steaming mug of coffee as he surveyed the lawn behind the Inn. Under the overcast sky, the grass shone with a vibrant green more brilliant than the rest of the surroundings.

The lake, on the other hand, was gray and angry. He shared an affinity with the body of water. The choppy surface reflected his inner turmoil. He'd done so much work for so long. She pinned her future on his departure.

He raised the mug and sipped, letting the dark roast wash the bitter taste from his mouth. For so long, she'd been his motivation. When she never contacted him about a divorce, she gave him the false impression she'd return one day.

The woman haunting the lighthouse wasn't the same that captured his heart. And yet, he wasn't dissuaded. She changed. He had, too. But they had this time together now. Whether Xavier intended to or not, he had brought them back together. Christopher wondered if they could find something better together than the emotional stasis they'd achieved apart.

Movement across the shoreline caught his attention. He raised his hand, shielding his gaze as he squinted. She might as well have been a mirage.

Dragging a mesh bag behind her, she set up the cones along the perimeter of the swimming area.

The lake wasn't the sole domain of the Inn. As much as he had tried to claim it, he couldn't. And Xavier hadn't wanted the monopoly on water sports and activities. While the Prims were frustrating, they ran a solid business alongside the Inn, catering to the guests. The Inn and the Prims squabbled over the years, but Xavier had been happy to keep the uneasy partnership.

Maybe he'd been correct. Adding a whole new set of costs to the business when it wouldn't necessarily increase revenue was a poor choice. Christopher wanted to be the undisputed ruler of all. She wasn't wrong when she'd called him out for micromanaging.

But now she surprised him. She'd read the schedule and didn't need to be roused to start her work. He couldn't fault her punctuality. Maybe she had made some changes. She remained bullheaded but listened. He strode toward her. He couldn't be complacent. She might not be his enemy, but she was not his friend either.

"Hello." He called, cupping both hands around his mouth as he approached.

She straightened, stretching her back and waving. "Almost set here."

"You'll need to wheel the lifeguard chair into place."

"I'm on it. Once I finish setting up, I have a break. Figured

I could take initiative and lead activities. I'm happy to be helpful."

Sure, she was thrilled to help him off the property. If she needed fire to smoke him out, she'd grab the matches in a heartbeat. He darted his gaze, checking all the fire pits remained covered. "Let's not rush into anything."

"You don't think I can work with the guests?"

His mouth twitched, a smile threatening to reveal itself. "Let's review your efforts so far. How did the movie matinee go yesterday?"

She sighed. "I burned the popcorn and popped all the balloon animals."

He swallowed his triumph. He didn't want her humiliated, just humbled. Working at the Inn wasn't complicated but demanding. Customer service hours were long and seldom rewarding. After standing and smiling for hours, he fought through the pain and frustration to get up and do it all again the next day. No breaks. He never vacationed.

"Sorry if I didn't appreciate the hands-on nature of your work." She folded her arms over her chest and eyed him from head to toe. "My mistake. I guess I pictured it as more of a leadership position on offer, considering your grand spot at the top of the world."

He rolled his eyes. *You should.* "Let's start fresh today. I gave you plenty of time off in the schedule so you can head over to the boardwalk shops and poke around. Gauge the responses as you greet old faces. Maybe your ghost will reveal themselves."

"Fine. After I finish the manual labor, I'll do your dirty work. Just tell me the truth. Are you inspecting the lighthouse?"

"I'm headed there right now."

"Good. Leave the door open. Just in case."

In case your ghost is still there? He was almost touched by her concern. But he wouldn't give her even the hint that he believed in her fake spirit. With a wave, he turned toward the lighthouse and headed that way, sipping his coffee.

Crossing the wooden bridge, he set his empty mug on the ground and scrubbed his hands over his face. This wasn't his first inspection of the building following the fire. But he wanted to approach it like it was. What wasn't he seeing? What clues had he overlooked? Touring the inside of the lighthouse, he stared up at the beacon light overhead. He wasn't going to test the strength of the metal stairs to inspect up close. From his perspective, he didn't see anything amiss.

He pulled out his cell and powered on the flashlight app. Shining the light in every direction, he saw no change from any other walk-through.

The walls remained sound. The renovation project wouldn't require a complete demolition and new build. The building wasn't perfect, but it contained historic charm in its original construction that he'd hate to lose.

Named Fred's Folly, the inoperable lighthouse had been a popular spot from the moment it opened. Tourists loved climbing to the top for a view of the whole lake. Without any extra capital for maintenance and repairs, the lighthouse transformed into a ticking bomb ready for the detonation of wrongful death and injury lawsuits. The lighthouse had been built to lay claim to the island before the Prims could build a dock off it in the 1920s. The Hales strong-armed the town's then-mayor into signing over the deed, and construction began before the Prims knew about the change in ownership.

While a feud hadn't erupted—most generations working well together—bad blood simmered between the families lingered. By extension, growing up on Hale property, Christopher learned to always be wary around a Prim even though he never had a reason for his vague unease.

Xavier, Ashley's father, had closed the lighthouse in the

late nineties. Then he developed the cursed treasure legend as explanation and, in doing so, inadvertently drummed up more interest. Christopher had chased off his fair share of lookie loos. By some miracle, none of the trespassers had ever been injured and sought restitution. During the Inn's financial lean years, a single lawsuit could have threatened the entire business.

With several decades of history behind it, Christopher could understand how the line between myth and reality blurred over the years. Longevity lent credence to even the most ridiculous tale. A big part of him worried that particular story was now haunting him.

He didn't see shovels or crowbars. No one was looking for loot that didn't exist. And, thankfully and more importantly, he saw no evidence of sabotage.

As he exited the lighthouse, he became aware of a disaster unfolding in slow motion. Standing alone on the tiny island, he was helpless to do anything but watch in horror and shock.

The lifeguard chair rolled down the sloping lawn from the storage shed. Picking up speed, it didn't stop on the sand or topple over. The chair rolled into the lake, only stopping as it slipped under the water's surface. The top of the umbrella barely visible.

The scene was like a pirate riding a sinking schooner into a Caribbean port a la Hollywood. He turned toward the shed and spotted her. Her eyes were as round as her opened mouth. With his luck, the Prims' boat would hit the thing, and then he'd have to pay for repairs. Knowing overbearing Carl Prim, the man would steer every broken-down vessel into the hazard to fleece the Inn into paying for a new fleet.

He jogged toward her. "What happened?"

"I guess I didn't set the brakes for the wheels." Her tone was low. Her whole demeanor shocked into stiffness.

He shook his head. "I don't get it. You worked here in the

summers. You weren't helpless then. You were always so capable and confident."

"Well... you know I wasn't great about doing as I was told."

He swallowed, appreciating her honesty. Back then, she had balked at every rule and regulation. Unless she came up with the idea. But he also remembered a girl who flitted through the Inn from one task to the next with ease. He could picture her here, there, and everywhere. Always smiling and charming the employees and guests. He didn't remember any complaints from anyone besides Xavier.

"I don't think I officially worked a full shift. Ever." She sighed. "Guess I really am as helpless and aimless as Dad said."

Christopher hated the edge in her tone. While she was often self-deprecating, the reluctance and acceptance of failure didn't align with the capable person he knew. "We all start at the bottom."

She snorted. "Some of us keep slipping down no matter how hard we climb." She smoothed her hair behind her ears and pressed her hands to her cheeks.

Was she trying not to cry? He wanted to comfort her but wasn't sure how or if she'd welcome his consolation. He wasn't pleased to see her at a disadvantage, especially not if he stood to benefit. "Okay. You've done enough today here. Maybe go to the boardwalk and see what you can learn."

"You promise you're not mad?" She wrinkled her nose.

He hated when she was so adorable. He was justifiably mad. She'd cut him off at the knees, losing a lifeguard chair. His beach had to close to his guests on an afternoon that was finally forecast to be warm enough for swimming. Guests would be displeased. His day was exponentially harder.

But how did he stay upset when she was so disappointed in herself? "I'm frustrated. It's the second costly accident you've had in a week. I don't quite understand how either happened." He sighed. "I'm not mad."

And he was surprised at the truth in the sentiment. But now he needed to find a couple strong swimmers to help him retrieve the chair, or he'd be in worse shape.

Chapter Nine

Ashley wasn't leaving the Inn because she'd given up or because she was following his orders. It just so happened that his suggestion to take the rest of the morning off and stop at the boardwalk had been her plan all along. Or so she'd repeat until the sentiment became a mantra as she headed on foot toward the shops a couple miles away.

Joggers and cyclists passed her as she followed the path along the shoreline. It was too early for other leisurely strollers. She filled her lungs with fresh air and let the cool morning breeze chill her hot skin. The morning couldn't have gone worse. She'd been doing a decent enough job until she sank the lifeguard chair in the lake. *Did he suspect her of sabotage or foolishness?* She didn't know which option was better.

At least he had taken the time to inspect the lighthouse.

He might not believe her fears about a ghost, and with another night in a warm, cozy bed, she wasn't sure she believed it either, but he still investigated the scene. As she finished setting the cones, she lost sight of him. She'd returned the mesh bag to the shed and grabbed the lifeguard chair and umbrella. She wheeled the white chair out of the shed when motion caught her eye. Standing on tiptoes, she'd craned her neck to watch him exit the lighthouse and stepped away from the chair. Then disaster struck from a careless oversight.

It was the third mistake since Christopher handed her the folder yesterday. She hated to admit she was probably in over her head with the Inn. If she couldn't run the resort, what else could she do? On her own, she hadn't exactly blazed a trail to success. Rather, she'd slunk off and licked her wounds, waiting to return.

She shook her head as she reached the boardwalk, climbing the steps to the raised walkway and shops along the curve of the lakeshore. She wasn't meant for menial tasks. As the boss, she'd be great, utilizing her skills of managing and charming people as the moment demanded. And she'd show him by interviewing the shopkeepers.

She wouldn't mind a couple scoops of rocky road for breakfast. She wasn't sure forcing him out was best for the Inn. And if she did, she wasn't prepared to lead a mob of angry villagers behind her. But she wanted to hear what they said about him.

Pushing up the door of Scoops, There It Is, she was greeted with nineties R&B. She hummed along to the music. The decade of her birth was old enough to inspire a retro ice cream shop. When she was a kid, the store had been called Dig This and was decorated with flower power and groovy motifs. It was a rather depressing thought to realize her memories were now sepia-colored and vintage.

"Just one minute," a deep voice called from the back.

The setting was photogenic enough for a prominent feature on her social media. Bright colors and nostalgia were always a hit with her followers. She froze. She hadn't posted in weeks and hadn't mentally composed anything for days.

I don't need to.

She didn't want to curate Loon Lake for the outside world. She didn't want to stage and choreograph her life here. When she assumed control of the Inn, she'd utilize her skills for the benefit of marketing. In her day-to-day? She wanted to live.

She approached the counter, strolling by the display freezer at the tubs. Brightly colored bubble gum and mint cookie contrasted with the standards of chocolate, vanilla, and cookie dough. She scanned the names, spotting the selection of sorbets and sherbets, and frowned. Where was the rocky road?

"Yo! It's a fresh day to keep it real. What may I—Ashley? Hey, didn't know you were back."

She lifted her head and spotted Zach Jenkins carrying a huge tub marked Rocky Road in loopy script. His uniform, a fluorescent-green t-shirt under bright-white overalls, one snap undone, followed the shop's theme. She smiled at the blinding ensemble.

"Hi, Zach." She smoothed her hair behind her ears. "Yep, just got back yesterday." The lie tickled her tongue.

"Sorry for your loss. I know things were... complicated." He frowned, depositing the tub in its place.

A few years older, Zach had been a senior when she was a freshman. She had always treated him as something of an elder statesman. With his love of giving opinions—or passing judgment, as Christopher often said—Zach had strong convictions and was always ready for a verbal fight.

"Thanks, I appreciate the sentiment," she said smoothly. "I love the revamp." She regretted tossing her old clothes. Her pleather boots would fit right in with the ice cream shop. She pulled a brightly colored scrunchie from her back pocket and tied her hair in a side pony.

"Nice." He nodded slowly, dragging the word out. "You fit right in here."

"Is it too early for two scoops?"

"Never." He grabbed the scoop and a bowl. "Rocky Road?"

Home is where everyone knows your favorites. She hated agreeing to act as a double agent against the first person offering her a warm welcome. "Yes, please. Best way to start the day. So, how are things here? I've only been back a few days, but it seems…"

He stuck a spoon in the bowl and handed over the ice cream. "Different? Does the general vibe seem off?"

She nodded, grabbing the bowl with both hands. Digging in, she savored the sweetness on her tongue and crunched the nuts.

"Start of the season is always rough. This year is even more so than usual." He strode down the length of the counter to the register, ringing up her purchase.

She followed and paid in cash, grabbing a ten-dollar bill from her back pocket and stuffing the change in a tip jar. "Because of my dad?"

"Not exactly. The weather has been off. Climate change is Lonnie's go-to scapegoat for why he's having trouble with his fudge." Zach rolled his eyes. "The Prims haven't started their tours on the water yet. They probably have a legitimate reason. Losing your dad has shaken up the community, too. How are you doing?" he asked, softening his tone.

A flare of emotion tickled her nose and enflamed her throat. The earnest sincerity touched her. She shrugged. "I'm okay. Thanks."

"If you need to talk, you can come here."

She nodded and stuffed another scoop in her mouth. The good and bad part of coming home was the shared history.

Zach had had a contentious relationship with his own late father.

"Okay, enough small talk." He rubbed his hands together. "Are you staking your claim to the Inn? Asserting your rightful ownership and kicking out your husband?" He shook his head. "I sure hope so. We all would."

"Really? What's been going on?"

"Your husband." Zach released a world-weary sigh. "He's run the Phillips family out of the arcade. It's been taken over by someone new."

She widened her gaze. "Why? What happened?"

"Short story is your husband's tyrannical demands. He pretty much expects us all to kiss the ring," Zach said. "If you're interested in the full details of the last five years, I've been blogging about it."

She wasn't sure what was more horrifying: that her husband's micromanagement had extended beyond the perimeter of the Inn, seemingly with her father's blessing, or that she was expected to sift through a personal website for the details. She liked Zach but he had a pretty big opinion of himself. The blog was probably a navel-gazing page devoted to him. Inwardly, she winced. She was guilty of the same on her accounts. "What's your blog called?" she asked, forcing a smile.

"The Jenkins Report. I've detailed the whole affair from the beginning. He acts like the king of Loon Lake and lords over us mere shopkeepers like we're serfs."

She pressed together her lips. Zach needed to sort through his analogies. Was Loon Lake in the modern era or the Middle Ages?

Technically, the boardwalk shops were part of the Inn. Christopher had every right and responsibility to ensure a smooth operation. Only the Prim's business was its own enterprise. Christopher had seemed off-balance by Steve's proposal. *Because he had gotten used to ruling everyone else?* "Last five years? Can you give me the condensed version?"

"He changed the terms of all of our leases. We can't transfer from one family member to another." Zach crossed his arms over his chest. "Each year, to renew, we have to present a formal business plan. He wants to know our costs and plans for growth. Often, he asks us to reevaluate and update. He'll stop in to see that we're sticking to our plan."

She scooped up a large bite of ice cream, stuffing it into her mouth to give herself time to think. Christopher was always overly involved in business. She remembered giving up on the lemonade stand they'd started because he became obsessed with optimization. She wanted to make some money to go to the arcade and get an ice cream.

He was a micromanager to the nth degree. Over the past twenty-four hours, he'd watched her complete mindless tasks like he didn't trust her to get on with it. He might have a point in light of the minor disasters she'd caused, but still she commiserated with Zach.

She swallowed her bite. "I always forget how good the ice cream is here."

Zach smiled. "That's because I make it from my family's basic recipe and work with a local dairy. Being a small batch company means I focus on quality. That was one of the things we fought over. He thought I should change for the sake of profits." Zach crossed his arms over his chest and leaned against the back wall. "I had a different idea." He pointed over his head.

Ashley lifted her gaze to a row of brightly colored T-shirts on the back wall. A neon green shirt was emblazoned with the Scoops, There It Is logo on the front pocket. Next to it was the shirt displayed in reverse with the phrase "A day without ice cream? As if!" in white letters. A neon yellow shirt had the same front logo design. The back read "Full PHAT ice cream."

"I've done a lot of online sales from my merchandise. Tourists love the slogans."

"What a great idea." She stuffed another spoonful into her mouth.

The merchandise was cute. Pun-based slogans and throwback styles popped up on the social media accounts she followed. She wouldn't be surprised if T-shirt sales cleared overhead costs for the ice cream shop.

"Another thing your husband and I disagree on. He doesn't get what I'm doing, and he definitely doesn't respect my process. I deliver product I'm proud of whether its buttons or mint chocolate chip."

While she savored the result of his efforts, she couldn't stop wondering what was wrong with making a profit. Christopher would have suggested ways to optimize production, increase efficiency, and cut costs. He was predictable and steady. While his micromanaging ways could feel oppressive at times, she knew from experience, he wanted the best for others.

Zach balking at Christopher's ideas wasn't a surprise. He'd been their town's undisputed golden boy for years. She remembered Zach ignoring advice in their youth.

They'd all grown up, but maybe the two men reverted to childish patterns without a referee. Zach and Christopher fought the same battle, to stay in business. Together, they could be a formidable team.

Zach sighed heavily, shaking his head. "But then again, why should he? He's never been a creator. He isn't in his family's business. He swoops in and focuses on the bottom line."

He's been successful. Without a doubt, what Zach described was overstepping. Somewhere between the two sides of the story lurked the truth. Was she that middle ground? She could defend her husband and help ease some of his harsher rules and regulations. At the moment, that didn't help her plan or his. If she stayed...

"Hey, have you heard anything about a ghost at the lighthouse?" she asked. A complete change of topic was her only option to save the meeting.

"A ghost?" He wrinkled his brow.

"It's closed. Looks like something happened there."

"Hasn't it always been closed?" He tipped his head to the side.

"When we were kids, visitors were allowed inside." Her voice cracked. She hated the forceful fragility.

"Were they? I don't remember." He shrugged. "I haven't heard anything about a ghost. Why would the lighthouse be haunted?"

"Why not?" She almost flinched at the defensive edge in her question.

"The building wasn't functional. A ghost in the Inn would make way more sense."

"The Inn has never had a mysterious death."

"Except your father?" Zach stroked his jaw. "A healthy man doesn't wake up? Seems like he'd have unfinished business he'd want to hang around and resolve."

Only regarding me. Dad would have wanted to rub her nose in his being right. She'd never given him that satisfaction. Her victory was hollow. "No, the Inn is fine. But really? You haven't heard any mysterious sounds or bright lights from the little island?" She really had failed as a spirit. No one was talking about her. She had made her haunting very specific for one person. But she had experienced something else. Had she been the only one?

"I mean, the Prims are always talking about stuff like that." Zach dropped his arms to his sides. "If anyone would know what happens out there, they would. They drive their boats past that island all the time. I can't really see much of the lighthouse except for the top. But I do hear a lot. Everything carries over the water. The lake is practically an amplifier. I couldn't pinpoint the direction of the whispers and laughter. I suppose the sounds could have come from the lighthouse."

She shoveled another large scoop into her mouth. If what Zach said was true, she might have announced her uneasy partnership with her husband to the whole town. She'd never realized how far the sound could travel. At least she knew Zach Jenkins wouldn't hold back if he thought she was in league with his enemy. Zach came straight out with every argument and opinion. It was, at times, frustrating and refreshing. But at least she knew where she stood.

She'd like such clarity with her husband. Or was it her soon-to-be ex? "I'll be sure to look through your blog. What you're describing is mind-boggling overreach. He's not the king of Loon Lake. What on earth could he be thinking?"

"You've got hours of reading ahead. We're starting a little newspaper, too. Maybe it's more of a circular, but we'll write a few articles."

She wanted to ask who was included in *we*. She needed answers about who was against her husband to come up with her best course of action. "Will you offer sales and coupons in the paper?"

She could have kicked herself as soon as she asked the question. It was such an unimportant detail. But she struggled to make sense of the information Zach told her fast enough for a thoughtful response.

He nodded. "Absolutely. Good deals drive a lot of business."

"What a great idea," she said.

"Glad you're back." Zach grinned, a broad cheek to cheek smile.

He'd stepped off of his soap box for long enough to show

an expression of genuine gratitude at the presence of a peer and potential ally. She hadn't ruined his impression of her. "Me, too," she said. "Thanks for breakfast."

The door opened, jingling the bell.

"Good morning, Zach. I've got more stickers." Seth Boyd strode in, carrying a box.

With blond hair that always needed a trim and a perpetual smile on his handsome face, Seth was someone she'd know anywhere. The nicest guy in town. No one else came close to his genuine kindness.

"Ashley?" Seth asked, shutting the door with one leg.

"Hey, Seth." She grinned. "How are you?"

Striding to the counter, he set the box on the ground and embraced her in a quick, one-armed hug. "I'm good. Sorry about your dad."

His sincerity tugged at her heart. Seth had graduated with Ashley and had always been sweet and caring. He was as comfortable alone as he was in a group. She remembered him sort of drifting from one club to the next. She stepped back and rubbed a hand over her itchy nose. "Yeah, it sucks. I was sorry to hear about your dad, too. Mr. Boyd was the nicest guy in town."

"Thanks. He left big shoes to fill at the print shop. But tell me more about you. Are you back for good? Taking over the Inn?" Seth asked.

"With any luck," Zach said significantly.

She studied Zach from the corner of her gaze, fighting to keep her expression neutral. Christopher wanted the town on her side. She couldn't jump to his defense over every petty comment someone said under their breath. "What are you up to? Stickers?"

Seth smiled. "Just a side hustle. I'm great with slogans, so I started selling motivational bumper stickers. Zach is my best salesman."

Zach crossed his arms over his chest and nodded. "He has a special way of looking at the world that connects with people. I've been glad to offer my guidance."

She darted her gaze between the pair. She hadn't realized they'd become good friends. Of course, a friendship age gap didn't matter after they had all graduated high school and started working. Zach acted like a sort of advisor to the younger man? He and Christopher had more in common than either would admit.

"Oh, that's fun. Can I see a couple?" she asked.

"Sure thing." Seth pulled two stickers out of his pocket and handed them to her. "I always carry a few. It's nice to cheer someone up, you know?"

She grabbed the stickers. "Be the winningest you," she read aloud. "Dream harder." Huh. She must not be the target audience if she couldn't understand the meaning. She lifted her gaze to meet Seth's hopeful expression. "Very cool. You said it's a side hustle?"

"I took over the print shop from my mom. She moved in with my sister in South Carolina. I'm having a smidge of trouble with the Inn." Seth lifted a shoulder.

If she turned around, would she see some smug, knowing look from Zach? "I'm sorry to hear that." She shook her head. "Not about your mom. I'm sure she's happy about leaving winter behind. I mean about the Inn."

"It's okay. I understand. I'm not upset about the Inn. I don't take it personally. Christopher is a perfectionist, and the new menus aren't quite hitting the mark for him. I'll get there. Printing is my job, and I enjoy it. My real work is something much bigger." Seth widened his eyes.

This time, she couldn't help but frown. She'd been a dreamer once. Now she couldn't imagine why. She'd left with her wings spread wide only to fly straight into power lines.

Her stomach tightened, waiting for the impact of whatever came next.

"I'm on the hunt for Soupy, the Lake Superior monster," Seth said.

Ashley blinked. "I'm sorry. I didn't catch that. Could you repeat it?"

"Soupy," Seth said again, slowly. "The Lake Superior monster."

Who? The speed of the delivery wasn't her issue. Her brain didn't understand the words he said. She had never heard of a monster roaming the lake.

"Soupy lurks in Loon Lake, coming in via the channel to Lake Superior," Zach said.

The explanation clarified nothing.

"Seth encountered the beast near the boardwalk and at the mouth of the channel," Zach said. "Seth has been on the hunt for Soupy for decades but only recently shared his search with the public."

Seth shrugged. "Zach thought the more people that know, the better the chance for finding him."

"And a creature like Soupy is a real draw for the whole community," Zach added. "A lake monster draws an eager crowd of tourists ready to discover the extraordinary. As word spreads, we anticipate that the shops will do more business than ever."

"Have others spotted him as well?" she asked.

Seth shook his head. "Not yet, as far as I'm aware. I've only had three encounters. The first time, near the boardwalk, was in the winter. My dad and I were ice fishing. I'm guessing hunting brought Soupy close to the shore. I think all the noise and usual activity in the warmer months scares him off."

She nibbled her lip. Seth established his own logic about this creature and was passionate about its existence. She wasn't likely to dissuade him with questions.

Instead, she studied the other man. Zach was a skeptic about her ghost. She accepted his disbelief but could not understand why he'd encourage Seth's folly. Clearly Zach supported his friend, which was admirable, but if he backed every bad idea, was it only to spite Christopher?

Realization sunk in. The town accepted a myth as long as the Inn wasn't involved. Zach was glad to make money without Christopher's input.

She turned toward Seth. "I guess I'd never heard about a lake monster before."

"I've been on the hunt my whole life with my dad."

"Why now?" Because her father was gone? How did Christopher feel about the idea? He was probably against it. Should she be in favor then?

"After I lost my dad last year, I was telling Zach that I worried I'd never make progress on finding Soupy. He encouraged me to go public with my hunt so I don't waste any time," Seth said. "If everyone knows, we'll have tons of eyes on the water, looking for the unusual. I want to record every unexplained encounter."

She pressed her lips together. She understood having deeply personal matters unresolved with a deceased parent. And she was relieved Seth's search wasn't to spite her late father or husband. He was honoring his dad.

But she wasn't sure she agreed with Zach's encouragement to commercialize the lake monster. Did anyone else have an experience with a figment of Seth's imagination? *I believe in a ghost based on scant evidence.* "I'm intrigued. Tell me about Soupy."

"He's a mosasaur who spends the bulk of his time in Lake Superior. More room to swim and hunt for fish."

"Why a mosasaur?" she asked. "Jumping on the dinosaur movie craze?"

"No, I spotted him a long time ago. I didn't know what he

was initially. It took a lot of research to identify him," Seth said, standing straighter. "Plesiosaur fossils were mostly found in England. Mosasaurs have been discovered in the Badlands, and the theorized ancient sea would have included the Great Lakes." He lifted his chin, staring down his nose for a half second.

Ashley crossed her arms. While the mosasaur might be more accurate, the creature was also exponentially more terrifying. And seemingly harder not to spot. Loon Lake wasn't nearly as deep as Lake Superior. If a mosasaur lurked in the water, it could eat most of the fish and swimmers in a few big chomps. "Hmm."

"What?" Seth asked.

She should leave well enough alone. Christopher always lectured her about the importance of minding her own business. The presence of a mythical sea beast didn't lessen the impact of her ghost encounter. Perhaps two supernatural experiences strengthened the likelihood of the unknown happening in one town. "Humor me. Legends and myths have to have a shred of believability."

"Exactly," Seth said.

"Wouldn't a mosasaur swim into Loon Lake, eat everything, and then swim out? If it stayed, wouldn't it have died?" Zach avoided her gaze. If she wanted to poke holes in Seth's story, she'd be on her own. "Soupy needs a food source."

Seth stroked his chin. "Good point. Perhaps I should shift focus and resources to studying the mouth of the channel. I do think the timber triangle could hold the key to where he lives and breeds."

Timber triangle? The phrase sounded foreign to her, but Zach's non-reaction indicated its place in the local vocabulary. "Part of Nessie's success might be the long neck and flippers aren't nearly as frightening as the teeth," she offered. "The toys are adorable."

Seth nodded. "I have to be true to the creature. I can play down Soupy's carnivorous tendencies a little bit. I don't want anyone to be frightened when he has never approached a human with deadly intent. He is a smaller mosasaur that has adapted to his surroundings. Although to be fair, the first time I saw him, I was terrified." He chuckled.

"I'd never venture out on the water again, if I had an encounter," Zach said.

She studied first Seth and then Zach. Their expressions were authentic. They dismissed her paranormal experience but believed an extinct animal lurked nearby. *Am I lacking a sense of humor?* She missed some component. She'd find the situation easier to process if they were joking.

After so many years of absence, she missed a lot. Her shared history recalled an almost distant past; she'd have to build new connections in the present. Laughing wasn't in her favor.

"Or her. Soupy could be female." Ashley smiled. "It was nice to see you. Both of you."

She exited the ice cream shop before she said anything she couldn't walk back. With her morning off, she'd wanted to reconnect with her old neighbors and not jeopardize her good standing with anyone. She strode along the boardwalk, slowing in front of each shop to see if she recognized anyone inside the businesses.

Busy with customers, the shops were filled with life and energy. She couldn't fault Christopher for wanting to keep the area thriving. The Inn and the shops did more than coexist. They elevated each other. Conversely, they had the power to drag each other down. His method wasn't surprising but did threaten both sides.

She could bridge the gap. But she had to stay, and she wasn't sure he wanted her to.

* * *

Christopher wasn't much for pensive silences only broken by heavy sighs. But that had become his norm since his wife's return. He couldn't figure out if she wanted to team up, to take over, or to ruin the business. Maybe she was crafting a toxic concoction of all three.

He turned away from the window and strode to his desk. The lawn was torn in a pair of deep slashes, marking the crane's path around the building to rescue the chair. Now, he'd have to fix the formerly lush lawn with a fortune spent on fresh sod.

He hadn't really had much option to do anything but solve the problem. He'd closed the beach and called in his groundskeeping team. After a few failed attempts to drag the chair out with chains and a truck, it became clear the situation required a heavy hand and not delicate maneuvering.

So, he'd called for help. As he had watched the work from the lawn, his brow deeply furrowed, he compared the chair with his wife. Ashley shouldn't be trusted with any equipment for the safety of herself and his sanity. He wanted to best utilize her charm with the guests. *She could tell campfire ghost stories as long as someone else controlled the flames.*

She'd scare herself and the guests. He couldn't determine the best path to dealing with her on the lawn. But in the process of standing outside, he had made everyone involved nervous with his glowering. He retreated upstairs, eating a sandwich brought to him by a shaking server before spending the rest of the day at work.

Now, as the sun hung low on the horizon, he couldn't help but question himself. Perhaps his straightforward strategy to fix the situation was the problem. If he was more creative and free-spirited, like her, he might choose to leave the chair and umbrella submerged in the lake as an offshore oddity in case anyone snorkeled.

He snorted. The murky freshwater lake wasn't conducive to exploration. Which was probably for the best. A sunken obstacle could be a danger. He did his best to keep his guests safe and happy. Once one lawsuit was served, others would follow. No matter how baseless, he'd have to fight every claim. He'd lose a fortune in legal fees.

His business was set for its most profitable year yet. But there was never a moment in the hospitality industry that wasn't rife with worry. To properly staff and run the resort, he had a lot of overhead costs. In addition, maintaining an old building wasn't inexpensive or easy.

If he wanted an easy buck, he was in the wrong profession. While he was aware of his miserly persona to the community, he didn't focus on the bottom line for his profit margin and hadn't taken a bonus in years. He remained because of his passion for continuing the Inn's legacy.

A knock sounded on the door.

"Enter," he called and scanned his planner for his next meeting.

"Oh, good! You're here," Ashley said, slightly breathless.

From the climb or enthusiasm at seeing him or both? He met her bright-eyed gaze and smiled despite himself.

She stepped over the covered tray outside the door and breezed into the room.

He frowned. The cleaning staff never left room service trays in the corridor. He'd call downstairs and ask why no one had cleared the trays in the hallway. He was looking for trouble. In it strolled.

"Sorry, is this a bad time?" She stopped, frozen in place in front of his desk.

"Just a long day." He scrubbed his face, wiping away his scowl and waving to his chair. He'd give the staff a break. They weren't the source of his frustration. Ashley claimed the role. "Please, sit down. What did you want to discuss?"

She pulled out a chair, scraping the floor.

He ground his molars together. He would not wince. He was interested in what had her so happy after her disastrous start to the day.

"I was fully undercover at the boardwalk. I stopped in and chatted with just about everyone," she said.

"Good. Learn anything useful?"

"Did you know the sounds are amplified on the water? It's clearer to hear someone across the lake rather than someone whispering next to you?"

He widened his gaze. He hated to think what he might have said that was overheard. He mostly kept his thoughts to himself. She'd been his confidant. Once she was gone, he adapted to holding in every thought.

"And you were right..."

He straightened. He liked hearing that.

"They hate you. They really, really hate you."

He hunched in his chair. So much for feeding his ego. "I guess you went to see Zach Jenkins?"

"He was my first stop. Is he their leader?"

"In a way, I suppose."

"I would have defended you, you know. I think there must be some middle ground between you and the shopkeepers. But I didn't really think it would help our case if I did. I'm supposed to be coming back to lay claim."

"What would you have said?" he asked, suddenly realizing how important her answer was. He felt just as fragile and unsure as he'd been as a kid when he learned he'd have to pay his own way. She might always have it easy. And he never wanted to make life hard for her. But he hated retreating into that scared little kid, the one that motivated his every choice for stability and security.

"I would have said you probably were too enthusiastic about the idea, but it had some merit." She smiled. "You want the best for everyone."

Her sad, shy expression tugged at his heart. It hinted at shared memories and that he wouldn't need to explain his reasons.

"But I didn't need to. Zach conceded as much."

"How'd you manage that?"

She chuckled. "You know people just sort of pour their hearts out to me. I listened, and he spoke freely."

She did have that gift. Her warmth invited an immediate sense of trust. Had she ever met a stranger? While he wouldn't trust her not to burn down the property, he put his faith in her ability to charm people. She was far better in that regard than he was. Too bad he'd never learned or gleaned her skills.

"What's next? Wait for the ghost?" she asked.

"Did you ask Zach and the others about it?"

She nodded. "I did, and no one believes in it. Except for the Prims, although I didn't have a chance to ask them specifically."

He rolled his eyes.

"What? You have issues with them, too?"

"Not quite." He loosened his tie. "I don't understand how such a gullible family has kept their business going for so long."

"Did you analyze their business plans?"

His ears burned. His throat squeezed shut. He'd done that for the advantage of the business owners. He wouldn't take money from someone failing. Especially if they couldn't see they were in trouble. He'd helped the arcade owners get out while they could and salvage a nice retirement down south. But everyone latched on to the angle he ran them out. It didn't do him any favors to defend himself. "I don't have any involvement with the Prims business or vice versa. It's been a mutually beneficial relationship."

"Except for the dinner cruises?" She arched a brow, curling her lips too.

"I'm glad you're amused."

"Maybe I think brand ambassador is a better use of my talents. I could be the liaison between the Inn and the local businesses."

A compromise? He drew back his chin. "Have you given up on your plans to take over the Inn?"

She threw back her head and laughed. "Try again. I meant instead of working on your checklist in the interim. Before I rightfully inherit my legal property."

He wouldn't give her an easy out for learning every role. She'd need a better working knowledge of the day-to-day to oversee the Inn. "We're not having that discussion. As far as the Prims are concerned, I have no reason to change. And I won't put you up to interviewing them. It'll be a lost cause. Carl's mean and Steve's naive. You wouldn't get answers. Although I would love to know why they keep delaying the start of the boating season."

"You're in charge. You tell me what to do. I'll go ask them why they're disappointing our guests."

She would. He admired that bit of backbone. But he wouldn't force her to interact with the pair. "Let's settle our business first." Did he imagine her sharp intake of breath? Or the fluttering at the base of her neck? He didn't want to proceed with a divorce. But dragging the situation out wasn't in anyone's best interests. And he had to protect his future. He'd already lost control of his heart. "About finding your arsonist."

"I didn't make headway with any living persons."

Not the ghost again.

"But I do have a few questions, I'm hoping you can

answer. I wasn't sure how to ask without alienating myself. I'm curious," she said, her tone low. "About Soupy?"

"The lake monster? Did you see the merch? It's not half bad. *Society of Soupy: the truth always surfaces.*"

"SOS? As in a cry for help?" She rolled her eyes. "I didn't realize what a community project the beast is." Her voice was tense. "Seth brought in a couple of his motivational stickers for Zach to sell. He's busy."

Christopher wasn't sure what to make of her reaction. The community's shift towards embracing conspiracies and the extraordinary must be sudden and shocking. He'd had plenty of time to witness the transition from the staid to the unexplained. But he downplayed her insistence on a ghost encounter.

"You're having problems with the menus?" she asked. "Maybe he should focus. He's dividing his attention. Only one is his actual, profitable business, and he's giving that the least of his time."

Christopher waved a hand. Once Seth figured out what he was doing, he'd be great at the print shop. He needed time. Christopher was happy to give him that. He was curious about her response. Before her return, the version of her he'd created in his mind would have jumped in and helped. He'd offered his support because he figured she'd want him to be encouraging. "You don't support Soupy?"

"I've never heard of a lake monster. I grew up on these shores. Why is the legend taking off now?"

Her question held shades of regret. *Did she not believe? Or did she feel left out?* He didn't have a fear of missing out. If he didn't do something, he didn't waste a thought considering *what if?*

She suffered from major FOMO. Did Soupy symbolize the length of her self-imposed exile and the distance between herself and the community? The town wasn't quite the same as she left it. Loon Lake had room for two dreamers. "Your concerns are about his workload? Or are you against his mythologizing? Because I don't quite follow your argument."

"Don't turn this around with logic."

He almost smiled. "Give Seth your encouragement. That's all he needs."

"You know I support others. I gave him a few ideas, but I'm sure Zach realizes I'm not a believer."

"You're creative. Help Seth. Soupy is a way to ingratiate yourself with him and everyone else. Dealing with loss isn't easy. I think we are all offering support by embracing Soupy."

"I don't need a way to make friends, thank you."

"I know you don't. But Soupy isn't a business. Seth is quite sincere about Soupy." Christopher leaned forward, interlacing his hands. "While he has only come forward recently, he didn't launch the creature out of nowhere. Talk to him. Learn more. You'll change your tune."

"I can't imagine I'm the only person in town that doesn't believe in Soupy." She exhaled a heavy sigh. "Elise isn't a believer. I'm sure."

Christopher bit the inside of his cheek. He didn't want to burst his wife's bubble. Nor did he want to get into a discussion about Elise.

Ashley widened her eyes. "She is? The one time I actually hoped I could count on her. Ugh." She groaned. "Why must I always adapt?"

Christopher would have snorted if he hadn't spotted genuine frustration in the set of her tight mouth. She had spent her childhood in a kingdom of which she was the ruler. Coming back might be an adjustment, but she had never experienced the typical growing pains of becoming part of a community. She'd been adored.

"How does Soupy stack against your ghost?" He leaned his chin in a palm.

Her cheeks reddened. "Initially, the ghost was fake. But I'm telling you, the lighthouse is really haunted. It's always been a creepy spot."

He laughed. He wasn't sure he'd ever disagreed about something more. But he'd give her a win. This time, it didn't take away anything from him. If only they weren't trapped in a zero-sum game playing each other, they'd actually have fun.

Chapter Ten

Ashley slept in the next morning. Or, at least, she flipped the door hanger to "do not disturb" on the outer door and firmly bolted both locks. She pretended to not hear him knock. She probably had someplace to be according to his get-to-work schedule.

Too bad.

She was sorting through an influx of information, none of it particularly good or helpful. She was worried that the shopkeepers planned some sort of uprising. Maybe they weren't out sharpening their pitchforks and threatening death and dismemberment, but as a group, they had more collective power than they might currently be aware.

But that truth wouldn't remain hidden for long. And if they caught wind that she was working with Christopher to learn the saboteur's identity? She would be their next target.

Unless his implication about finishing their business meant meeting with a lawyer and starting divorce proceedings, then everyone would know exactly where she and her husband stood.

Her heart slammed into the front of her chest. Under the

covers, she rubbed the heel of her hand over the general area housing that useless organ. She'd been lying awake for hours now. As long as she remained here, she gave him plenty of time and opportunity to ambush her.

No thank you.

She slipped out from under the covers and dressed quickly. She gave his schedule a half-hearted glance. He'd given her time off today for *rest*. She rolled her eyes. Peace wasn't to be found alone with her thoughts.

He'd floated the idea of her helping with the lighthouse renovation project. That seemed as good a place as any to head. At least then she'd have a purpose for her wandering and wouldn't give the appearance of the truth. *Lost, lonely soul*. She needed to conduct her own investigation of the sight.

But something else bugged her from yesterday's revelations. She wasn't the only imaginative person in town. Maybe Christopher was right to call her out for not supporting Seth's lake legend dream. Seth deserved friendship and not skepticism. She found her cell phone. Pulling up the print shop's website, she called the number.

"It's a great day to print your way," Seth greeted. "How may I help you?"

"Hi, Seth. It's Ashley Hale-Lewis."

"Hi, Ashley. I'm almost done with the latest batch of menus if Christopher is having you check up on me."

Did everyone know her husband put her to work doing grunt jobs? "Oh, that's great. I'm sure he'll be glad to hear. But no. I was calling about that other thing." She cleared her throat. She'd let Christopher into her head and couldn't escape until she made amends. "Soupy?"

"Really? You seemed like a skeptic yesterday."

She frowned. She hated the truth in his words. "I'm sorry about that. I was sort of taken by surprise. And I had a few ideas about Soupy. I was wondering if you wanted to meet up?"

"Well, I'll be at the coffee shop around two. I'm meeting up with Elise McKenna to discuss a project for the historical society."

"Two sounds great. I'll see you there. Bye." She hung up the phone and sighed. Now, she had to find time to draft something about Soupy that sounded convincing enough to get back on Seth's good side. Hopefully, she could figure it out on the fly. In the meantime, she had someplace to be where she could sneak around without getting Mr. Willie's or Christopher's attention.

Pocketing her phone and room key, she tugged a ball cap low over her head and exited the room with her chin down. Incognito, no one stopped her as she made her way down the stairs and past the hospitality tray set up in the lobby. She grabbed a granola bar and poured herself a coffee.

"Ms. Hale?" Mr. Brixen called across the room. "Is that you? Mrs. Lewis? Ms. Hale-Lewis?"

She drew her ears up to her shoulders. Her disguise hadn't been enough to conceal her identity. Sipping from her coffee, she slowly made her way to the concierge desk at the end of the front desk. "Hello."

"Sorry, do you want to be called Mrs. Hale-Lewis?" Mr. Brixen frowned. "I should have asked."

She forced a smile across her features. "Please don't worry. Hale-Lewis works. How may I help you?"

"I have an envelope here for Mr. Lewis. I was wondering if you might deliver it to him?"

She gritted her molars. Everyone knew Christopher treated her like an unpaid intern at the moment. She almost reminded Mr. Brixen that the role was only temporary. She would assume her rightful place as the boss soon. He might think twice before asking her to be a messenger.

"I have to run out for a guest, and I gather you're meeting with Mr. Lewis?" Mr. Brixen asked, his voice shaking. "I'm sorry to impose. I would so appreciate if you would deliver it to him?"

She was glad he was able to read her thoughts. She softened her expression. "Of course, I will. Our meeting is later, but I'll take it to him. I appreciate how you devote your time to our guests first and foremost."

Mr. Brixen beamed. "Thank you, ma'am." He extended the envelope.

She widened her gaze and accepted the thick package. The thick envelope was decorated with sparkly white hibiscus flowers on a white ground. In the upper right corner, she spotted the return address.

Hawaii. She nibbled the inside of her cheek. He had some nerve planning a trip to celebrate his victory over her. They'd talked about visiting the Hawaiian islands for their ten-year anniversary. She'd missed it, and he booked a vacation alone. She never pictured him on a beach without her forcing him to put his toes in the sand. However, if he had thrived for the past decade without her, he was clearly capable of all sorts of behavior she couldn't have anticipated.

Or maybe he's got a job lined up. The sudden thought was rational and reasonable, given her husband's work hard, never play personality. If he left, he'd solve a lot of problems. Still, her stomach dropped, and she stuffed the envelope into her oversized, tote-style purse. "I'll take care of this."

Mr. Brixen nodded.

She retreated to the doors, gripping the bag tight. Inside, she carried something or nothing. She wouldn't know which for a while. If he ever told her... She pushed the worries to one side.

Outside, she surveyed the lawn but didn't see him. She didn't have time for distractions, but a montage of everything that had happened and all that could never be played in her mind. She'd imagined a big wedding on the lawn. But once Xavier told her she was too young to be engaged, she'd run off to the courthouse with Christopher. She'd pictured spending the Fourth of July out here, laying on a blanket and staring at the sky with her children as fireworks erupted overhead. But then she'd run, and Christopher hadn't followed her.

She sipped her coffee and made her way down to the lighthouse. Crossing over the wooden bridge, she didn't see anything out of order around the perimeter. She approached the door and pushed with her fingertips, holding her breath as she did.

Please be a nice ghost. On tiptoes, she entered. And saw nothing.

She spun in a circle and frowned. Besides the melted and burned debris of her air mattress and ruined sleeping bag, nothing else took up space on the floor.

If someone else had been inside and digging for a supposed treasure, like Christopher supposed, the floor would have been disturbed. Evidence would be left. She spotted nothing.

No one else had been here.

She shuddered, and her whole body quaked as a chill swept her from head to toe. Besides fire damage, the lighthouse remained otherwise undisturbed. Saboteurs could have returned and covered their tracks. She'd left the lighthouse for several days. But some trace of disturbance would be visible.

No human was capable of lifting floorboards and shifting dirt without a hint of their activity. The perp or perps had plenty of time to return to the scene and continue whatever their end goal was. But they hadn't. Her ghost theory strengthened. *What is a ghost's end game? Unfinished business? Companionship?*

She refused to pursue that morbid line of thought. She

was hardly in a place of critiquing someone else's end goal when she wasn't sure of hers. Last night, she should have talked to Christopher and asked him what he meant by finishing their business. Hiding today didn't help. They had a post-nuptial agreement that would make the divorce process relatively straightforward.

In the current circumstances, the document would serve her husband far better. Instead of the fifty-fifty split, winner would take all. Perhaps Dad would have wanted the exact outcome. She couldn't deny the improvements Christopher had made. Her logical, careful husband had focused all his attention on eliminating waste and creating opportunity.

But he missed some chances for fun. Maybe he had forgotten how to enjoy himself in her absence. She hoped so. Because she wasn't ready to say goodbye. They could take the Inn from a quaint hideaway to an entertaining destination if they worked together. Or at least they'd enjoy the time spent together. He couldn't fake the glow in his amber eyes or the warmth of his smile.

A cold chill snaked down her spine like an ice cube traveled each and every vertebrae. The effect was so peculiar. As the goosebumps rose on her arm, she curled her toes.

The sensation wasn't the same as she'd experienced the night of the fire. Then, she'd been trapped and almost suffocated. This feeling was lighter, more of a tickle than a taunt.

Zach was right. Dad was the only person to die on the Inn's premises, and he hadn't been anywhere near the lighthouse. He'd been found in his bed. While she hated the unfinished business between them, she wasn't sure he'd been impacted enough to stick around and try to contact her from the other side. Now that she was here, she couldn't ignore the facts anymore.

She stumbled forward. From a perfectly still position, knees locked, she'd been pushed to the ground. The shove was sudden and forceful. On her hands and knees, she was turned away from the windows, staring at the ground.

And then came the blast.

The single panes of glass shattered. Dust rose. The walls crumbled like a sandcastle on a windy day. The building was collapsing. *How?* She scrambled to her feet and raced outside. Shielding her gaze, she stared up at the building, and then came another boom, and the stones toppled in on themselves. A force pushed her backward.

She tumbled into the lake: splashing, kicking, and trying desperately to make sense of the unfolding situation. Bobbing up and down, she reached her arms out, grasping for anything. She strained her neck above the water, dragging in air. Her head spun, and she couldn't sort up from down. A life ring hit her in the head. She grabbed onto the orange circle and waved.

"Ashley?" Steve Prim called.

She coughed and nodded, gripping the life ring tight.

"Hold on, I'll pull you up." He tugged the rope attached to the life ring.

The icy water chilled her like a thousand tiny needles pricking her skin. The longer she remained in the lake, the less she was in control as her body went numb. Then she felt like she was engulfed by invisible flames, her limbs scalding as she burned from the inside out.

At the swim platform, she reached for the boat with one hand. She hit the slatted wooden platform with her fist, unable to uncurl her fingers. She forced her hand flat and pulled herself onto the boat. Drenched to the bone, she curled into the fetal position.

Steve approached with a thick towel. He moved his mouth.

Why wasn't he speaking? What was he doing?

He reached for her and lifted her over the back of the boat, wrapping her tight in the towel and rubbing her arms.

She couldn't stop shaking. Ashley wanted him to let go of her. She was fine, but her body wasn't delivering the message. Her chin wouldn't stop trembling long enough for her mouth to form words. She raised her palms and gently pushed against his chest.

He stepped back.

She sank onto the bench and cleared her ears by blowing her nose. But the sounds remained distant and waterlogged. "Hi, Steve. Thank you."

"Are you okay? What were you doing at the lighthouse?"

Heat crept up her neck. She owed him no explanation. Christopher deserved the truth of how she spent her free time. But she wouldn't talk about her ghost to anyone else.

Her teeth chattered, the rapid-fire motion uncontrollable. *Was she suffering extreme embarrassment or a fever?* She hoped neither.

He stood over her, staring down.

She tucked a leg underneath her. She had never known Steve to be judgmental or opinionated. But she couldn't help the skin-crawling feeling he was assessing her now and found her extremely lacking in character, common sense, and courage.

He took a few steps back and settled in the captain's chair, scrubbing away whatever expression marred his typically sun-kissed, smiling face. He was a good-looking guy. Golden and glowing. But he had depths she hadn't guessed at. "I don't want to sound like I'm telling you what to do."

So don't. I have a husband for that. She pressed her tongue to the roof of her mouth.

"I have to discourage you from taking selfies for your social media in dangerous places. You know this lake is deep and dark. Please take care of yourself. We just got you back."

Now she really didn't know how to respond. Did he think she was only driven by curating her life? Until a few days ago, that had been true. She was home, and she wanted so much more. Instead of an argument, though, she'd try a different angle. "Don't suppose you saw what happened?"

"It looked like a dynamite explosion or something. It was like a movie. Are you sure you're not hurt?"

She tested her muscles, twisting from one side to the other and extending both legs. "I think I'll be okay."

"That building should have been condemned years ago. It nearly collapsed on you. What if I hadn't been going by? Why is there no lifeguard at the Inn? You could have drowned."

She knew why the beach was closed. That was entirely her fault. Until a replacement chair arrived, the one she'd sunk was broken after its retrieval, the Inn discouraged swimming.

"Was it the ghost?"

She stared. Finally, someone believed her. She couldn't celebrate or commiserate.

But his acceptance was off. He rattled off the conclusion in a second like a prepared remark. His family believed in the made-up story about treasure, and Zach had told her Steve mentioned odd sights on the island. She didn't like his answer. But she didn't have it in her to question him. "I don't think a ghost can demolish stones like that."

But a spirit could have saved me. She would have been standing directly under the windows if she hadn't been shoved. She hated the deadly possibilities. Her throat sliced by shards of broken glass. Or her head smashed by a falling stone.

"Maybe Soupy?" Steve asked.

She stifled a groan, avoiding that minefield.

Why was everyone so eager to buy into a lake monster concept that made no sense? For a legend to endure, some logic was required. At least she presented a solid argument for her apparition. She crossed her arms over her body, rubbing her shoulders. She was icy down to her bones. "I'm okay. Can you take me to shore?"

"No. You need to get checked up. You might have a concussion or something. The Inn will want to brush this off. You need to file a report and get this cited." Steve turned away and revved the engine of the idling, bobbing boat.

Don't I get a say? She wouldn't mind a checkup. As an adult, she could make her own choices.

Steve took charge of the situation, not asking her opinion or desires.

She hated the loss of control. Because she would have agreed to a check-up if he had asked. *Why is he so invested in getting me to the hospital?* Once again, she missed some bigger part of the whole picture, a connection that would make sense in hindsight.

Arguing with a determined man never achieved her goals. Ashley would placate Steve but get some much-needed support, even if asking her husband for back-up meant he'd insist on a trip to the lawyer to officially decide property ownership before further damage could be done.

"Can you get my purse?" Ashley shouted, her voice breaking. She pointed a shaky arm to the bag a few feet away near the rubble.

Steve nodded and steered the boat close. He retrieved the purse with one swift movement, barely lifting out of the captain's chair. He tossed the bag in her direction.

If she wasn't so cold, she'd stare. Instead, she grabbed the purse off the ground and pulled her cell phone out of her bag. With her cold hands, she fumbled with the device.

OTW to hospital with Steve Prim. Hurry.

She sank back against the seat cushion. She wasn't sure if she'd added enough panic in the text or if she'd scared her husband too much. A manual for etiquette in tense situations would be handy.

Slipping the phone into her purse, she crossed her arms over her chest and held on tight. She had too many questions swirling around her mind. At the top of her list, she wondered at Steve's proximity to the Inn in his personal watercraft. Why float around near the lighthouse if he wasn't leading a tour?

Unless, he's my ghost?

Fred's folly had been built to establish ownership of the disputed land. Now it might serve to bring down the whole empire. She'd resolve to do the impossible. Not say a word until Christopher showed up at the hospital.

* * *

While living without her had been hard, Christopher always had hope for their future. If time could heal all things, he kept the faith for their reconciliation. In his mind, they were destined for each other.

After running off and eloping, they had returned to her very unimpressed father. Having grown up on the property alongside Ashley, he had known and respected her father the same as his own. Christopher had watched her manipulate every situation to her benefit. He hadn't given the rushed marriage a second thought, figuring, like every other occasion, she'd charm everyone into accepting her decisions.

Only, this time, she hadn't.

He'd gone to Xavier Hale. Christopher had vowed to stand tall and listen if the old man wanted to berate him. But instead, Xavier had been shaken by his daughter's impetuous decision. He looked scared by the lengths she'd go to get her way. In that moment, Christopher didn't see the institution but the human. And they'd forged an uneasy bond.

Slowly, day by day, Christopher proved to Xavier that he was worthy of the daughter and valued the business. But then he'd strained his relationship with Ashley. She wanted to be the center of his world, the only Hale he spent time with. She couldn't appreciate what the unofficial apprenticeship meant. And he'd never been good at explaining.

Suddenly everything changed. While she had expressed frustration with her father for not training her, she had never told Christopher of an ultimatum until she was packing the car. One day, she was her usual, bubbly self, and the next, she was leaving. He didn't take her decision seriously, figuring she said something rash to her father in the heat of the moment and would turn the car around as soon as she calmed down. By the time he realized he should have listened to the hurt in her tone over the angry words, he had lost her.

In the kitchen, he finished his salad while leaning back against the stainless-steel sink. If he stayed on his feet and kept moving, he could almost run away from his problems. Last night, when he had said he wanted to finish their business, she hadn't flinched or tried to stop him. She hadn't reacted at all.

He wanted some response. From a typically heart-on-her-sleeve personality, her stare was particularly chilling. Where was her fire and fight? He was starting the process of ending their marriage. It wasn't in his best interest to remain financially tangled together. With a hefty payout, he would end the monthly allowance. He could start fresh.

Did he want that?

He had been okay with the status quo because at least it gave him the illusion that she still loved him. When she had brought up Elise, she had almost given him the impression she was jealous.

In a town full of superstitious people, he and Elise were the only skeptics. They shared some of the burden of asking the obvious questions and pointing out the irrational antics. Elise was close with Seth, and it would never have occurred to Christopher to question her beliefs about Soupy. Logic and reason weren't the basis for attraction. And he'd never been drawn to Elise the way Ashley pulled him. She had been his sun.

He'd avoided her all day. His head urged him to start the talk with the lawyer, but his broken heart couldn't handle going through with it. Without her, he had hidden under a cloud. In only a few hours, he had forced himself back into the shade and withered. He hated it. He needed her. She was quite content on her own.

In his back pocket, his cell phone buzzed.

He reached for his phone with one hand and set the bowl in the sink with the other.

He swiped the screen with his thumb and froze. As the text popped up, he was colder than ice, his blood chilling his veins.

My wife: OTW to hospital with Steve Prim. Hurry.

The message didn't give him enough information. Was Steve hurt? Or was Ashley seriously injured? What had happened?

The side door crashed against a wall.

A fresh-faced teen, dressed in the logo-emblazoned green polo the summer groundskeeping staff wore, rushed in.

"Sir, the lighthouse collapsed."

Christopher's jaw dropped. He looked from the teen to his phone and back again. Ashley must have been inside. His throat swelled, threatening to cut off his oxygen supply. He coughed, forcing the airway open. He'd focus on taking action. "Get Mr. Willie and tell him to block off the area. The lake is already off-limits. I have to be somewhere right now. It's urgent."

The pimpled-faced kid nodded. But his gaze slid to the side.

"Now. Go." Christopher never yelled at his employees.

The teen needed the verbal push. He raced away.

Christopher had never been so directionless and in need of

a firm hand to guide him. Although, he'd had two. Xavier and Ashley. The strong-willed Hales took charge of him for most of his youth. His past didn't matter. *She's hurt, and it's my fault.*

He exited the building without another glance at the staff and hopped in his SUV. He depressed the accelerator to the floor mat, driving as fast as he could. If a deputy stopped him, he'd explain the situation and probably earn an escort. Staying in one place a person's whole life had a few benefits.

He reached the hospital in record time, parking in the main lot and racing inside.

"Christopher?"

He stopped inside the automatic doors, his shoes squeaking against the tiles and turned.

Behind the main desk, Lauren Jenkins waved. "She's in room 213."

He nodded and jogged past the elevator banks and up the stairs. In a small town, he couldn't escape the people causing him trouble. Bumping into their siblings was inevitable. Pushing Zach Jenkins out of his mind, he raced ahead. He reached her room, doubling over as he dragged in every burning breath he could.

"Christopher?" Ashley asked.

He straightened, his chest heaving from his exertion, and saluted her.

In a hospital gown, she sat on a bed with a sheet covering her legs.

Superficially, she looked okay. The surroundings added a sense of drama, but she wasn't visibly bandaged and had no beeping machines attached to her. Appearances could be deceiving. In this case, he wouldn't guess the extent of her trauma.

She was admitted for observation. Whatever it was, he would support her. He'd stand by her and help her get through it. *For better or worse.* He hated to think this was how they found each other again, but he would not waste the chance to prove himself. "Ashley, let me say I—"

"Shh. He's only just stepped out to make a call," she hissed.

"Who?"

"Steve Prim." She waved for him to approach.

Christopher rounded the bed. Facing the door, he could monitor the entrance. He leaned close.

"I was in the lighthouse. It was fine. Barely touched by the fire."

"I know. I checked it out, too. It's odd. I didn't see anything noticeably out of place." *Almost like there is a ghost.* He wasn't sure what he had expected to find, but besides smoke stains in the dusty interior, the building was at its same level of disheveled. If the structural integrity had been compromised, shouldn't he have noticed? He wasn't an engineer, but he wasn't obtuse, either.

"While I was inside, I felt a chill and fell to the ground. Then the explosion came."

"Explosion?" He widened his gaze. Shouldn't a boom have shaken the Inn? Wouldn't the glass rattle in the frames of every window following a detonation? "How long ago?"

"A few minutes before I texted."

At that time, he had been inside the kitchen. The noisiest place on the whole property. He didn't like that he hadn't heard a loud pop. Or glass breaking. He'd been oblivious to a major catastrophe only yards away. He'd have to think about how to do better, so he was always aware. "So... what happened?"

"I don't know. I think there is a ghost. But a friendly spirit who saved me. I made it out before the stones collapsed. Another blast came and knocked me into the water. Steve was going by on his boat and fished me out."

"His boat?"

"Yeah. Not with tourists." She stretched each word. "Like a personal boat. An old Supra."

Her tone was unmistakable. But was Steve's behavior suspicious? Christopher didn't understand why the Prims continued to stall opening for the season. If their boats had problems, surely Steve was better off fixing up their fleet at the boathouse and not cruising around the lake near the Inn's property in a personal vehicle. Something was off.

Right now, however, Christopher had to focus on what mattered. Her. Not the Prims. "How are you feeling? Did you hit your head?"

"No, I'm fine. Steve insisted, and he's trying to get the police involved. He wants me to file a report. Against the Inn."

If she did, she would have effective legal documentation against him. She might even take the property back as damages. He'd accept it. First and foremost, he wanted her safe. "What do you want to do?"

"Get out of here before he comes back."

She didn't want to take action against me? He wouldn't push her one way or the other. The opportunity to use the explosion to her advantage shouldn't have risen to the top of his concerns. But it did. He realized he wouldn't fight her if she pursued legal action. More than anything, he needed her healthy. "Are you sure you can?"

"Yes. Can you guard the door? I'm going to change. The doctor said I could leave. He told me once Steve left, but I didn't have a ride. I'd like to be gone before Steve returns with a cop."

So, you just needed a lift? She popped him like an overinflated inner tube. He was glad she wasn't hurt. But he'd wanted to be something more than a ride. He wanted to be a husband.

He turned and strode toward the door, shutting it and

leaning against it in the hallway, standing sentry. He'd never quite been a full partner to her, not in the meaningful ways he imagined. Did he fight for another chance? Or was it time to take flight and let her go and find someone who could make her happy in all the ways he couldn't?

Chapter Eleven

Ashley hadn't worried about her appearance. In the chaos of falling into the lake fully clothed and being admitted to the hospital, she hadn't cared. When she arrived, she had readily accepted the dry hospital gown. Getting out of her wet jeans and soaking bra was her top priority.

The back of the garment was open, so she had gotten under the warm covers. If she was being evaluated for a concussion, she might as well be as comfortable as possible. She could be here for a while.

When Christopher had entered the room, he had paled and quickly covered his mouth with a hand. She jumped off the bed, tossing the blanket in the process, ready to assist him in case he vomited or fainted. She almost asked who had died. She knew that answer. Her dad. And then, today, she'd been close to joining him.

Cool air fanned her through the open back.

His eyes widened at her outfit, and she crossed her arms over her chest.

She sobered in an instant and quickly explained the

current predicament. She had to get out of there before Steve Prim raised the stakes.

Whatever happened, she wouldn't ruin Christopher. Pulling her damp jeans over her legs was a process. While no longer soaking wet, the heavy denim stuck and clung. She didn't manage much better with her T-shirt. Worst of all, however, was slipping into her canvas sneakers. She squished and squelched with each step. She wanted nothing more than a hot shower and a warm bed.

Had Christopher looked bereft because of me? Her heart skipped a beat. She wished.

Childhood best friends turned lovers wasn't anything extraordinary. It had been dumb luck, as she would describe most of her kismet moments. The sweet, cute kid who always followed along with a plan grew into a caring, sexy man before her eyes. He could have fallen for anyone. He should. He'd be so much better off with someone who listened twice as much as she talked.

The first time he'd kissed her, he had needed a little push. She'd flung herself into his arms. She had been desperate to press against him, to feel his lips on hers. The heady romance was buoyed in part by her father's displeasure at it. But not solely. She loved Christopher because of who he was and the man he would become. She loved his past and present and longed to be his future.

That was over. He'd made his choice. And it wasn't her.

She grabbed her purse and traced the outline of the room key in the interior pocket. That was a miracle she could thank the ghost for. She shivered and strode across the room, opening the door.

He turned and frowned. "Ready?"

She crossed her arms over her chest. Her whole body was clammy. And chapped. Wet undergarments were a whole other level of torture. "Yes, let's go."

With each step, she held her breath. She wasn't exactly sneaking out, which was good because her wet shoes weren't conducive to stealth. She wanted a clean getaway before Steve came back. Not that she was threatened by Steve. He was sweet and sincere and conspicuous. He couldn't plot, plan, or scheme. That's why they'd never work and why she had turned him down in middle school.

But she worried why he had stepped out of the room. He had probably called Carl. If she could avoid one man for the rest of her life, it would be Carl Prim. That was another reason for emphatically checking the *no* box in seventh-grade math when Steve had slipped her a note asking her to be his girlfriend.

She followed Christopher out of the hospital, stopping for her official discharge papers at the front desk. She was forced into a wheelchair. He left to get his car. An orderly wheeled her outside to wait.

She fought to keep from sighing or rolling her eyes. She wouldn't fuss or fight. She wanted to leave, and any prolonging wasn't helping her cause.

Christopher parked the SUV at the curb. He hopped out of the vehicle, leaving the engine idling, and opened the passenger door.

She smiled, pleased by the little courtesy. Until she spotted the towel spread over the seat. Not so much a gentleman that he didn't put his car's interior above her pride. She knew where she stood. She hopped in and buckled. In the same position, she might have behaved similarly. But she would have given the terrycloth to the person for warmth and not to shield the upholstery from a soggy bottom.

He climbed into the driver's seat, reversing from the parking spot and driving toward the Inn.

For several moments, she drifted in the silence. She'd finally found someone who believed in the ghost. Steve's fervent attitude frightened her. She wouldn't try to pretend nothing had happened.

And at least the latest incident stalled any sort of real talk for a little while. *Did the d-word linger on his tongue every time he said hello?* She could stall with a topic he'd dismiss. But the longer she stayed, the less she could explain away the odd goings-on. She turned in her seat, studying him. "Do you think there could be a ghost? I was alone in the lighthouse today, but I had some sort of... And just before the fire. I still have questions."

"You started the fire by accident," he said slowly. "I didn't notice any structural issues at the time, but I'm not a fire marshal. The blaze must have done more damage than either of us realized. The stones were weakened and fell apart like dominoes."

She scrunched her nose. That answer just didn't work. She knew what she'd felt. Her mind didn't invent what she had heard. A loud pop or bang. A clear, deliberate noise. For several moments after the blast, she'd listened to the world like she was underwater. Her hearing had returned. The explosion hadn't been fatal at least. It had definitely been intentional.

She stroked her chin. "To what end would someone sabotage the building?"

"You mean besides yourself. Now that you're not there trying to scare me off."

Her cheeks burned. "Who else could possibly gain anything from bringing us both down? Because either way, one of us owns the resort."

"I don't know. I can't think this was anything more than a terrible accident. Thank goodness you weren't hurt."

She half-listened, turning to stare at the passing scenery. The old treasure story poked up in the middle of every explanation. Besides ghosts. "I just don't get why someone would do that in broad daylight. Wouldn't someone looking for treasure wait until nighttime?"

"Unless they know what they are looking for is under the lighthouse, and destroying the building during the day allows them to search through the rubble at night."

She faced him and grinned. Finally, they were on the same page. And shenanigans had been one of the hallmarks of their relationship. She might not get more than one last chance to share a little fun. If they solved a mystery in the midst, all the better.

His stomach growled. Hers joined in.

He pulled into the parking lot of the hotel. "How about I'll grab us some food and bring it up to the office, okay? We can discuss upstairs."

She liked that. She'd like it even more if they could plot at a fancy restaurant. A curl of anticipation and nerves settled low in her belly. In the past ten years, she'd forgotten the sensation. At an off-property place, she could flirt with her husband properly. After all, she could segue into being a double agent. Zach would most likely approve.

But Christopher wouldn't. He'd have some well-thought-out counterargument ready. So, she'd take what she could get and run with it. "After I take a hot shower? Maybe put on some dry clothes." *And makeup. Like a date.*

His amber eyes flashed, burning bright.

She almost added the suggestion to the end of that question. She wouldn't put herself through the pain of his rejection again. No matter how sweet the potential pleasure if he accepted. It made everything about the last few weeks almost bearable. Like dealing with the fervent townsfolk and Soupy.

Her stomach dropped. She forgot about Soupy. If she put off her meeting with Seth, she wouldn't win him to her side. Not that she was so sure how she was playing anything anymore. Who was a friend? A foe? Why pick sides if her homecoming was forever? Couldn't she have it all?

"Everything okay?" Christopher asked, frowning.

She shook her head, plastering on a smile. "Yes, everything is fine. It's just... Can I get a raincheck? Can we meet in your office later? I have a meeting that I almost forgot about. I'm late."

"You do?"

"It's a Soupy development meet-up at the coffee shop. Figured it was a good way to ingratiate myself, and you did seem a bit surprised I wasn't a bigger supporter."

He chuckled.

Her heart squeezed. The sound was as warm and inviting as logs popping on a fire.

"I understand. You'll have even more to share later. I'll look forward to it. I'm wondering if maybe we should pull an all-nighter. We can watch the lighthouse from my office. Maybe we need a little more surveillance to catch our culprit?"

Feeling his steady gaze, she turned away. She didn't want to give away too much of her turmoil. She hadn't come back to rekindle anything. He stoked the embers inside her back into flames. With more alone time, she might do something desperate. Like throw herself in his arms again ala their first kiss. He was giving her a chance. "Yes. Thanks. I'd love that. I'd better get going or I'll be late to meet Seth."

She pulled back her shoulders and fumbled with the seatbelt. She had returned to claim her inheritance. Nothing was settled. Would it be? Finally, her icy fingers pressed the button and released her. She hopped out of the car and didn't look back, leaving a trail of wet shoe prints and taking only her memories.

* * *

Christopher did the gentlemanly thing and let her get out of the car and leave him first.

He hated doing that. But it was inevitable since he was incapable of walking away from her. They had plans to meet up later. He sighed and tapped the steering wheel, tracking her progress inside the hotel.

Would she have turned him down if he asked her on a proper date? He couldn't remember the last time they dressed up and shared a meal in public. She loved the ritual of dates, carefully selecting her outfit and styling herself. And he loved how every tiny movement was imbued with extra flirtatious behavior. With nothing and no one else to distract their attention away from each other, they had often gone to dinner at seven and stayed until closing. He missed that.

The painful truth he couldn't escape was that he hadn't known she wanted to leave until too late. If he had understood every moment was final, he would have done things differently. He would have held her closer, kissed her longer, and told her everything. *Except, I wouldn't.* He'd promised her father he'd keep his silence about the business.

At least they avoided discussing the final details of settling the estate. And while he might miss her company, he couldn't be mad at her destination. Meeting up with Seth, she could encourage him. The pair could create something new, big, and inventive. Each had a talent for seeing the possibilities in any given situation. Ashley's boundless imagination always shocked and delighted. Christopher would approach the same scenario with a sense of dread and despair. She always found a spark of something exciting and positive. Over the years, she'd given him hope countless times.

Today, he'd almost lost her for good.

He gripped the steering wheel tight, staring through the insect-crusted windshield in the direction she'd gone. The smear of bug guts blocked any movement in the distance. At the moment, he'd swear he had x-ray vision thanks to the adrenaline rushing through his veins. She could have been killed. All because she was looking for a ghost she had invented and convinced herself was real.

Steve Prim believed her, had rescued her, and the while he'd probably stared at her with those adoring eyes. Christopher curled his fingers into fists. Steve had a very punchable face. Naturally, Steve would be the one to save the day and make Christopher the bad guy. He groaned. He really hated the Prims.

Curling his upper lip, Christopher couldn't be mad at Steve. He endured a lot with his overbearing father. While the local business leaders might balk at Christopher's methods, he proved his dedication to the region and never resorted to harsh words. Carl Prim communicated to his son through thinly veiled threats and emotional abuse. His ugly words were public. *How bad was it in private?* It was a miracle Steve wasn't aggressive. But, also, he'd never be out from under the man's thumb.

Surely Ashley could see that? Of all the romantic choices in town, Christopher remained the best option. Kind, hardworking, caring, he added the qualities of loyal, steadfast, and true as a husband. He couldn't tell her more of his dedication without hurting her.

He remained trapped in an impossible situation, only for the Steves and Zachs of the world to swoop in and steal the girl. And then, as if he willed it, his peace was broken. In the cupholder, his phone rang, the name *maybe* Steve Prim flashing.

Christopher would admit to a small, petty pleasure in not adding Steve to his cell phone contact list. This call was forwarded from his desk. He was surprised he'd had this much peace. He grabbed the phone and slid his thumb over the lock screen. "Hello?"

"Hey? Is Ashley with you?" Steve said through heavy breaths.

"No." Christopher frowned. She was on her way to see Seth. He might have entertained the idea that she would bump into Steve or Zach, and years of friendship might develop into something flirtatious. But she wouldn't lie to his face about where she was heading. "Why? What's going on?"

"She fell into the lake, and I took her to the hospital to get checked out. And she's not here. I left and came back, and she's gone."

"She's an adult, Steve. She can check herself out if she's physically able."

"I know, I know. It's just. That wasn't the... She was supposed to wait."

For what? Steve rescued her and gave her a ride to get cleared by a doctor. She had no obligation beyond her sincere gratitude. *What more was he expecting? That she'd feel so appreciative she'd fall in love with him?* Christopher curled his upper lip, preparing to snarl.

"The front desk saw you," Steve said. "Or someone who looked like you. Oh, my word. Do you think she was kidnapped?"

"What?" Christopher shook his head. "Why would she be kidnapped?"

"Why would she leave?" Steve screeched.

Christopher pulled the phone from his ringing ear and took a deep breath. He pressed the cell to his ear again. "She is fine. She was with me. I picked her up. But she's not with me at the moment. She had someplace to be. She's getting coffee with a friend."

"That's a relief. I'm glad she's okay," Steve said.

The ring of sincerity in his tone struck Christopher. Steve wasn't the smartest guy, but he was kind. For the first time,

Christopher wondered if he should do something to help. His enemy wasn't Steve as much as Carl.

The man demanded top dollar from Inn guests for a subpar experience. Christopher had fought for improvements and better prices. But Carl knew that as long as Christopher didn't take the initiative to offer his own cruising options, the Inn would remain a steadfast partner.

Unless I hire Steve? Ashley wouldn't balk. She might encourage the idea. Christopher could picture her bright smile. Was her happiness enough to override the frustration inherent in dealing with Steve as an employee? The man was little more than a lackey. Carl browbeat his son into a pulp. Could Steve step up once he was free of his old man?

"Let me handle this," a gruff voice yelled on the other end of the phone. "You always mess things up. You mishandled this whole situation."

Christopher pulled the cell away from his ear. The sharp words cut through the nice image like a serrated blade, a crude hacking of the surface.

Carl wasn't even on the call, and he was loud enough for the listener to cringe.

Christopher didn't particularly want to hear more. "She's fine. I'll handle her bills. Thanks for your help." He ended the call. He didn't want to stay on the line and deal with Carl. Although, he did feel a twinge of guilt for subjecting Steve to that prospect.

What was there to *mishandle*? Steve's outlandish assumption, that Ashley was kidnapped, bothered Christopher. The situation had been serious enough without adding in foul play. *She could have been killed.* He'd assured them both that the lighthouse accident was an inevitable mishap. The building should have been torn down or fixed up years ago. He wasn't certain. *Had someone tried to kill her?*

The more he thought about the entire calamity, from

explosion to rescue, the worse he felt. Dread coiled around him, weighing down his arms with old iron chains. No, he wouldn't let Carl's sourness turn his mind. Carl was the worst parent in town.

Xavier had been hard to please. Ashley didn't understand how impossibly high the standards her father held himself to were only lowered slightly for her. But he had never been cruel. He'd been indulgent for too long and had put his foot down when he had no other choice. Pride had prevented him from being honest. Their relationship suffered.

Christopher's temples throbbed, and the car walls closed in. The tight quarters were cramped. He'd rather not sit in a tight box with his work calls—and thus problems—forwarded to him. If he had issues, he'd rather deal with them from the comfort of his office.

Christopher slid out from the driver's seat with a harumph, locked the car, and crossed toward the front entrance.

"Mr. Lewis," a gruff voice called. "A moment."

Carrying a rake and wearing coveralls, the groundskeeper scowled, the expression just perceptible through the silver beard. He looked formidable and fierce. However, anyone who knew the man was aware he only terrorized weeds. "Good afternoon, Mr. Willie. Did you block off the island?"

"Little good a rope will do." Mr. Willie snorted. "Dismantle the bridge. You must take serious action to deter lookie-loos. Someone getting injured is a big problem."

Mr. Willie was, as usual, one hundred percent correct. But Christopher wasn't dealing in logic at the moment. He was working with his wife. *After we catch the villain.* "Yes, I'll consider the suggestion. Any luck with the lifeguard chair?"

"It's dry. I've placed it back into position. Not that anyone is swimming this early in the season." Mr. Willie raised a hand to cover his mouth. "Perhaps you can give Mrs. Hale-Lewis chores that don't involve the grounds?"

The words were muffled but not enough to lessen the impact of hearing her referred to by her married name. Christopher pressed the heel of his right palm against his pounding heart. "Of course."

Mr. Willie tipped his head and strode back the way he'd come.

Christopher continued toward the entrance, nodding and smiling at the bellhops and valets as he strolled inside his kingdom. He'd grown up on the grounds and never imagined anywhere could come closer to heaven on earth. He'd left for college and returned as soon as he could. She'd wanted to keep traveling. He'd never been enough for her, and neither had Loon Lake. What changed? Was she here because she came to appreciate what she'd had? Or because she had nowhere else to go?

He wanted this to be her choice.

Inside the lobby, the Inn was buzzing with conversations and activity.

Christopher made eye contact with each staff member standing behind the registration desk as he passed. He reached the bottom of the stairs before anyone stopped him.

Mr. Brixen stood in his path. "Mr. Lewis, may I have a word, sir?" The concierge darted his eyes and nodded toward the front office.

"Of course," Christopher said brightly, following the man. He was always aware of being present and pleasant when in the Inn's public spaces and the community in general. Only in the attic could he be himself. Xavier had taught him the importance of keeping a calm countenance.

Christopher stepped inside the office and shut the door. "What's the problem?" he asked under his breath, careful and aware as always of ears everywhere.

Mr. Brixen tapped on his cell phone and extended it. "Look at this. It's only been picked up locally. But this isn't the sort of thing you want getting out."

Christopher raised the phone, squinting at the screen. A webpage with the bold headline *CURSED?!* appeared over his senior yearbook photo. He frowned. Using the worst possible publicly available image was a low blow, even for Zach Jenkins on his Loon Lake conspiracy blog, The Jenkins Report. He scanned the text, swallowing his sigh. The text mentioned some of Ashley's recent shenanigans, leaning into the ghost angle she was so fond of but twisting it from a friendly specter into a malevolent poltergeist.

Luckily, the post didn't include today's explosion. But it mentioned that access to the island was restricted recently. Mr. Willie wouldn't like that; it might spur some of the youths to sneak onto the island and poke around the rubble, potentially hurting themselves.

"Thanks for bringing this to my attention. I think I owe the author a visit. I don't want this getting any traction," Christopher said.

"Very good." Mr. Brixen wiped a hand over his brow.

"If that's all?" Christopher asked gently. He didn't like the relief evident on his employee's face. Was he scary? Would Ashley be a better boss? More approachable?

"Did Mrs. Hale-Lewis deliver your envelope? I gave it to her first thing."

Christopher frowned. "No, but it's been a chaotic day. I'll ask her about it."

Mr. Brixen nodded.

Christopher left, taking the stairs two at a time. Up and down, in and out. He was running in circles. Since she'd come back, he hadn't known rest or peace. He would love to stay in the office and ignore the latest round of problems. But that wasn't his style.

What envelope could be so important that Mr. Brixen asked Ashley to hand-deliver? Why hadn't she? *Hotel Lavande?*

He scrubbed a hand over his face as he breathed shallowly, heading back to his car and jogging across the front drive. Mr. Brixen would instantly know the contents were important. Would Ashley? Why hadn't she given him the envelope?

He couldn't worry about the package now or try to read into her inaction. He'd push it to the side until their meeting later. He needed focus.

When he had something to do that he'd rather not, he had to deal with the issue as soon as possible. And there was nothing and no one he would rather avoid than Zach Jenkins. But the time had come for a face-to-face meeting. He wasn't about to back down.

Chapter Twelve

Ashley tugged the cuffs of her worn sweatshirt over her fingers. Despite the change of dry clothes, dressing for comfort and not style, she still hadn't warmed up. Inside the vehicle with Christopher, the air had hung heavy and unmoving. Full of suspense and anticipation. But the moment she had slipped out into the pine-soaked fresh air, she'd been chilled to her bone.

She entered the coffee shop through the open front door, her steps creaking on the uneven pine floorboards. The smell of coffee and the whir of the bean grinder greeted her first. She scanned the interior, noting most of the tables were occupied.

Approaching the counter, she ordered a hot chocolate with whipped cream and stood to the side. She loved the warm ambiance of the coffee shop. Her stint working in one hadn't been enough to cure her of the good feelings. Despite her lack of skills, she'd recharged every time she met a smile or chatted with a new customer. Extroverts did their best in public, and she was no exception.

It was why the only way she could stay in Loon Lake was in the center of the action at the Inn. If he cared about her, he wouldn't deny her the chance. But if she cared about him, she wouldn't ask him to sacrifice his career. Her temples throbbed. The longer she stayed, the more confused her goals and motivations were.

"There you are!" A gruff, wheezy voice called.

She stiffened, lifting her shoulders to her ears and slowly turning toward the door.

Carl Prim shook a beefy finger as he approached, his ruddy cheeks shining from exertion.

Behind him, head and shoulders above, Steve mouthed *sorry*.

"Oh, hi, Carl." She forced a smile. "Hi again, Steve. Thank you so much for the rescue earlier."

"You were supposed to wait for us," Carl said. "Wait. Not leave. Stay."

When a man raised his voice at her, she knew the expectations. The man wanted her to go meek and boneless, nodding like a good girl and apologizing for nonexistent errors and faults. But she'd never been called submissive or obedient. Instead, she got angry. She was not a child, and she would not be told what to do. Steve had angled her into the hospital, and she'd been too stunned by his agreement about her ghost to push back and insist he take her home.

But she wouldn't be intimidated by him or his father. And she wouldn't be addressed like she was a stray dog. The last man who tried that had been sorely disappointed to learn just how stubborn and strong-willed she was. Her heart ached a little for Dad and the hollow victory. She widened her stance and lifted her chin. "No. I was fine. I appreciate your concern, but I am perfectly sound and was able to leave."

Carl sputtered, opening up his mouth again.

"And besides," she continued before he could speak. "I've already talked to Christopher about the dinner cruise. I think it's great. You have my support." She nodded at Steve.

Now, the younger Prim gaped at her. "You do?"

The barista called, "Ashley."

She turned grateful to be saved from a response or giving either man any more of her attention. Grabbing the hot chocolate, she took a sip and turned away. Surveying the room again, she spotted Seth at a table near the window.

She glanced back over her shoulder, ignoring Carl and smiling at Steve. It was a shame he couldn't escape from under his father's thumb. Couldn't the Inn somehow absorb the marina and bring Steve on board? He was too gentle to deal with the constant barrage of insults.

But maybe that was just Ashley feeling petty and wanting to take everything good away from Carl.

Lonnie Treacle appeared behind Steve and Carl. "Guys, glad you're here. Come join me." He eyed Ashley warily and tilted his head to a table in the window.

She understood. The last place she wanted to be was seated with that trio on display for anyone walking past the coffee shop. She wouldn't have paired them as friends. But perhaps being old-timers gave them a shared sense of purpose. She hoped they weren't plotting against her husband. She couldn't fight for him as a double agent on every front.

Could she find an alliance with the younger crowd? Today's meeting was a good place to start. She made her way towards Seth. But as she neared, she realized he wasn't alone.

He'd told her about his meeting with Elise McKenna. She'd forgotten. Ashley could only hope he had offered a similar warning to the woman in return as she approached the table.

With a starched collar that was buttoned to the top, pale white skin, a constant expression of boredom, and brown hair tightly pulled back in a bun, Elise, leader of the historical society and director of the town tourism board, made an excellent ghost. Perhaps she would have been a good recruit if she hadn't always looked down on Ashley's antics as childish. How strange now to see the woman sitting side by side with Seth, arguably an even more foolish dreamer, and a small smile tugging up the corners of her mouth.

Elise would have been a better match for Christopher.

Even thinking it squeezed her heart so tight, Ashley struggled to take a full breathe. She reached the table. "Good afternoon. Am I too early?"

Elise lifted her chin and frowned.

"Not at all," Seth said with a smile. "We were finishing up."

Ashley pulled out a chair opposite the pair and sat. "What are you working on?"

Elise's forehead wrinkles deepened.

The flaw in the woman's otherwise perfect façade encouraged Ashley to keep pushing. Elise was so calm, cool, and collected. She evaded every argument with polite manners. Her adherence to etiquette grated Ashley's nerves, because she only realized Elise's slights after the fact.

"I had a few ideas for next year's big quasquicentennial celebration," Seth said.

"Wow. It almost rolls off the tongue. I'm surprised you need much more than that," Ashley said, hoping her teasing tone was effectively delivered.

Elise remained unmoved.

Seth chuckled. "It is something. One hundred and twenty-five years. Elise is heading up the committee."

"Yes, I'll have lots more to share with the Inn soon," Elise said primly.

At least she hadn't fired a verbal shot by singling out Christopher as the sole decision-maker, even if her wary expression held steady. How strange to encounter another naysayer when she'd been so welcomed by the shopkeepers on the boardwalk. Now she had to wonder why she hadn't received more pushback.

Zach, Seth, Lonnie, and the others joined Team Ashley almost as soon as she returned. She reevaluated how much the response was due to her and how much was an angry show against Christopher. *Was she viewed as the lesser of two evils or the easier to manage?* She'd have to think about it more. Later. Now she squirmed in her chair for a meeting she'd arranged but had become the third wheel at. "Is there a theme?"

"Seth was sharing a few slogans."

Seth blushed.

That bad? Ashley could only blame herself for asking. She had to prepare to not react. "Oh really?"

"You can't choose other people's memories. Make good ones that'll last over a century on Loon Lake," Elise said.

Ashley gaped. The surprising sentiment touched her heart. She couldn't control the narrative or influence anyone's opinion. She'd been trying to do both her whole life, especially with Christopher. She feared her husband considered her the comic relief and not serious enough for a real partnership.

"Ouch," Seth whispered.

Ashley shook her head and rubbed at her watery eyes. "No. It's good. Really good. That just kind of..." She pressed her right hand over her heart. "Sorry, it hit me. I wasn't expecting that." She smiled at Seth. He was a hustler. His print shop was a full-time job. But he still pursued his other interests.

"I was talking to Elise about your online stuff. I suggested you as the digital liaison," Seth said.

Elise stiffened.

Ashley did her best to keep her reaction neutral. *Pitying the dreamer went both ways?* Zach must have asked Seth to help her in the same way Christopher asked Ashley to partner with Seth. She and Seth had more in common than she realized. *Why not team up?* "I'm sure there will be a lot of details to settle."

"And you'll have the Inn," Elise added in very clipped tones.

Somehow, she made the casual words threatening. Was she shy and uncomfortable around someone she hadn't seen in years and had never had anything in common with? Or was it something more?

Elise pushed back her chair. "I'll be in touch, Seth."

"Thanks." He stood and stuck out a hand.

He was all fumbling gestures and stiff points. Elise wasn't much smoother, raising one hand and then the other. Their handshake seemed overly enthusiastic and lingering.

Ashley glanced away from the awkward goodbye. Was this what she looked like around her husband? At least she could count out the other woman as a love rival. Ashley had to figure out a solution to a new problem. How did she make Christopher fall in love with her again?

"Goodbye, Ashley," Elise said.

Ashley lifted a hand and nodded.

Seth sat and leaned forward. "Hey, are you okay? We can reschedule if this isn't a good time for you?"

"Umm?"

"I heard about the lake. Are you feeling alright?"

He did? Heat swept up her neck as a shiver raced down her spine. In a second, she was back in her sopping clothes, feeling foolish on the Prim's boat. "I'm fine."

"You were at the lighthouse? Did you see anything unusual? Any strange movements in the water?"

She shook her head.

"That's too bad. Zach is going to write an article about your ghost."

"Oh?" Her response was more gasp than vocalization. She hated her initial reaction to question whether Zach believed her ghost story or wanted ammunition against Christopher.

"When I went public about the lake monster, I had an initial rush of leads. Maybe you'll get something positive out of it. Before we talk about Soupy, I was hoping you could drop something off at the Inn?"

"Sure."

He pushed a box on the ground toward her.

Bending, she was glad for the excuse to hide her face under the table and take a break from the conversation. "What's this?" she asked, reaching inside for a smooth faux leather portfolio before straightening.

"The menus for the Inn. It took me several attempts to stop the smearing and fix the formatting. But I hope Christopher will be pleased. Third time's the charm, right?"

She opened the menu and widened her gaze. The letterpress printing on textured paper invited her to run her fingers down the sheet. "I can't imagine he won't be. These are beautiful."

"Thanks. I invested in a new machine when I took over. I had to work through the kinks of the process. But now I have a handle on it. I should be good to go from here on out. I promise."

She closed the menu and held it to her chest like a talisman. Christopher would be the biggest supporter of anyone trying to better themselves. And he believed in Seth. It's why Seth had so many opportunities to fix the mistake and why Christopher encouraged her to help.

What memories had Christopher made? She'd always thought of him as her partner in crime. As the lead character, he was her equal and her foil. Never her sidekick. *Was reality totally different?* She slipped the portfolio into her purse behind the envelope.

In the chaos of the day, she'd forgotten to give the package to Christopher. She could have handed it over in the car on the drive home from the hospital. She was lucky her bag hadn't been blown apart by the explosion or tossed into the water. What had the delay cost him? A job? Would he have to stay?

"You said you had some ideas about Soupy?" Seth asked.

"Yes." She nodded, glad to push aside her worry over her husband's next act. "My impression from the other day is that you're leaning into the paranormal phenomenon with real facts about mosasaurs."

"Exactly. The book is informational about mosasaurs and the ancient history of this region."

"I think it's the wrong direction. It's not very endearing to hear about prey, especially considering you propose this creature is in the lake and could devour us all. That's not a positive for tourism."

"What do you propose?"

"Couldn't Soupy be more like Puff the Magic Dragon?"

He scrunched his face. "But Soupy is real. I've seen him. I don't want kids thinking they can ride on his back or pet him. Can you imagine the lawsuits?"

Her stomach twisted. She didn't want to stop the creativity, but Seth needed to be grounded in some reality, or the project wouldn't take off.

"I don't quite follow why you want me to turn him into a fairy tale," Seth said.

She was glad he cut through her thoughts. She wasn't sure where she was heading either. She cleared her throat. "What else can be said about history? You have something unique to offer here. Have you ever considered writing a different sort of book?"

"Sure, of course I have." He shrugged.

She relaxed, letting out a ragged breath.

"I've been working on a memoir for years. Nothing is written down. I just sort of think about what I would include.

I use my phone to record my thoughts sometimes. Dad and I researched for years. He motivated the whole project. He encouraged me every step. Sharing my experiences might be just what others need to explain their paranormal encounters. Give others tools to advocate for themselves."

It was hard to argue with sweet, sincere Seth. She'd probably love to read his book about searching for Soupy with his dad. The retelling of a wonderful parent and child relationship would only add to the ache and longing for something she'd never had. "A memoir is one angle. But I'm thinking about Soupy from a children's picture book perspective. That's your best bet for merchandising and scaling up. Good IP is priceless. Could Soupy teach a lesson?"

"He can explain about being a mosasaur. Also, hopefully he can shed light on some new research. Mosasaurs lived in shallow salt water, but there is evidence of freshwater mosasaurs, too. Did you know plesiosaurs lived in freshwater rivers? A lot of exciting developments."

She nodded, her lips straining under the weight of pleasantries. Had Seth missed his calling? He had a lot of enthusiasm. "Or maybe he's lonely? Having a hard time fitting it until he learns he has to stand out?" *Is that me?* The conversation was derailing. She came as a concession to Christopher and was now uncovering more of her insecurities than she had ever guessed existed.

"So... not roaming the lake?"

She shook her head.

"I'll give it a try. I want to stick to the facts about Soupy and not write some fantasy about the monster. But maybe I can explain how the prey has evolved as the landscape has changed? I'm sure the science could be really interesting to schools to help keep kids engaged in learning."

She held his stare. Was she this hard-headed about the ghost? An accident sparking the fire was the most rational explanation. Her memory wasn't infallible. She didn't think she could have caused the blaze, but how else could she explain it?

The explosion was simply the next step after the building suffered so much damage. Maybe she was wrong. The strange skin-crawling encounters were hard to explain. The emotions clogged her throat, and the moments were locked in her visceral awareness. Something lingered at that lighthouse. Christopher was on board to meet her tonight. She'd propose a stakeout. And she'd prove she wasn't making up the incidents. They could both be right.

She had to have him on her side.

"Yes, that would be a great start," she said. "I am curious about something. The other day at the ice cream shop, you mentioned an encounter with Soupy?"

"Yep. As a kid."

"Tell me more."

"Do you really want to know? You aren't worried you'll get too scared to get into the water?"

Not likely. She didn't want to discourage him. She had the sense Zach and Christopher didn't believe Seth as much as they supported him. She wanted more information before she got on board. Someone didn't claim to see a long-extinct dinosaur relative with no reason behind it nor did a person perpetuate the myth without having a strong positive or negative memory attached to the moment of discovery.

She wasn't seeking to make sense of the psychology behind Seth using his fervent belief for Soupy to process his grief. She'd admit to herself that she wanted to work through his encounter to help her understand her own otherworldly experience. "I promise I won't."

"My dad loved ice fishing. He made me go. I hated every second. It was cold and boring. We had nothing in common. One trip, everything changed. I was alone in the hut. A dark shape swam under the ice. I got off my seat and kneeled on the ground near the hole. It opened its jaws and displayed its massive rows of teeth. I couldn't explain it. For once, Dad didn't brush me off when I told him or tried to explain. He listened. We went back the next weekend and the next. I didn't make another sighting until a year later. But that didn't discourage me. Dad got into the hunt too. We researched and studied. Once, we traveled to Chicago for a special museum exhibit about Mosasaurs. Before he died, he asked me to keep going. He didn't want me to give up. I won't."

I miss my dad, too. She opened her mouth and quickly shut it. Her children's book angle wasn't wrong, but knowing what she did now, she'd admit her instinct had been dismissive. Seth had reasons for Soupy she could understand. She needed to support and not challenge him. Maybe someone would do the same for her regarding the ghost.

* * *

Christopher hadn't strolled along the boardwalk in a year. He'd been meaning to for a while. The Memorial Day kickoff was more chaotic than usual, with stormy weather that continued into the first few weeks of June. After losing Xavier, however, Christopher had operated in a fog. Now, with the start of an understanding between him and Ashley, the sun burned off the low-hanging clouds, and he could see the terrain again.

And he spotted Zach Jenkins blocking his path. Metaphorically.

At the ice cream shop, Christopher dragged in the deepest breath he could and pulled open the door.

The silky-smooth voice of a male R&B singer lured the unsuspecting inside. *Can we talk?* Christopher almost choked on an ill-timed chortle. If only a conversation could smooth over years of distrust on both sides. They were way beyond civilized discussions.

Zach wanted blood.

Christopher wouldn't claim innocence on his part of the long-simmering feud. From the start, he'd retaliated against every one of Zach Jenkins' petty remarks with some form of passive aggression from himself or his business. A mediator or a miracle were the only viable solutions.

Nineties R&B couldn't hide the sins of the proprietor of the shop, as much as Zach might wish.

Christopher strode toward the counter.

The wind had picked up, chilling the day. Ashley had probably encountered an afternoon crowd at the coffee shop, tourists seeking hot beverages. Less than a half dozen patrons savored a cold treat around two bistro tables in the front window.

"Yo! It's a great day to keep it real. How may I help you?" Zach asked with his typically brittle tone. He was the iciest thing in the shop. Dressed like a geriatric member of a failed hip-hop revival, he crossed his arms over his chest and his chin hardened. He assumed a tough pose for the D-list group's latest album cover.

It was hard not to laugh at a grown man in neon and overalls. But Christopher wouldn't dare provoke him, no matter how funky fresh the ensemble. Instead, he arched a brow. "Have a minute?" He was always careful in front of tourists. More than anyone, he was aware of his public image.

Zach dried his hands on his apron. "Scotty," he called without turning. "Cover the front, please?"

Sneakers squeaked on the tile, and a pimpled kid burst through the door to the backroom in a neon apron to stand at Zach's side.

"Let's step out back," Zach said.

Christopher nodded and strode the length of the counter

toward the exterior door. He pushed open the fire-rated metal panel and scanned the gravel lot filled with dumpsters and cars for the employees of each shop.

He wasn't sure this was a better place for the conversation. For his sake, his office would have been best. At least he didn't spot anyone with pitchforks waiting to march on the Inn.

The door slammed shut.

"How can I help you? Need more projections?" Zach rubbed his hands together. "Perhaps you want to see my dream journal, too?"

Christopher crossed his arms over his chest. He couldn't totally hide his incredulity, but he successfully held back an eyeroll. Not giving into his worst impulses to taunt back was going to cause him to develop a twitch. "I trust you want what is best for the community and businesses as much as I do."

"Of course."

Deep breath in one, two, three, and release. If Christopher hoped the breathing technique would slow the rapid race of his pulse, he was wrong. His fingers itched to curl into a fist and punch the smug grin off Zach's face. At least he hadn't been told to talk to the hand. "Then I have to wonder at your methods."

Zach rolled his eyes. "Always so formal and fancy. You love a ten-dollar word when a penny would do. Say what you mean."

"Why are you blogging about the lighthouse and a ghost?"

Zach shrugged. "Why not? Ashley seems pretty convinced there is something supernatural occurring at the property. Shouldn't her voice count?"

Not in this way. Christopher gritted his back teeth.

"She is your wife. Shouldn't you be supporting her?"

Christopher might have growled. He definitely curled his upper lip. He wouldn't have his honor called into question by this man. "Enough. I'm handling what is happening at the Inn. I don't need any outside involvement."

"You demand respect for your boundaries, but you won't do the same for us in return? Mind our own business and leave yours alone?" Zach wagged a finger. "Tsk tsk. Very unbecoming."

Christopher wanted to say a lot. Words like *criminal investigation* floated through his brain. But how much could he give away? Being provoked by a bully wasn't anything new. He wouldn't give in to the urge to silence his opponent and reveal too much. "I guess I don't understand you. What is best for the Inn is best for the whole town."

"We disagree about the definition of *best*."

"You think Ashley is the winner? Or do you think she'll be easy to control?"

"She'd definitely change things up. We could all use that."

She would. But without someone to reign in her flights of fancy, she'd be running from one ghost story to another. Chaos would ensue. If channeled properly, she was an asset. "The Inn is central to the town."

"Maybe it shouldn't be. Maybe we're tired of living in a dictatorship and want a democracy."

Christopher snorted. "Or you intend to set up a puppet autocracy."

"Well, the stories are interesting." Zach stroked his chin. "I didn't give Ashley any credit for her ghost theory. But now that she's supporting Soupy, perhaps I should give her idea another look. And, of course, there is still the treasure."

Christopher rolled his eyes. "There is no treasure. You know that. It was a marketing ploy."

"And it's still working. I get that you tried to set up Ashley as some sort of mole. But you're not the only player in this game."

Christopher couldn't shake his distrust or his respect for

the other man. While Christopher admitted he was guilty of trying to use Ashley's return for his gain, he had never worked against her. In his heart, he wanted to establish a partnership for their own best interests. But his attempts at controlling how he let her back into his life had failed. She owned him body and soul. He owed Zach no explanation. Christopher lifted his gaze to Zach's. "This all started because a savvy guy like you didn't want to write a business plan. Your anger and campaign against me started with numbers. Do you see how silly this has all become? And I think, deep down, you're grateful that I forced you to analyze your books. That makes you madder than anything."

Zach flared his nostrils like he'd breathe fire. "You know, I can't wait to see what Ashley does with the Inn. She is so creative." He turned and stalked back inside his shop, slamming the door.

Christopher stood in place. The longer he stared at the door, focusing on inhaling and exhaling, the more his vision cleared. He wasn't sure how long he remained. But slowly, the world came back into view, no longer tinged with angry red but the bright colors of the day.

And then he moved. If he stayed, he was likely to get hit by a bag of garbage Zach would gleefully fling at him from the ice cream shop.

Christopher strode along the gravel road connecting the boardwalk shops to the main street. The building's public entrances overlooked the lake. The back doors faced the road, making deliveries and garbage day out of sight from the guests' view.

It also gave the long stretch a false sense of peace. The pine scent was strong enough to cover the trash. Bird song echoed. The cool air refreshed even the weariest of souls.

Loon Lake managed to avoid much of the commercialization that overtook a lot of other communities. But it was a constant battle to maintain their way of life. The future held no guarantees.

Tires crunched over the gravel.

He lifted his head off his feet just in time to spot the SUV barreling down the road. Jumping back, he slammed into a dumpster, the lid hitting his back. He wrapped his arms around himself, tight, hoping compression might ease the sharp ache piercing him.

A door slammed shut.

The sound reverberated against his ribs, and he shut his eyes.

"Chris?" Seth Boyd asked, his heavy steps coming close. "Oh, man. I'm so sorry. Are you okay?"

Only one person used the nickname. Opening one eye at a time, Christopher spotted Seth.

Chewing his lip and nervously shifting his weight, Seth would probably offer assistance.

Christopher didn't need any help. He dropped his arms and stood as straight as he was able. "I'm okay. What's got you in such a hurry?"

"Hold on a sec." Seth held up a finger before racing to the trunk. He opened the back, grabbed a box, and shuffled over. With a big grin, he set the box down and pulled out a newspaper. "Check this out."

Christopher grabbed one, impressed by the feel of the print. "You printed this?"

"I did." Seth's grin broadened. "I had an idea, and the local business owners bought ads, so I could get going with it. This is sort of a test run. I'm dropping off a box at Lonnie's and Zach's to start. They've been really supportive of the whole thing."

Christopher stiffened. The project might not be in his best interest if those two were involved. He scanned the front page. "*The Summer of Soupy*," he read the headline out loud.

"Yeah, this was before I met with Ashley. We just finished up. She had a lot of great ideas about Soupy, but this was already complete. Can you give her a copy? I forgot to give her one when she grabbed the menus. I squeezed in a whole section devoted to her ghost."

From the very center of his being, Christopher radiated his displeasure with a deep, furrowed brow. What would an article achieve? He worried someone had taken advantage of an opportunity, the fire, and risked her life with the explosion unknowingly.

More attention on her ghost story wouldn't help. Curious onlookers would mill on the lakeshore and complicate his surveillance of the lighthouse. Should he call the police and file a report before his insurance company caught wind of the issue?

Why hadn't she asked him for his advice? He promised to discuss her sightings. Her lack of faith disappointed him, lodging a rock in his throat. "She wrote an article for you?"

"No, no. Zach did. But I think she'll be pleased. He's a good writer."

Christopher opened the paper, scanning the local calendar and ads until he spotted the article, a full page in the center. Words popped off the newsprint. *Conspiracy? Treasure? Danger?* Throbbing started in his temples and continued down along every nerve ending. Zach had done more than just blog on a page no one would visit. He found a way to bring the fight to the public and used Seth as a shield. More than that, he called Christopher's bluff.

If Christopher avoided the tabloid blog *The Jenkins Report*, he'd have a harder time ignoring stacks of print in every building in town, including his lobby. *Loon Lake Life* might be a newspaper to Seth, but it was an incendiary eighteenth-century revolutionary pamphlet to Christopher. Or so

Zach Jenkins would have it. Christopher wouldn't give in to his nemesis with an outburst.

"You'll tell her?"

"Sure."

A crash of metal on metal saved him from more response or having to gracefully decline to accept any copies for the Inn.

"Hey, Seth," Lonnie called from the fudge shop door. "You coming?"

"Yes, sir," Seth said, straightening the box in his arms. "Bye, Chris."

Christopher nodded. With a heavy sigh, Christopher decided on the long way along the gravel road back to the Inn. Maybe crunching stones under his feet would drown out the voices in his head. Or maybe he owed himself and her the truth.

Chapter Thirteen

Why did standing outside his office door feel so serious?

After a nap and a shower, Ashley had dressed for their evening activity. He was probably joking when he'd said *all-nighter*, but she prepared all the same. She was ready for vindication, looking forward to this chance to prove herself correct. But until she paused in the hallway, she hadn't considered that whatever happened tonight would impact her future.

She had grown up in this building. She knew every nook and cranny. Here, in converted attic space, she could see through the drywall and paneling to her spooky childhood memories.

His domain hadn't been her father's, thankfully. She had too many bad memories from the lectures and disappointed headshakes she'd received in that spot. She should have no qualms up here.

But it was like she had wandered onto the set of a beloved sitcom in time for a very special episode. Or, worse, a preachy public service announcement only vaguely connected to the other zany antics aired weekly. She was an outsider in her home. She hadn't considered the true cost of leaving.

She pinched her cheeks, adding a bit of color, before raising a fist and knocking on the door. She didn't want to look like she had gone to too much trouble with her appearance. But neither could she show up without making some sort of effort. She smoothed her hands over the extra-large black sweater, tugging the hem over her hips and leggings.

The door opened.

Christopher appeared on the other side.

Her heart flipped.

He was dressed in black, too, although his crewneck sweater hugged his torso like an expensive, tailored fitted suit. Inside her slip-on, canvas sneakers, she curled her toes. The white fabric was no longer spotless but faded and shabby. Like most of her life. She hadn't purchased anything new in years, only replacing what she absolutely could not mend.

She was focusing on the wrong aspect. He took the plan seriously enough to dress the part. Even if he still didn't believe in every facet, his outfit showed some real understanding.

A tiny flicker, a lot like hope, flared inside her chest. She rubbed her palms together before tucking her clammy hands under her arms. "Hi. Can I come in?"

"Please." He pushed the door wider, stepping back.

She passed into his sanctum and took a deep breath of the hint of pine and leather in the space. The room was calming because it was so high up, perched in the treetops. Climbing stairs was a wonderful exercise, and with such consistency, his butt must be rock hard.

She flushed. Why did her mind go there?

"How are you feeling?" he asked.

She whirled around.

He shut the door and crossed toward the leather chairs, waving her to sit.

She crossed the room, unsure how to answer. Her hot cheeks betrayed her.

"Any fever? I hope you didn't catch something from the lake water." He frowned.

"Oh, no. I'm fine." She waved off his concern and sat in one of the chairs, slipping off her shoes and tucking her feet underneath. She liked to sit twisted up and tight. Making herself small wasn't the goal. She liked feeling in control, holding onto herself. Sometimes, the physical was all she could restrict.

"Are you sure? If you don't feel well..."

He'd what? Get her a blanket? She was tempted to wait him out and hear what he intended. But she might end up with more than she bargained for or less of what she wanted. "I'm fine." She released a heavy sigh.

He pierced her with a knowing look.

"Yeah, sorry. That wasn't very convincing."

He lifted the corner of his mouth in a smile.

"I guess, if I'm being honest..." She nibbled the corner of her lip. Every truth she hid whirled through her mind. She wanted to reveal everything. But how much honesty could she share before he turned away and stomped on her heart?

"I've never known you to be anything otherwise. Please don't start pretending to be someone else now."

"Good point." She shrugged. "I feel sort of... silly."

"Why?" He narrowed his gaze and tipped his head to the side.

But he didn't stare at her with condemnation. He wasn't judging her. Instead, he studied her with contemplation and slight confusion, like he hadn't known her his whole life.

The idea of a fresh start was surprising and tempting, a hint of what they could have been if they'd met as adults without a lifetime's worth of baggage and experience between them. Like he hadn't been her first everything, and she was someone mysterious and worth getting to know. Like she wasn't his free gift with purchase.

She raised a shaky hand, pushing a loose tendril behind her ear. "I'm nobody's first choice. I've never let that bother me before. With the Inn, though," she exhaled a heavy breath. "I took everything here for granted. Coming back, I've had to reassess. Everyone is here but different. Mature. And me? I'm stuck. I guess I worry about you laughing at me," she murmured.

The soft words delivered a heavy punch in the silence that followed.

Bullseye. Her verbal arrows accidentally hit the truth with pinpoint accuracy. She wished she hadn't said anything. She wanted to crawl inside her sweater and disappear. She fought the urge to do just that. Only since coming back did she fully appreciate what she had relinquished and could never get back.

He'd always been there. She'd taken him for granted, too. She'd been so blind that she missed the incredible person who —at one point—had loved her and devoted himself to her. He agreed to her whims and plans for years. Now she couldn't trust that she wasn't tied up in his ultimate goal of owning the Inn because of the games she'd played. With her previous departure, she'd done the hard work of removing herself, his obstacle, from the path to his success.

"I'm not laughing at you." He reached a hand over to her chair, resting on the arm. "I've only laughed with you."

"You didn't choose me," she whispered, too scared to speak louder. She stared at his hand so close. She placed him in the center of an unwinnable situation. As someone who had prided herself on setting him up for the easy answer, she'd tossed him into the middle of a storm without warning. "I'm sorry for... what happened. I shouldn't have put you on the spot."

"I am, too."

She met his gaze. "You are?"

He nodded. "I should have picked you."

"I didn't make that a compelling choice." She scrunched her nose, fighting the burning sensation. She'd wanted him to follow her without question. Would she have respected him for doing so? She'd put them both in an impossible position that produced bad results no matter the decisions.

She'd needed a decade to understand that. And she couldn't tell him what she'd realized, or she'd lose him. She glanced at her purse. Inside, the mysterious envelope sat. She imagined it beating like a heart under the floorboards. She should want him to go. He broke her heart years ago. Realizing he still had the power to shatter the pieces was an awful discovery.

"Mr. Brixen stopped me in the lobby earlier. He said he handed you a package?" Christopher asked.

She flushed with embarrassment. How clearly he could read her face even after all these years. She opened her bag and slipped out the thick envelope, extending it to him.

He grabbed it. "Thank you."

"What is it? A job offer?" she asked, unable to stop herself from getting at least a few clear answers.

"Is that what you want?" He studied her as he dropped the envelope to the table.

No. She forced her shoulder to lift in a lame attempt at nonchalance. With any luck, he didn't notice the shake in her hands. Winning would be a hollow victory at best. She understood now how much she stood to lose by claiming the prize. He'd leave. She'd had a life without him. She didn't want that again.

He wiggled an eyebrow. "Maybe I got you a job offer."

She lightly jabbed him in his shoulder.

He chuckled, low and long. "I'm kidding, of course. You

were right to come home. You belong here. You're part of the fabric of this place."

"I'd say the same about you."

He shook his head. "Not really. I only belong because of your family. No one will miss me."

I would. I already lost you once. Don't make me live it again. Starting over hadn't worked out the way she'd wanted. Could she move to Hawaii and try again? The new setting would only hide her pain for a little while. She probably should offer to leave but couldn't bring herself to consider it.

"On to other topics. You went to the coffee shop today. How was Soupy?" he asked.

She met his pleasant smile with a fake one of her own. He'd given her the cue, and she'd follow suit. He wanted to back away from real talk. If she stopped, she wouldn't push him away. She could survive a little longer without any progress or answers.

* * *

Seated on one of the two leather club chairs, Christopher studied the arrangement again, wishing he could pretend he hadn't just asked such a pointless question. He'd really had no choice. Fear forced him to stick to the plan and avoid anything even hinting about *them.*

Too easily, he could picture her at the Hotel Lavande. She'd run it with aplomb. He'd teased her about finding her a job far from his domain. But he couldn't argue the merits. She could soar anywhere. She'd shine in Hawaii. He could help her financially. He'd do anything. He could buy the resort for her, taking on the mortgage.

Because he couldn't bear listening to her tell him he was her default and never her choice. He'd shouldered a lot. But he could never come back from that.

Treating her like an equal, he should fill her in on Zach's machinations. She should know how the man attempted to manipulate her. He didn't want to weaken their fragile bond by sharing painful information. He wasn't much better than Zach, and Zach at least gave her ghost far more credence.

Christopher had placed two flashlights, two walkie-talkies, two notepads, and two pens on the low coffee table. A neat and tidy pairing of items for their mission. Before they could use the tools, they'd first need to work out the details, and discussing their feelings wasn't part of it.

He was relieved to have something to focus on because he was more confused than ever. He'd never claimed to understand women. Any man who did was a clown. At one time, however, he'd known her heart better than his own.While he couldn't claim expertise anymore, he'd swear he heard an invitation in his SUV. Of course, he had to be wrong.

What he needed was time to get himself organized. He needed a plan. His lawyer would have plenty. First, however, he needed to understand what she wanted. He'd have the lawyer draw up paperwork with a payout that would be more than generous. She considered the property a winner-take-all scenario. He wanted to fight fair.

But now he wasn't sure what to do or say.

In such situations, he typically kept silent. But she hated quiet. He had uttered the ridiculous question that popped into his mind. And then he decided to repeat it. "How was Soupy?"

A knock sounded at the door, saving her from an immediate reply.

"Sorry, I ordered some food. I hope you're hungry."

"I am." She licked her lips.

He got up from the chair and crossed the room, glad to put some space between them.

A uniformed server stood on the other side of the door,

holding a tray.

"Thank you," Christopher said, grabbing the wooden handles.

With a nod, the staff member shut the door.

"Can you clear a space on the table?"

She nodded.

He crossed the room and lowered the burden to the top, lifting off the silver lids on several plates piled high with meats, cheeses, dried fruit, and crackers.

"No candied pecans? Or the rosemary-cured olives?" she asked.

He frowned and stared at the tray. *It* was a plate of food to him, nothing more and nothing less.

She crossed to the desk and picked up the phone, calling in a request to the kitchen.

"Sorry. I guess I'm out of my depth."

"It's okay. I love food. But if I'm going to eat, I don't want to just mindlessly consume. I want to enjoy my meal. Bring out flavors with contrasts. Sometimes, the most surprising combinations make the most delicious treats."

He liked hearing her talk like that. He was curious about the changes she would make if she stayed.

Another knock came at the door.

She answered and accepted a smaller tray.

He made room on the low coffee table and grabbed a plate, serving himself some sustenance. He'd been a fool to think a salad was enough to keep him going. He hadn't wanted to trouble anyone by asking them to make him a meal outside of regular kitchen hours.

She looked at his plate and added a few things here and there to it.

"Maybe you should stick to your strengths," he said. "You like food." And he liked the glow on her skin. More than the late afternoon light, she shone from the inside out.

"It's nothing." She waved him off and gathered food for herself.

"It's something. If I don't eat in the kitchens here, I'm great at making a bowl of cereal. I don't know how to feed myself. You have a passion for food."

"Hardly. I just think life is too short not to enjoy every second, including meals. What's stopping any of us? Worry about tomorrow and a few extra pounds? Who cares?"

Or fear of losing those we love. She was right. He glanced away, grabbing a skewer of olives and stuffing it in his mouth. Unintentionally, he had encouraged her into danger by not taking her ghost story as fact. She'd put herself in harm's way because she hadn't had his full support. At the lighthouse, she could have been seriously injured.

He probably lost a few years of his life after the stress of seeing her so fragile and tiny on the hospital bed. He had to go with her, even though she'd try to dissuade him. He wouldn't waste the energy or the words. He'd keep tabs on her and watch her as close as he dared. "It's something worth considering."

She shook her head. "No, working in the food industry isn't my future path. I'm not sure what is. But I don't want to devote years to something I'm not passionate about."

Coming up with off-the wall ideas. Reinvigorating these old walls. People. He had a list a mile long of her strengths. "Let's talk about tonight," he said. He hated to jump topics, but he didn't want to linger on her weaknesses. She was so creative and inventive. She saw everything from a different perspective. There was a value to her eternal optimism. But he knew he'd only fluster and frustrate her if he continued the discussion. "This office has the best view of the lighthouse. I'll order some coffee, and we can take turns keeping watch after ten. I don't think we'll have long to wait. If someone is going to head to the lighthouse, they'll go early or lose their nerve."

"Do you still think the ghost is a human hoax?"

Her flat delivery didn't persuade him to drop his beliefs. She had no proof of a ghost. The destruction of the lighthouse left tangible pieces of evidence. He failed to understand her grip on the story she told herself. *What am I missing?* "I want to take every precaution we can. We can't protect ourselves against an other-worldly being. But we can be prepared for a mortal."

"Fair enough." She smiled. "But, if it's a ghost?"

The little tilt of her mouth, the self-deprecating charm, tugged his heart. He'd been tempted to chase along with her for years, following every scheme, because of that effervescent quality he couldn't quite pinpoint.

She included him in her jokes. It was always the two of them against the world until he'd suddenly had grown-up responsibilities. She'd had no clue about the weight on him.

Slowly, one secret at a time, he chose the real world over her. He couldn't go back, no matter how much he longed to. She had no idea what it meant to stay.

"Why do you think it's a ghost?"

"Because why not?" She arched a playful brow.

But he'd hit her armor, missing the bullseye but piercing the protective shield all the same. Was she swamped with regret? Was that the feeling holding her down? He wouldn't burden her on his behalf. He'd prefer a fresh start if possible. "I actually ran into Seth. He's started a local paper of sorts. He wanted you to know he had it in production before your meeting."

"Why is that important?"

"Because his lead headline is about Soupy in his current, awe-inspiring murder spree self. But inside he found space for something you'd be interested in. Zach wrote an article about your ghost."

Her breath caught. "Oh. He did?"

Christopher turned to study her then. She looked unsteady and unsure. "He brought up the old treasure rumor and alluded to a conspiracy on the part of the Inn."

"Of course, he did." She shook his head. "I don't want to be used in a game between the two of you."

I'm not using you. But he wasn't sure that was entirely true. At the start, when he knew she was back, he wanted to manipulate the situation to his best advantage. He was still trying to work every angle. Zach was doing the same, albeit from a different side. If it was a game, though, Christopher would admit one thing. He played for keeps.

* * *

Maybe it's my dad sending me a message. If Ashley told him why she needed, more than anything, to believe the ghost was real, would she be brave or pathetic? Putting her heart on the line with him never really got her to where she wanted or expected to be.

She wanted Dad to be watching out for her. Desperately. Otherwise, she had to accept the truth. He was gone for good, and she never had a chance to say goodbye.

Right now, however, she needed to find some sort of common ground. Their shared interest in the resort probably qualified. "Hey, what's going on at the old sawmill."

A few yards away from the mouth of the channel stood a crumbling sawmill and dock. From its stone foundation rose a three-story timber structure. The original planks had been patched and covered with vinyl siding, creating a patchwork, rectangular eyesore along the shoreline.

Christopher didn't care because it didn't directly impact the business. She knew he should. He might not be able to see the building now. But if the land sold to a developer, they'd probably be able to see the condos, mansions, or whatever monstrosity was erected to capitalize on the space. At the least, the dock jutting out into the lake would become crowded and noisy.

They'd been downstream from a sleeping giant. Once awakened, all sorts of trouble could erupt. The region didn't have any specific building code restrictions. The area thrived on community spirit and a system of respect and shame that served better than any formal legalese. Could it last?

"What do you mean?"

"It looks almost abandoned. Has the old lady passed?"

"She's in hospice. She moved out of the building six months ago. Should I send a team by? Did you spot trespassers?"

Ashley shook her head. "I'm sure it's fine. I didn't see anything out of the ordinary. It was more like...a feeling."

"Like your ghost?" He narrowed his gaze.

Exactly. She didn't pretend to be an empath or somehow attuned to the supernatural. But buildings gave off energy. And the sawmill emoted sadness. She couldn't remember a time it had ever been operational. The industry had moved on from the old methods practiced at the Maguire Lumber mill since the nineteenth century.

If she wracked her brain, however, she remembered the cheer of the building. Colorful planters overflowed with petunias and impatiens, dotting the façade and outlining the private dock every few feet. The flowers brightened an otherwise green patch of the shoreline.

She remembered boat rides with the Prims past the tallest structure on their shore. She imagined it as a tower fit for a princess. Now, the building was shuttered and closed. The planters were empty. The whole space looks vacant. "She hasn't appointed a caretaker? Has she considered selling the property?"

"She has too much respect for the history of the place to

let it go to a developer. Of that, I'm one hundred percent certain. I'm sure she's considered who will inherit and has a plan in place after her passing."

"She should give it to the historical society and be done."

"Maybe. Elise has been working that angle for years." He shook his head. "If anyone can convince her, it'll be Elise. She's tenacious." The corners of his mouth lifted.

Ashley didn't like his smile at the mention of another woman. Nor did she much care for the melodic sound of the other's name on his tongue. "I guess tenacious is one word for her." She lifted her shoulder.

"You and Elise could probably be friends. If you tried..."

She let the statement hang heavy in the room. Elise was everything Ashley wasn't. They'd been rivals in school because neither could understand the other. Ashley had no desire to suddenly become the woman's friend, especially not if she was after her husband.

"The old legend could hurt all of us," he said. "Some call it a curse."

She rolled her eyes. "*A Maguire in possession is prosperity for all*? You think the reverse is also true? Without a Maguire, we're doomed?"

"The community is superstitious. Old lore has a habit of becoming a self-fulfilling prophecy here."

She crossed her arms. "I'm surprised you support the legend. Isn't there some sort of rumor about treasure tied up in the mill? I would think you'd be team no treasure on all fronts."

"I don't mind a Maguire treasure hunt. That would restrict the explorers to the opposite side of the lake. Specifically, the Timber Triangle."

"That's another thing I'd never heard before that everyone acts like it's a part of our town's founding." She hated feeling so out of the loop.

"Seth's revelation about Soupy led to a series of confessions about strange occurrences in and around the lake. The Timber Triangle was actually Elise's contribution based on her research."

Why did everything include Elise? "What? Like the Bermuda Triangle? Did aliens abduct a plane flying in the area?"

He grinned. "Not quite. A ship sank out there. And other reports of malfunction have appeared in various maritime records. But if you start probing, you'll probably learn somebody had an extraterrestrial abduction. In Loon Lake, everything is possible."

Why not her ghost?

"Maybe," he dragged the word, "something is out of the ordinary at the lighthouse."

"A ghost?"

"I don't know. I like that it protected you."

Good. Because she needed every ounce of safety she could get. If a spirit from the great beyond wanted to help, she wouldn't turn it away. She'd feel safest with her husband on her side. "Well, I find the Maguire legend a bit ridiculous. The mill has hardly been prospering. Are the rest of us supposed to be quaking over what happens if the ancient laws of primogeniture fail?" *Because the town won't have to wait long.* She didn't see much purpose in further explaining the situation. Without her blood claim, she'd be out of luck. She was a hypocrite to argue the other side.

"Why do you pick and choose which myth to believe in?" He leaned his chin in his hand.

She almost sighed in relief that he hadn't jumped on her argument to turn her words against herself. "I have to accept all or nothing? Like you? No middle ground?"

He frowned.

And she dropped it. Because they'd both hit too close to

the heart of the matter for the other's comfort. "If I support Soupy, will that make you feel better?"

He groaned.

And she chuckled. Her first real belly laugh in years, the tickle in her throat turned into a bending over, holding her stomach guffaw. "I have offered opinions. I think we had a good meeting. Seth is clever. It's up to him now. If he can hire an illustrator, he might be okay."

"Illustrator?"

"Children's book is the best way to market the creature." She pressed a hand to her heart. "In my humble opinion."

He chuckled. "Yes, very self-deprecating and modest. I don't think he'll take you up on that. He seems convinced he has to educate everyone about Soupy. But I'm glad you've come around. Dreamers need each other."

"Soupy wouldn't be the worst thing to happen to town. Not like the idea to have a Fourth of July regatta." She grinned.

He groaned. "Oh, don't remind anyone. They'll want to do it again."

The regatta had been Christopher's first attempt at getting involved in the Inn during their teenage years. He'd pitched it as a fun, community-wide parade. In the end, a handful of boats had been pulling rafts of various buoyance in the frigid water. She could still remember the calls to the EMTs for help warming up the passengers on the rafts when one of the Prims tour boats got too close and soaked everyone with their wake.

Had that been his last creative idea? She wouldn't accuse him of quitting when he struggled with trying something new and met with disaster. She hated if he'd missed opportunities to think outside the box over the years. Soupy might be his way to make up for his years of hard-nosed management and embraced a little fun. She hoped so.

"Elise and Seth seemed to really hit it off. He's working

with her on the new slogan." She paused, waiting for a reaction.

Christopher stuffed a bite into his mouth.

Had she misread his feelings about Elise? She hoped so. "Seth has a catchphrase I like."

"Really? What is it?"

She was toeing the line between them, inching towards the dangerous topics they seemed so much better off avoiding. But whatever happened, wouldn't they need a reckoning of the past? *Maybe not. Maybe we can just pretend we start over.* "You don't choose other people's memories. Make good ones together."

"Wow. Seth came up with that?"

She nodded. "He did. It gives me hope for his work with Soupy. That and the connection with his dad." Understanding what the lake monster meant to Seth helped. What must total parental support, despite the illogical conclusion, feel like? Her dad loved her but didn't really believe in her, dismissing her ideas as frivolous. Her nose itched, and unshed tears stung her eyes. She sniffed. Better to focus on the present. "I dropped off the final batch of menus in the restaurant. Do they earn your approval?"

"Whole-heartedly, he did a great job. He's working through the process and learning. Without anyone else to guide him, he's got to take ownership of every step and the end result. But he'll get there. Seth's a good guy."

Takes one to know one. She tucked the blanket more firmly around herself. "Stop distracting me from my job, please. I've got to catch a ghost."

Christopher chuckled and faced the windows. "Right you are."

Chapter Fourteen

With her legs tucked underneath her on the leather armchair and a blanket thrown over her lap for good measure, Ashley should be falling asleep. She was warm, dry, and full. She'd had a companionable evening, laughing about old stories and avoiding any serious talk. She'd come so close to unburdening her heart, only to have the good sense at the last second to hold her tongue. Following the day's excitement, she should be exhausted. She shouldn't be awake and replaying every moment of the day.

But she was too wired to sleep.

At ten on the dot, Christopher had ordered coffee. She had slurped almost the entire carafe on her own. He'd fallen asleep an hour ago.

The chairs were angled to face the windows.

Outside, the sky was a rich, dark velvet studded with diamonds. The moon shone bright as a spotlight. The world was resting.

His deep snores threatened the quiet peace. She smiled. For a long time, she'd been unable to sleep through an entire night alone. It wasn't missing a warm body next to her. She produced enough heat to sleep without covers through winter.

She'd missed the snoring. She could fall asleep but couldn't stay asleep without the white-noise machine effect of his breathing. She wouldn't rouse him to stop. The noise was reassuring and comforting.

If he knew he snored, he'd do everything he could to stop. He hated to be an inconvenience to anyone. She'd miss the imperfection.

She narrowed her gaze back toward the windows. The lights in the office were turned off. She was sitting in the dark, but her vision had long ago adjusted to the night. She scanned the lighthouse, now covered in caution tape and scaffolding.

The spiral staircase remained but the rest of the building was a pile of debris. He'd need to knock the whole thing down before going further. The metal risers held no historic significance. Starting fresh made the most sense. And not just about the building.

She was becoming her own worst enemy with a self-fulfilling prophecy that she couldn't do anything without help. She'd grown up with every need and most wants fulfilled. On her own, she still had someone else to rely on. She'd come back and done nothing but cause trouble.

What if she really tried? Could she go somewhere and start over and find success? Did she want to?

Stay. The force of the word reverberated from deep in her chest, shaking her. Maybe believing in the power of a fresh start was part of the problem. Why would she want to reinvent herself? In Loon Lake, she was the sum total of her actions from birth. It was, at times, painful and embarrassing. Any acquaintance—no matter how casual—could recall some of her worst moments in a few seconds or an off-hand phrase. She still didn't laugh about the time she got stuck to a totem pole, the thick tar nearly taking off a layer of the skin on her palms as Lonnie Treacle had to help Zach Jenkins' dad peel her off.

But she also knew she could count on anyone for help. Even if she did something ridiculously, epically ill-advised. Like pretending to be a ghost and setting fire to a town landmark.

She wouldn't accept ownership of that accident. She'd replayed the situation hundreds of times in her head and couldn't work out how it could be anything *but* a ghost. Batteries could combust. But how would a tiny votive cause such a spark? The community wouldn't believe her but neither would anyone think poorly of her for her conviction.

With people who knew her, she had family. They had lived a shared history and still could have many struggles and triumphs to celebrate and endure together. Giving up and moving on wasn't in the cards. She'd tried. She'd never found happiness with any relocation. Belonging was far more valuable than a first impression.

Movement caught in the corner of her eye.

She untucked her legs, leaving the blanket in the chair and tiptoeing to the window. Her muscles ached from too long in a pretzel-like twist. Her ankle cracked. She froze and turned.

Back on his chair, Christopher shifted but continued to snore.

At the window, she squinted and looked at the lighthouse. She couldn't see anything or anyone. She didn't have the skin-crawling sensation that preceded every encounter with the ghost. Honestly, she wasn't sure what to think about the entity. While the ghost had started the fire, the spirit had saved her from the building collapse. The fire secured her a nice warm bed. Maybe the ghost cared about her. *Why?*

Looking at the lighthouse again, she still saw nothing unusual. The water's dark surface was smooth as glass under the bright moon. She didn't see any shadows and heard nothing. Reason stood that all remained as it should. But she couldn't shake her certainty either.

She crossed to his chair and grabbed his shoulder, gently shaking him. "Christopher. Christopher," she murmured.

He opened his eyes and yawned. "Hmm?" A lazy smile spread over his face. "Come back to bed." He reached for her.

Fool that she was, she almost swayed into his touch. She longed to be held, safe and secure. But they wouldn't find peace until they got to the bottom of the treachery at the lighthouse.

She stepped back. "We're not in bed." Her voice cracked. She coughed. "Wake up. I think someone is at the lighthouse."

He scrubbed his hands over his face. "Ashley? What time is it?" His voice was low and gravelly, and he blinked several times, twisting his neck from side to side.

"Not very late. Maybe eleven fifteen?" She glanced at the clock on her phone and snorted, showing him the screen.

"Eleven forty? How long have I been asleep?"

"I don't know. An hour? Come on." She grabbed the blanket off his lap and tossed it onto her chair. "We have to go."

He got to his feet and brushed past her, his shoulder rubbing hers in a whisper of a touch.

She sucked in a breath, achingly aware of his nearness. Her skin electrified from the accidental contact, zinging down to her toes. She had never wanted anyone in such a maddening, all-consuming, fiery way as she wanted her husband. From the first hint of puberty, she couldn't seem to shake her addiction.

"Let's take the flashlights." He strode to the desk and grabbed them, tossing one to her.

She caught it and followed him to the door in the front corner of the room. With a shake, she tamped down her hormones.

He opened the door and flashed the light on the handrail. "Hold on as you go down. I don't want to turn on the lights."

"This is like a secret passage." She followed behind him, the stairs wrapping in a tight spiral.

"Or my own personal escape hatch," he said, his voice threaded with something dark and funny. "No one is allowed to use it but me. Saves a lot of time when I'm needed downstairs."

At the bottom, he held out his hand.

She grabbed it. Her stomach flipped and fluttered at the contact. Her body eased into the muscle memory of his warm touch. He'd always been her safe harbor. Even when he was taking her to places she'd never dreamt. She trusted him. Her faith remained steady.

He opened a side door and gently tugged her alongside.

The contrast of the chilly night air against her flushed skin was sharp. But not painful. Her senses were heightened. She breathed in pine and his aftershave.

Silently, they picked their way close to the lighthouse. As they neared, sounds came into play.

The gentle lapping of the water against the shore mixed with something metallic and out of sync. Nature wasn't so discordant. It had to be man-made. The scrape of a shovel?

In a few yards, they'd reach the wooden bridge. The sounds of their steps over the planks would give away their location.

Squeezing his hand three times, she tugged him back.

He frowned.

Hide, she mouthed. She dropped his hand, turning for a place to conceal them. She spotted a pine tree near the shore. Erosion had created a hollow to one side, exposing its roots and providing a perfect person-sized hole.

She turned back to him. He was gone. Rubbing her eyes, she scanned the area and spotted him.

He'd dropped to the ground and held a pine branch in front of his face.

That was hiding?

She swallowed her sigh and grabbed his hand, pulling him to his feet. She led him to the tree she'd scoped out. She dropped into the hole, pulling him down with her.

Almost on top of her.

Her heartbeat thundered in her ears, drowning out all other sounds. She stared up at him, licking her very dry lips as she did so. In the beginning, falling for him had been so easy. Two friends who knew each other better than themselves. A pair who spent all day, every day together and still wanted more. Before the complications of family and expectations, they'd been two people hot for each other. Her skin burned. She parted her lips.

His intoxicating scent of aftershave and fresh laundry mixed with sweat. His eyes flashed. He licked his lips and lowered his head.

She arched up, drawn to him like a magnet. Every muscle in her body strained. Her skin was on fire.

"I thought this was supposed to be easy?" A male voice said clearly.

In a second, she shrank. She knew that voice. Betrayal from a friend was like a bucket of ice water tossed on her, smothering the fire with cold, hard truth. In the years since she had been gone, her neighbors continued to live their lives. She hadn't returned to a fairy tale town frozen in time by a curse. Which left her with horrible questions.

Why had someone she'd known forever tried to kill her? How did Zach act normal when the explosion didn't succeed? Who else was involved?

* * *

Christopher knew Ashley's *kiss me* face. The memory of the first time she looked at him *like that* had been imprinted on his soul. They'd been in high school, laughing about something as they sat on the boardwalk. And then she'd turned and looked at him like he was everything.

Even now, his chest expanded, and his chin lifted. She had that power over him, to elevate or eviscerate. And he'd forgotten just how heady the sensation.

His fingers twitched, his palms burned to touch her, hold her, kiss her.

She'd pressed into him, rising out of her hiding spot and flooding his senses. Her lavender smell, her parted lips, her dazzling eyes, her shallow breaths teased him to claim her. He wanted her. He'd missed her. In the days since her return, he realized how he'd trapped that part of himself in a deep, dark, and desolate dungeon.

She was the only woman who had ever stirred such passion. With her, he was possessive and obsessive. He'd forgotten how much until she'd returned. She belonged with him, not to him, but at his side. He'd been a fool to ever think he could pay her off and somehow get on with his life. She was his life.

In the seconds he'd come awake in his office, he had turned and seen her face and instinctually reached for her. Like a thirsty man grabbing a cup of water. She had reminded him of their circumstances, and he pushed aside the desire lingering just under his smooth façade.

Not now. Now he was here, and she was arching into him. He licked his lips and lowered his head.

"I thought this was supposed to be easy?" A familiar male voice complained.

Christopher swallowed the groan building in his chest. If he released it, he'd hear rumors of a bear now circling the property. He wanted like five more minutes before he'd been right. He could have kissed her. He should have because now she was wrong.

Her ghost wasn't real.

Part of him had hoped the spirit couldn't be so easily explained. He harbored a wish that Xavier lingered on the earthly plane, helping his daughter to atone for his unfinished business in life. But no. Christopher's assessment that humans manipulated the situation was correct. And for his victory, he'd claim an unhappy wife who would not want to make out.

He dropped his chin to his chest, taking several deep breaths.

"Keep your voice down," another man said, his voice strained and wheezy.

That voice sounded familiar, too. He knew both men. And that was the worst piece of news he'd had in years. It was Zach and Lonnie.

He didn't want to think that the people he'd grown up with hated him enough to try to kill his wife and destroy his business. Sure, they'd argue something else but they had been caught red-handed. Lonnie and Zach plotting to destroy him as thoroughly as a man could be ruined.

He lifted his gaze to her face.

Her expression clouded, unreadable. Her wrinkled brow and scrunched face assured him he'd missed his chance. Well, perhaps that was for the best. He wanted to kiss her with every ounce of his being. But did she reciprocate his feelings or had she been swept up in a moment? He owed her a clear choice if he considered himself a gentleman.

Their marriage had probably been that for her, although he'd been honest about his commitment. She'd disregarded the vows almost as soon as she could, running off. She'd made her choice years ago. He'd been an idiot to imagine any different.

Even if she could somehow forgive him, she would never forget. When it counted, he'd made a choice against her. She'd never truly appreciate the circumstances he'd been put in, and he wasn't sure he'd ever been able to rationalize what he did as being in her best interests. Not truly. He'd picked safety over love. Her return was hollow.

He wasn't the victor. He'd just lost again. This time for good. He wouldn't put any pressure on her. He'd see the lawyer in the morning. He'd buy the *Hotel Lavande.*

He leaned close. "Go back to the Inn and call the police," he murmured into her ear. He fought the urge to bury his face in her neck. She was everything he'd ever wanted and never could hold on to. Pulling back, he met her gaze.

She nodded. *Be careful,* she mouthed.

He scrambled backward and, on hands and knees, rounded the pine tree. Once in the open, he ran, leaping over the bridge. "Come out with your hands up."

"Crap, I told you!" Lonnie Treacle, the taffy and fudge shop owner, shouted.

Christopher rounded the lighthouse. On the backside of the small island, away from view of the Inn because of the pile of rubble, the sixty-something-year-old man leaned on a shovel.

Kneeling on the ground with a trowel, Zach Jenkins met Christopher's gaze.

Christopher saw red.

While Lonnie was part of an older generation, Zach had only been a few years ahead. Zach knew Ashley. Throughout the years, he'd spoken of her in glowing terms. Friendship hadn't stopped him from attempted murder.

"Stand up now. You've got some nerve showing up here," Christopher hissed. Rage pounded through his veins, curling his fists at his side.

"Why?" Zach stood, dusting his hands on his pants and crossing his arms. "Because we're taking advantage of an opportunity?"

"Nearly killing my wife is an opportunity? How dare you." Christopher lunged forward.

Lonnie pulled him back. "Stop. What are you talking about? We're just looking for the treasure. Heard the lighthouse was in ruins. Figured this was a good time. We never hurt anyone."

Christopher wheeled around. "The treasure doesn't exist. The gold isn't real. It was a marketing ploy from the 90s. Why is everyone in this town so gullible? I have bad news. Santa doesn't bring your presents either. You can be as good as you want, and if your parents don't have any money, you won't get a thing." His voice shook, long-repressed emotion flooding him.

Lonnie dropped his grip and held up both hands, sliding his eyes to his partner.

"Why can't people in this town face facts?" Christopher roared. "You make choices, and you accept the consequences. There is no grand scheme to save you. Hard work doesn't always mean success. Life isn't fair."

"Oh, are you, once again, on your high horse trying to force us to your will?" Zach curled his upper lip. "You always know what's best, right? You're the ultimate boss. You rule your little subjects and act so gracious in letting us peasants stay on your property."

"You've got some nerve. Everything I've done has been in the best interests of this town." Christopher poked himself in the chest with his index finger. "I love this place. I've never tried to run or hide or lurk in the shadows. I've worked my whole life for this community. Can you say the same? As far as I can tell, you've always been out for yourself."

Zach scowled.

Christopher turned toward Lonnie. "And what about you?"

The older man shook his head.

"No. Because both of you are out for your own good. Most people are. But some people actually care about their community and put in the work whether it is cheered or jeered," Christopher said.

Clapping sounded.

Christopher spun.

Ashley stood behind him with Sheriff Hanks and a deputy, her hands raised as she applauded.

"Officers, please arrest these men," Christopher said, holding her gaze and enjoying a split second of justice.

"For what?" Zach cried.

Christopher spun.

The officers approached the pair and handcuffed each man.

"For attempted murder and trespassing," Christopher replied coolly.

"Attempted murder?" Zach turned ghostly white.

Good. He was scared. Christopher would have cheered if he didn't long to slug the man. He didn't want to get hauled in for assault. Instead, he clenched and unclenched the fists at his side. "What else do you call setting fire to the lighthouse while my wife was inside? Or the explosion that destroyed it the other day?"

"We didn't do this." Lonnie sputtered, tilting his head to the dilapidated lighthouse.

"That wasn't us." Zach darted his gaze between Ashley and Christopher. "Please, you're my friend. I would never have hurt you." He focused on Ashley.

Christopher's blood pounded. Now he really wanted to slap the man. He gave a good show of fake shock. He should try out for the local community theater. If he was out of jail by then.

Christopher stood in front of Ashley, shielding her from the farce. He hadn't done enough, but he could do this. He could protect her and get out of her way. "Evidence says otherwise. And you're still trying to steal from the resort that has supported you and kept your families clothed and fed. How dare you. Get out of here." He nodded at the officers, grabbed her hand, and strode away.

He needed a strong drink to clear his mind of every thought plaguing him. Because he'd come so close to losing her, and he hadn't understood how deeply he'd been impacted until he had a chance to confront the perps. He didn't want to go through with the divorce. But didn't he owe her? He'd see her safely inside the hotel and spend the rest of the night torturing himself.

Chapter Fifteen

Ashley grabbed a molasses cookie off the tray and bit into it while pacing his office. She couldn't sit still, not even to attempt to eat. As it was, she barely tasted the rich, sugary cookie, the crackled top giving way to a perfectly soft center. She focused on the wrong things. The scrape of the granular sugar on her tongue and the too-strong aftertaste. She couldn't look at the positives.

Like Christopher still wanted her. He couldn't hide his reaction under close quarters. She might have convinced herself she was mistaken before, but not when she felt him pressed against her.

The reverse was true as well. He wouldn't doubt her feelings any longer. Every attempt at playing coy had evaporated in the heated moment. And his fiery response to confronting the foes only solidified his feelings.

She was shaken at the depths of Zach's hatred. Lonnie's too. She'd always imagined herself safe with anyone in the community. Since she was a tiny girl, she had treated everyone like a member of her extended family. She fooled herself into believing the same of them.

214

Am I collateral damage to Zach in his plot against Christopher? Zach had the audacity to smile and greet her like a long-lost friend. All the while, he suppressed a white-hot anger against Christopher so explosive that he'd kill her without a second thought. She shuddered, stuffing the rest of the cookie into her mouth.

She wasn't sure she could truly believe that of Zach. Lonnie maybe. But not Zach. Some other part of the whole affair troubled her. She wouldn't give up on her ghost just because evidence and common sense told her otherwise. Neither could she continue down that path with her husband.

She needed action, a distraction, or anything other than listening to the next part of his plan. Because now they'd reached the real talk portion. And she couldn't handle the truth.

The door in the corner opened, and he appeared.

She spun and lifted her hand in a wave only to freeze midway through the motion. She pulled her hand back, wiping the crumbs off her face.

"Do you want a drink?" he asked. But he didn't wait for an answer. He strode toward his desk, pulled out a drawer, and set a bottle of whisky and two crystal tumblers on the soft, leather inset top.

"Where did you get that?"

He shrugged. "I keep it in the bottom drawer." He opened the bottle and poured two glasses. He approached her, holding out a glass. "For emergencies."

She accepted, her fingers briefly touching his in the exchange. "Have you had many of those?" She laughed and lifted the glass in cheers before sipping.

The liquor washed away the remaining cookie, burning her throat. She wasn't much for straight alcohol. Her preference was something fruity and frozen while lounging around poolside. A beach was definitely head and shoulders above a dimly lit office after midnight. They'd reached the only conclusion they could have for their ill-fated romance. The never part of now or never.

An apology tickled her tongue, but she struggled with stringing together a coherent, unemotional speech. *How do I voice my regrets*? That she understood how wrong she'd been to put him in the middle. That leaving only hurt her. That he was so clearly better off without her. But she wanted another chance though she didn't deserve him.

She wanted the ghost to be real so she could fool herself into thinking Dad hadn't given up on her. He hadn't died in his sleep without a chance to put their differences aside. She told herself a story to make everything okay. She couldn't keep up the tale anymore. She'd lost the plot. She had no spin to make her situation pretty for social media.

He eyed her warily.

She crossed to the chairs, still facing the windows. Sitting, she tucked her legs underneath, resting the glass on her knees. "Thanks for the drink. I'm not one to rely on alcohol to unwind. But today has been exceptional."

"Can't say I've ever had a day quite like today." He lowered himself into his chair, stretching his legs out in front and crossing his ankles. He sipped.

She wanted to ask how he acted so calm after the charge in the air and if he would have kissed her. She wanted him, but, if she put him on the spot now, she'd force his hand. The most alarming revelation wasn't her continued attraction. In the aftermath of the arrest, she had to focus on what had just happened.

"Are they..." She wasn't sure how to phrase her question. She had never been afraid for her safety. After the fire, she'd come to the Inn. Following the explosion, she'd more or less walked away. But this? Their denials only scared her more. If Lonnie and Zach could convince themselves they hadn't attempted to kill her in order to steal a non-existent treasure, what else were they capable of?

She cleared her throat. "Are they taken care of?"

He frowned. "They were arrested and are currently on their way to our local jail. I'll fight hard against bail. They don't deserve to go about their lives in town after trying to end yours."

She nodded. She believed him. He'd been a fierce opponent in the aftermath. When she'd hung back to call for help, she'd accidentally tested Zach's theory. Every word spoken on the tiny island carried as if delivered through a megaphone. Christopher had said *my wife* with so much emotion. He couldn't have been faking. He'd never been a good enough actor to get them out of trouble as kids. Why lie now?

"I can't believe I was right." He sighed.

From the corner of her eye, she caught him, shaking his head and taking another sip. "You're rarely wrong. Isn't that one of your strengths? Finding the winning hand?" *Letting the losers drop.*

"For the record, I think they must have started the fire to get you out of the lighthouse. I'm not sure how. Lawyers will find out. I don't think they intentionally tried to kill you with the collapse."

No, two men she'd known her entire life hadn't set out to kill her. But her murder would have been incidental to pursuing their own goals. She shuddered. "Not exactly the warm and fuzzy homecoming I expected."

Why had she thought, for a second, she could come back here? *Because I love him.*

She faced him and drained the rest of the whisky like a shot. As soon as she swallowed, she sputtered and coughed, raising her elbow to her mouth.

"Yeah, my thoughts exactly." He drained his glass and reached for hers, setting both on the coffee table. "I'm sorry,

Ashley. I'd be lying if I didn't admit I wanted to see you again. I never imagined you'd have to endure so much on my behalf."

She cleared her throat and tucked her hands under her legs. If she didn't get a hold of herself, she'd do something reckless and irrevocable. Like using the liquid courage that hadn't even hit her bloodstream yet as an excuse for a kiss. A real one. With tongue and hands and moaning. Instead, she threw a bucket of ice water over them both. "Do you think, if I would have come back earlier, he'd have become my mentor? Do you think he ever would have accepted me as his apprentice?"

Christopher frowned. "Are you sure you want to go down this path?"

"No. But I am." She smiled, leaning her head back against the smooth leather chair. A surge of self-annihilation pumped through her. She'd nearly died at the hands of a neighbor. Truth was all she'd accept. He'd answer her and then she could circle back to the other sore subject.

"I don't know," he murmured.

Christopher's softly uttered uncertainty shook her to her bones. Maybe she shouldn't have asked if she wasn't prepared for honesty. She had no choice. She needed answers. Continuing in ignorance wouldn't help her in whatever future she approached.

"He missed you," Christopher said with the surety she expected. "I won't pretend he asked about you. I knew pretty quickly not to mention your name. But I'd catch him lingering near your pictures, at the cottage, in the attics, along the shore near the bridge. Any spot that reminded him of you drew him like a magnet."

She scrunched her ticklish nose. She'd missed Dad too. The problem with being an almost exact clone of one's parent was in the shared stubborn willfulness. Neither of them would ever yield an inch. If either of them had weakened, the other would have raked them over the coals mercilessly until the end of time. She accepted her blame in the estrangement. Learning to say *sorry* or *I was wrong* would have been invaluable.

"What do you want to do, Ash?"

Start over. "I don't know."

"I want to come up with a compromise you can accept. I won't try to keep you here. You've always wanted to fly."

His sad smile tugged at her heart. She had. But only because she thought the nest would always be ready for her return. She hadn't appreciated what she'd had. And now she was going to have to say goodbye to it forever.

"What do you want? What is fair?"

To be partners. When she stripped away everything, she had one desire left. Asking him would be exposing every last trick. She had no more games, no more ideas, and no more plans. Running her life as she saw fit had left her empty and alone. She was tired of hiding and faking.

"I have nothing." Her voice cracked. "I don't want to take from you. The Inn is truly yours. You've devoted the time and care. It's your vision and sweat equity. I guess I'm just jealous. I need something."

* * *

Christopher regretted finishing his drink so fast. He shot a longing glance at the coffee table. He never expected honesty from her. He'd known her forever, longer than he'd known himself, and filled in many of the gaps on his own.

She wasn't the sort to speak with such candor, or she'd have to listen to it.

She didn't flinch or shudder or try to hide in any way. She was open, vulnerable, and fearless. He needed to be just as brave. Or he'd live with regrets for the rest of his life.

For too long, he'd held a fear so close to his heart he'd

begun to believe the lie. That marrying him had been one more way to get back at her dad. He'd been in love with her for as long as he could remember. He worried about being a pawn between father and daughter. But he'd been so young and overwhelmed with hormones he hadn't cared.

In the wake of her departure, he'd been swamped by all the rational, reasonable thoughts he had buried. He'd awoken from a dream to find himself all alone. With her return, he discovered he was just as wild for her as always. She could come in and sweep him up in her chaos, and he'd gladly follow. Before the interruption, he'd nearly sealed his fate of being at her beck and call until the end of time.

While he ached for what could have been, he was grateful for the break. The cold air and icy realization of what had been happening under his nose had snapped him from his lust-filled haze. They could discuss their future rationally. Although, with each second in her company, he felt his grip on logic and reason slipping away.

"I have another option," he said slowly, ignoring the thump of his heart with each second. *Let's stay together. Let's reconcile.* The love hung in the air between them, shimmering with the passion that had never waned.

He pushed aside the feelings. He'd do the smart thing and offer her a clear choice. He didn't want her beholden to him or anyone. Because he wanted her to want him for himself. Not for the way he could help her or provide for her, or provoke her now-dead family. He wanted her to choose him.

"What is really inside the package I brought?"

He frowned. Package? From her? He wracked his brain but came up empty.

"Hawaii?" she asked. "Is it a job?" Her chin trembled. "Could I take it?"

"Would you want to move? You just got here."

She shrugged. "It would solve a lot of issues."

Not for him. Her father accused him of eloping to satisfy his lust. Xavier had asked what would happen when Christopher grew tired of the physical side. The truth was the physical only enhanced and deepened their emotional connection. Christopher found his other half in every way with Ashley. "Not a job offer as much as a buyout. The hotelier wants to retire. He's offered to sell it to me. I could go. And you could stay and takeover the Inn.

She rolled her eyes. "Do you want the property to be haunted for real?"

"What does that mean?" He drew back his chin. Her abrupt comment was as moment-shattering as an open-palm slap. *How could she be so cavalier after I offered up my livelihood?*

"I appreciate your thoughtfulness and caring," she said, lowering her voice and reaching a hand to cover his.

His thumb itched to trace her hand; he wanted to flip their grip and cover her hand in his. She softened the blow with her gentle delivery.

"Dad would come back from the grave and shake the walls. He'd rather have this place destroyed than let me be involved in its operation." She smirked and shook her head, drawing back her hand.

"If you believe that, how do you make sense of him giving you the option of claiming in the Inn at all?"

"Appearances. He cared a lot about what other people thought, especially as the first family of the lake." She scrunched her nose. "I suppose I do, too. I've definitely focused on curating an image over the past decade to the detriment of really living. I'm not scared anymore. I'm ready to try. But I don't want to push you out. And I don't want you to go to Hawaii."

"Wouldn't my leaving solve your problems?"

She shook her head.

Good. Because he didn't want to go anywhere without her. "What will you do?" he asked.

"I haven't figured that out quite yet. I don't know what I want."

"What about me?" His voice cracked. He coughed, clearing his throat. "Do I get any say? What about what I want?"

She shrugged. "You don't want me involved. You don't want me around. Your life was much easier."

"Of course, I want you. I've always wanted you. Who do you think funded the allowance?"

Her skin assumed a pale, green pallor.

His stomach dropped to his knees. He didn't want to hurt her. He was only trying to illustrate his point. His love never wavered. He was patient and steadfast.

He'd been a jerk.

With her chin down, she looked so small.

His gorgeous, glorious, gregarious wife shrunk to the size of a doll. She looked like a toy to be picked up and played with or tossed aside at someone else's discretion.

Had he been guilty of using her? He'd never intended to tell her the truth. However, once the words slipped free he wouldn't pretend she misunderstood.

Her reaction validated his worst fears. "I'm sorry."

She shook her head.

"He never stopped missing you. I'd catch him on his phone, scrolling through your posts. He'd walk to the light-house every afternoon. I caught him there once. Crying with a picture of you. He couldn't apologize. I don't think he knew how to start."

She turned to stone, her features hard and carved. "But he didn't look out for me. He wasn't worried about how I'd provide for myself."

Xavier wasn't the only Hale too proud to be happy. She

knew the truth now. There were no more secrets between them.

Christopher reached for her icy hands and squeezed. Groveling wasn't his style. But he could learn from others' mistakes. He wouldn't let pride ruin him. "Stay here. Please. Let's take a real chance. Nothing and no one is holding us back now." And he meant it. His parents had passed years ago. Her father was gone. He had reached an age where he no longer cared about any outside opinion.

Except hers.

It was the two of them against the world. He'd fight everyone. But he couldn't battle her.

"What would I do?"

"Whatever you wanted." *Just stay.* "Cook, come up with special events, just be here. Be you."

"Would we be partners?"

He leaned forward and brushed the hair off her face. With his thumb, he traced the gentle line of her cheekbone.

He wanted no more secrets. No more hiding. Just the truth from both of them forever. But he wasn't sure they could coexist in a business. Was that the only way forward?

Under his touch, she trembled, leaning into his palm.

She couldn't make herself more vulnerable and open to him.

He held back, unsure he could do what she wanted and relinquish control. The town would cheer. Zach might lead a parade down the boardwalk if the charges were dropped and he was released from prison.

From the corner of his eye, a burst of light caught his eye. He turned and stared outside. The sky brightened as an orange glow expanded, bright as the sun.

For a long moment, he didn't breathe. Was this a sign from the heavens pointing him the direction Ashley wanted? She had been his sunshine. Improbably, a new day dawned.

And then came the sound. A bang followed by several loud pops like the delay of the Fourth of July fireworks shot from the same spot. Gunpowder. The remains of the lighthouse exploded.

This wasn't symbolism. The Inn was under attack.

Chapter Sixteen

Ashley thought they were finally having a moment. Learning that what she had feared most was true—Dad had abandoned her—hadn't crushed her. She lived, she breathed, and she found a surprising inner calm. Because Christopher hadn't given up on her.

Something had eased in her heart. Her relationship with Dad was over and done. The only reconciliation would be making peace with his memory. She had to search within for forgiveness.

Her husband remained. She had resigned herself to letting him go, and then came a flash of what they'd had. If she could release herself from the guilt over not making amends with Dad and walk ahead with her husband, she'd remove all the obstacles from their path. *Did he still love her, or had his allowance been about pity?* She needed the answer. In a second, she decided to scare herself and him. She asked for something better than sole ownership of the Inn. She asked for a partnership.

Why didn't he say anything?

The longer the silence stretched between them, the more

tension rose in her stiff limbs. A lump clogged her throat. Instead of lightness, she turned to stone inch by inch.

Maybe because she had said something neither of them would have anticipated, he hadn't really heard her. Her chin trembled. She darted her tongue over her dry bottom lip. She'd have to put herself out there again. Her mouth opened.

He turned away.

The loss of his attention became a physical ache. She wanted to protest. Her question demanded an answer. She deserved a reply.

As he stared, rapt, focused on the window, a loud boom shook the Inn.

She followed his gaze. Her eyes widened.

The lighthouse was gone.

Against the dark sky, angry orange flames engulfed a pile of stony rubble.

From the safety of the office, she stared at the fire. They had been there on that spot not too long ago. Lonnie and Zach couldn't be involved. The bad guys were in the back of a cruiser headed to jail. *Was this an accident? Or arson? Was someone after them? What if the fire spread? How was it set? Was the entire property in danger?*

An alarm sounded.

She heard it from a distance, not quite processing the noise, the scene, or the feelings. Frozen. Immobile. Horrified. Her brain and her body weren't working in tandem.

"Ashley. Come on. We have to get out of here." He stood, moving away.

Her skin chilled without his touch. No. He couldn't move away. He needed to stay and answer her question. He had to agree. Because she couldn't keep living her life without him. No more unknowns.

When he returned, he grabbed her hand. She almost

sighed at his touch, relief making her boneless. She stood, and he pulled her to the secret staircase.

She bobbed along behind him, floating down the steps. Her brain didn't process the locomotion necessary. Numb and cold, she was so very tired of running. She wanted to stay here with him and give them a chance. Waiting for his answer wasn't her style. If she started doing that now, she'd gain nothing but maybe lose everything.

At the bottom of the stairs, he didn't stop. He continued through the hall to the side door.

On the damp grass outside, she slid, thudding into him.

With a hand, he steadied her and gazed into her eyes. She had to ask him again. No, she'd tell him. They were going to be partners. They were not going to be idiots and lose each other in some misguided act of chivalry.

But she could hardly hear herself breathe. The Inn's fire alarm system blared louder outside than on the top floor.

Guests milled on the lawn in various combinations of coats and pajamas. Employees raced through the chaotic, noisy scene. Conversations and cries mixed into a deafening sound.

The siren from the fire trucks echoed in the night.

"I've got to go. Stay here, okay?" Christopher asked.

No, don't leave. We have to stick together. We're a team. Her brain buzzed, processing the scene at a rapid pace. Her body didn't match the speed. She couldn't speak or move.

She was immobilized.

He squeezed her hand. "I'll be right back. Stay here. Stay safe. Okay? We can talk later."

She stared at their clasped hands. His warm palm anchored her in the moment. She nodded.

He leaned close and kissed her forehead.

His aftershave lingered in the air.

Then he turned, racing away.

When he disappeared from view, she let her shoulders drop. In a crisis, she was powerless.

During the lighthouse fire, she'd narrowly escaped the flames. Incapable of dousing the flames, she'd run into Christopher's arms. Within minutes, he stopped the fire.

Again, on the day of the explosion, she probably would have drowned, too shocked for her survival instincts and years of swim lessons to kick in, if Steve Prim hadn't been nearby. Was damsel in distress her true identity?

She felt so helpless. She hated that. It wasn't just Dad or Christopher. It was herself.

She needed to prove her value and her worth. Not just to Christopher or the community. To herself most of all. If she didn't want to be a joke, she had to be serious. Starting now. He hadn't responded to her question. She would prove herself to be a capable partner and take charge in the midst of the chaos.

In the distance, above the buzz of furtive conversations, another siren echoed.

The emergency vehicle came closer with each passing second. She took a shaky breath. Help was near. Above the crowd, she heard the crack of breaking branches. Paramedics and the fire department must have arrived.

Turning toward the sound, she saw movement in the darkness just past the light cast from the Inn. She squinted and narrowed her gaze. Nothing in particular stood out. *A person? An animal? A ghost?* She gulped. Not a ghost and not a joke. She needed to be serious and assess the threat.

On tiptoes, she raced toward the dark tree line, skirting the shrubs at the perimeter of the property, following the thick forest towards the spot where she hid in wait for a warm dinner all those nights ago. Funny how moments came full circle. She would have laughed if fear hadn't slid its fiery grip around her throat and squeezed tight.

Did anyone see?

A low murmur came from a few yards ahead.

"No. Too focused on the Soupy fools," a familiar voice said.

Steve. She started to shake, her teeth chattering. She clamped a hand over her mouth, an ineffectual attempt at subduing her fear. She knew the voice. She'd known it for years. What were the chances on having two such betrayals in one evening?

"Well, that was an unexpected piece of good news. You can't control every detail. Maybe it's better not to have that ability." Carl Prim chuckled a horrible, raspy laugh. He coughed, a dry, hacking sound.

She strained for more. *What was the unexpected good news? Why are they here?*

"You okay, Dad? Let's get out of here. We can come back and finish up in the morning."

Steve was the voice of reason? She'd always thought him as the stooge. Had it all been an act? Under the guise of friendliness, did a killer lurk?

Ashley didn't like her proximity to the pair. She inched her way back, unseeing. She faced her foes, hoping her shocked but familiar expression might save her from a gunshot to the back of the head.

Snap.

She froze, squeezing her eyes shut. She'd stepped on a fallen limb in Christopher's otherwise meticulously manicured manor. Her bad luck continued.

"What was that?" Carl rasped.

"Who's there?" Steve called.

Her lungs burned with the breath she held. Could she somehow disappear? Her body refused to move as her brain whirred with terrifying scenarios at top speed. Would they kill her? Take her somewhere? How long before anyone looked for her?

The crunch of sneakers against the fallen pine needles was as loud as roller skates gliding over a sheet of bubble wrap.

"Ashley?" Steve asked.

"Oh. Hi, Steve." She opened her eyes and smoothed back her hair. "Pretty wild night, huh? I was just upstairs when I heard all the commotion and came down. Thought I'd see if I could be useful, you know?"

Steve shook his head, rolling his shoulders forward. "Oh, Ashley."

"What's this?" Carl asked in his gruff tone, stopping at his son's side. "Better take her with us."

"Me? Where? Why?" She belatedly added a gasp. She'd never been subtle. Her biggest role in high school came as an actor in the background of *Bye Bye Birdie*. She'd been told to tone down her performance, that her pantomime distracted from the rest of the scene.

"Enough of your nonsense," Carl said. "Grab her, Steve."

Steve gripped a hand on her elbow, jerking the arm up.

She flinched. "Hey. Ouch. Listen. Think about this. I don't know anything. If you take me, you're in huge trouble. Do you really want to get arrested for kidnapping? Christopher is litigious. He'll go after you no matter what happens to me." She shivered, hoping *"no matter what happens"* was a metaphor and not about to become her destiny.

"We have a plan. It was better without you here, but now we can use you to our advantage." Carl rasped and coughed.

Carl was cruel. She'd heard rumors and had been shielded from knowing him personally. Growing up, she'd felt sort of like a kindred spirit with Steve. She had a difficult father, too. But Xavier had a heart.

"Steve, think about this," she murmured.

Steve held her tighter. "It's my plan, Ashley. If you're gone and Christopher is run out of business, the Prims can finally claim the land that should have always been ours. Let's move."

Carl strode ahead.

Steve tugged her away from the Inn and into the darkness.

She let him lead without any comment. With her heart pounding, she wasn't sure she could have formed a sentence without choking. Finally, as her eyes adjusted to the darkness, she uncovered where she'd hidden her backbone. She'd humanize herself to them. Give the pair a false sense of security that she was on their side. "Where are we going?" she whispered.

"The boathouse," Steve replied.

She nodded. Okay, she knew their destination. Knowledge was power, right?

They'd drag her through the woods separating the properties. Unfortunately, in the dark forest, she couldn't grab the attention of a bystander. But maybe Steve and Carl would have to move her somewhere else. They wouldn't kill her inside their family-run business. She had some time. "And you've been behind everything?"

She found an odd sense of relief in the midst of her terror. Perhaps Christopher was right to stick to logic and reason. Without an imagination stoking all sorts of thoughts, the world was remarkably flat. Predictable. Boring. Nothing to do with a ghost.

Dad was gone. She couldn't hold out hope for a reconciliation. She reached a place of reluctant, emotional peace.

"Define everything?" Steve asked.

"The fire?" she asked.

"No. You did that," he replied.

And now she was shocked all over again.

Was the ghost still hanging around? Could Dad help? She prayed hard that her father would stay and save her. She was running out of options.

Christopher. He'd been the answer all along. She'd run off without asking him for the truth. He'd finally told her, and her instinctual response had been to push back against him, to deny and continue to accept the lies she told herself.

Why? Because she was her own worst enemy? She had to take action to rescue herself. Now or never.

She slipped off her hair tie with her free hand, glad she'd used a bright loop to secure her ponytail. The scrunchie was a throwback to her youth. Zach Jenkins wasn't the only fan of nostalgia. Could her love of mall accessories help save her?

When her captors stared ahead, she dropped it behind her. Please let it be enough to grab Christopher's attention and realize she was in trouble. She hoped not life or death.

*   *   *

Christopher hated standing by and watching.

He'd spent so much of his early life at the mercy of others' whims, that staying silent was second nature. As a teen, when he had first started seeing Ashley as something more than a friend, he slipped into his old patterns of letting her call the shots. However, in the years since she'd been gone, he had assumed control of his life.

And now, as everything he'd so carefully worked for hovered near total ruin, he had to take charge.

She didn't fight him about staying put.

He gave her hand one last squeeze, instilling his touch and smile with every promise he had. They couldn't go back. He was sorry to ruin her final impression of her father. But if doing so cleared the air for them to move forward, he could be grateful for the chance.

She was safe.

He strode toward the burning island. He wasn't foolish. He wouldn't attempt to fight the fire himself. If Lonnie and

Zach had set the explosives to cover their tracks, they would be in for bad news. As soon as the fire department had the situation under control, Christopher intended to level additional charges against the pair. Trespassing, arson, and attempted murder. He hadn't thought Zach hated him enough to kill. But he'd been wrong.

"Mr. Willie," Christopher called as he neared the groundskeeper blocking the bridge with his crossed arms. "Thank you."

With a nod, Mr. Willie turned and faced the smoldering ruins. "Never thought I'd see this."

"Me either."

"D'you suppose there is a ghost?"

Christopher stared straight ahead, unseeing. He didn't want to respond to the man. While he appreciated Ashley's creativity and whimsy, he didn't need her working the whole community into a frenzy. He had been a hypocrite to her, berating her for the ghost while encouraging the myth of Soupy. Ashley deserved his sincerest apology.

"Stand back," a voice called.

Christopher stepped to the side, breaking from Mr. Willie to allow several volunteer firefighters in full gear to race down the bridge, carrying a hose. He made his way back toward the crowd, reassuring the guests that the Inn was safe, the fire was under control, and that they could all return to their beds.

He was eager to do just that but waited to be sure the staff had corralled the guests back inside. Exhaustion crept up his body until it threatened to pull him down to the ground to curl into a little ball on the soft grass. He dragged his heavy feet and hung his head, too weary to lift his chin, too tired for more pleasant small talk.

She must be exhausted, too.

He reached the side of the Inn. Away from the curious gazes of visitors and staff, he lifted his head and smiled.

Coming back to her felt good, natural, and cozy. Like coming home. But where was she?

He rubbed his eyes and looked again at the spot where she had been. The side of the building was empty. No one loitered nearby. Perhaps she'd gotten sleepy and went inside to rest after the truck arrived. He pulled open the door to an empty back hallway and darkened stairwell.

The hair on the back of his neck rose on end. She hated being in the building without the lights on. If she'd headed upstairs, she would have left the switch for him to turn off. No, she wasn't inside. He shut the door and strode around the building, first taking large lunges. By the time he reached the front door and still hadn't found her, he was jogging. His blood pumped through his veins at top speed; the sluggish feeling evaporated in the wake of the horrible pins and needles sensation pricking every inch of his skin. At the back of the Inn, on the patio, he nearly collided with Mr. Willie.

"Have you seen Ashley?" he shouted at the groundskeeper, panting.

"What?" Mr. Willie twisted his head from one side to the other. "Ashley? Ashley Hale-Lewis? Your Ashley?"

She's never been mine. For a second, he'd stood before her with no more secrets. They'd approached either the end or the beginning. And disaster struck, killing his second chance. "Yes, my wife." He bit out the words.

"No. Haven't seen her."

Oh no. Christopher couldn't lose her now. He couldn't come so close to getting her back to miss out on the rest of his life with her. And he hadn't really said everything, had he? Fear held his tongue. Regret would be his constant companion.

"Sir? Are you okay?" Mr. Willie grabbed him by the shoulders. "You look like you've seen a ghost."

In another circumstance, Christopher might have laughed

at that turn of phrase. All he wanted to do was cry. "Come with me." He continued around the side of the Inn toward the spot where he'd last seen her. Had he missed her? Was she curled up against the building?

He pulled out the flashlight from his back pocket, glad he'd kept it after the commotion, and powered on the thin beam of light, shining it in every direction.

Mr. Willie turned on the flashlight app on his cell phone and did the same on the other side, facing the trees. "Over there. I see something." He headed into the tree line edging the lawn.

Christopher followed and felt his heart drop.

Mr. Willie held a brightly colored, fluffy hair tie.

The same kind Ashley was always pulling out of her pockets to get her hair out of her face quickly. Someone took her. Christopher hated the feeling sinking into his bones. Certainty was a cruel sort of torture.

He stared, unseeing and unblinking. What if he'd been wrong about everything? What if the fire and tonight's explosion hadn't been Zach? Perhaps worse, Christopher needed the other man's help. Zach knew too much. Could he harness his gossip for good? "Mr. Willie, I need to go to the sheriff. Can you please check on everyone inside?"

"Do you need me to come with you?"

In that moment, Christopher almost said yes. He didn't have any friends, none besides his wife. But he could count on a few people. And the groundskeeper was one of that select number. "I'll be fine. Please, look after the Inn." Without waiting for acknowledgment, Christopher slipped out of the forest, crossed the lawn, and jogged to his car, glad he'd taken his keys with him when he'd left his office.

He drove at top speed, reaching the station in a few minutes and bolting out of the car to bang with both fists on the locked door.

A uniformed deputy approached the glass door with a puzzled expression. He unlocked the door and pulled it open a crack. "May I help you?"

"My wife..." Christopher panted. "She's missing. Abducted, I think. Are the two men arrested at the Inn earlier still in custody? Were they bonded out?"

The deputy shook his head. "No. They are still here."

"I need to speak with them. I think they have information about my wife."

The door shut.

For a second, Christopher considered pushing his way inside. Getting thrown in jail alongside the trespassers would only delay him. He needed help. Now. He had to save her.

Then, mercifully, the door opened inward, and the deputy waved Christopher inside.

The door shut behind him, and he could hear murmurs coming from an open doorway. Following the sound, he spotted Lonnie and Zach in the holding cell.

Lonnie sat on a metal bench, his back against the wall.

Zach rested his forehead against the bars, straightening as Christopher entered view. "Are you coming to drop the charges? We can't get anyone to answer our calls tonight and bail us out. Did you call a town meeting? Lure everyone away from their phones?"

"You don't..." Christopher stopped. For once, he had more information than his nemesis. He would savor the victory if it wasn't so bittersweet and tinged with even more ignorance. "There's been an explosion."

"What?" Lonnie gasped.

"The rest of the lighthouse was obliterated. Like that." Christopher snapped his fingers.

The men turned pale and green.

Was it fear? Relief? Worry? Christopher hoped for a little of each. "What were you doing there? Setting explosives?"

"Never. We were trying to get photos of Soupy," Zach said.

Christopher rolled his eyes. "On the island, you said you were digging for the treasure. Pick a lie and stick to it."

Zach pulled a little toy out of his back pocket. "It's true. We thought we could stage something to help launch the legend."

Christopher crossed his arms over his chest. "I'm supposed to believe you now?"

"It sounded childish. Hunting for treasure was the better reason if we were going to be arrested for trespassing," Zach said. "It's why we brought shovels. I could only find a garden trowel."

If that was their excuse, it was pretty slim. "Where is Seth?" Christopher asked.

"Elise asked him to meet her by the old sawmill dock. It's a full moon," Zach said.

"The Prim family reported a couple odd occurrences over that way," Lonnie added. "She's not part of what we've been doing."

"Weren't those sightings all related to a sturgeon?" Christopher's patience, already stretched thin, was near to breaking.

"Soupy isn't harming anyone." Lonnie shrugged. "Helping a friend isn't a crime."

"I wish that was still true." Christopher didn't know what to believe in anymore. Legends, myths, and oaths. All he knew was he trusted Ashley, and he needed to save her. "I might consider dropping the charges. If you help."

"Why would we help you?" Zach curled his upper lip.

"Ashley's in trouble." Christopher's voice cracked, emotion choking him.

Zach turned a ghostly pale. "What do you mean?"

"She's gone. Taken." Christopher ran a hand through his

hair. "And if it's not you two. I don't know who it is. I can't lose her. Please."

Lonnie stood, approaching his partner in crime. "Maybe you do understand the bonds of family."

Christopher darted his gaze between the pair. "Of course, I do."

"We weren't so sure. We all thought you only cared about profit, not people," Zach said.

"I care about profit because of people." Christopher bit out the words. He didn't want a reckoning now. He wanted a rescue. "Listen, I admit to overstepping the interests of my business. I can take my approach down a few notches. But after saving the resort from near ruin, I couldn't let the shops go down, too."

Zach stuck a hand through the bars.

Christopher shook on a truce.

"Get us out, and we'll take the secret path to the boat house," Zach said.

"Boathouse?" Christopher asked.

Lonnie sighed. "Yep. If Ashley's missing, it'll be the Prims. They're the only ones with anything to gain from her disappearance."

"And they aren't clever enough to think of another hiding spot. Most gullible, naive people," Zach said.

But in his arrogance, Christopher underestimated the real foes and imagined the danger lurked elsewhere. And now she was at risk. He had so much to say and apologize for.

He needed more time.

<h1 style="text-align:center">Chapter Seventeen</h1>

shley tripped over every tree root she could. She was not about to go quietly. However, she didn't make any voluntary sounds. Having a dirty hand clamped over her mouth or a piece of tape was not her goal. She did her best to thwart the kidnapping by slowing them down.

Steve was a patient person until he wasn't. After the tenth stumble, he yanked her hard. He lifted her off the ground. She couldn't drag her feet.

Her ribs connected with his belt and holster. She winced, swallowing the groan. Was he wearing a gun?

"We're here," Carl said.

Light spilled onto the ground.

She blinked. They'd made it out of the woods to the boathouse.

"Inside," Steve said, lifting her arm again before flinging her forward.

She righted herself in time to hear a gun cock. Hands raised, she stared at father and son. Did she look scared? She hoped so. Hiding her anger from them to portray herself as weak went against every instinct she had. But she had to survive.

Steve waved the gun towards the door.

With a nod, she turned and stepped over the threshold, entering the building and skirting along the back wall. If they wanted to shoot her, she planned to leave blood splatters on every surface she could. Her DNA would speak on her behalf. She would be avenged. She shivered. What a horrible thought after a surprising evening. *I should have kissed Christopher when I had the chance.*

The truth about her allowance stung her pride. She'd wasted valuable time with her husband by feeling sorry for herself. She couldn't change the past. By focusing on what she couldn't fix, she'd lost track of the most important part of the explanation. Her husband loved her and never gave up on her.

Unfortunately, her carelessness would lead to her death. Did she value righting the wrongs in the afterlife more than apologizing to the living? She hated the dire circumstances that forced her revelation.

Carl strode toward the office, passing the two tour boats, and opened the door.

With faded paint on the hulls and battered and scratched awnings, the tour boats didn't look like the once gleaming vehicles she remembered. In her memory, the boats sparkled under the sun, their decks filled with smiling tourists.

Ashley glanced over her shoulder. "I don't see the new dinner boats."

Steve continued to wave her on.

She assessed the bigger threat. Carl was a known hothead. But Steve's cold behavior was an unwelcome discovery. Her survival depended on her correct calculations of their dark souls.

"Sit," Carl said, pointing at a chair opposite the desk. He

walked around behind the solid piece of furniture to claim his spot.

She did as she was told, sinking into the seat and darting her gaze. She spotted a desk calendar and froze. She'd been home for a little over a week. In sixteen days, her husband could claim the Inn free and clear. If the Prims killed her, she'd really clear Christopher's path to her inheritance. In her heart, she knew he wouldn't want it.

Steve entered the room, shut the door, and stood with his back against the solid panel.

The office had no windows. No other means of escape besides the door behind the armed man.

Steve frowned and motioned for her to turn.

She shifted in the chair, turning toward Carl.

Now you're meek and mild? Now you do as you're told?

As clear as if he stood opposite, Ashley heard Dad's voice. She dug deep, infusing her backbone with steel. If she had to charm her way out alive, so be it. Her story wouldn't end here. "Listen, don't do this. Let me go. No one will notice I'm gone."

Steve's hardened gaze softened. The man she'd known since childhood lurked somewhere inside him still. Good. She had a chance. She turned toward Carl. "We can pretend this never happened. I support your family's business. I believe in your new idea. We can be great partners."

Carl rolled his eyes. "The dinner cruise? That wasn't real."

"It wasn't?" she asked.

"No," Carl snapped. "We wanted to egg on Christopher. Get him to act rashly, show he's unhinged without the old man steering the ship."

She bit her lip. The old man hadn't had his hands on the wheel for years. Admitting that wouldn't buy her time or safety. She needed another stalling technique. "Okay. You riled up Christopher. Mission accomplished. What happened next? Did you put Mr. Willie on your payroll?"

"Mr. Willie?" Carl threw back his head and let out a sharp bark of laughter. "I wish. That man is practically a guard dog, constantly prowling the perimeter. He made our reconnaissance so much harder. As did you with your lighthouse stunt."

Reconnaissance for what? She was missing some deeper part of the play. "The treasure was never real."

Carl scoffed and rolled his eyes. "We're not idiots. We know that. Something was taken from us almost a hundred years ago."

"By my family?" she asked. Her stomach twisted. She didn't shy away from her feelings. She embraced every ounce of emotion, savoring the end of her life as she stalled for more precious seconds."

"Stole the land the lighthouse sits on. The island had been the site of operations for the Prims. But the handshake agreement was voided by one of your ancestors." Carl sniffed.

"What would you do with it now? You've set yourselves up here very nicely. Why go through the hassle?" she asked, hoping she'd instilled enough empathy and concern into her tone.

"Because the island is an asset, and we need every one we can claim," Carl said.

"How could you possibly take over property that is legally part of the Inn?" she asked.

"Eminent domain." Carl lifted an eyebrow. "We have a shell utility company ready to stake the claim for the land."

"Another ploy?" She curled her lip, unable to stop herself.

"No, it's very real," Carl replied. "It's under the guise of updating infrastructure and getting the town up to modern standards for internet connectivity."

"And you think you'll have town support?" she asked.

"I won't need it, but I will have it," Carl said, smirking.

"We thought everyone in Loon Lake played by the rules. But not your family. They take and take. We're reclaiming what is rightfully ours. The town will understand."

"They took from me, too." Her voice cracked. "My family, I mean." She cleared her throat. "I'm not like my father. I didn't even go to his memorial or whatever it was." She swallowed the awful, sour taste in her mouth, forcing down the rising bile. Lying to save her skin. She'd never thought her character would crack, but in this life-or-death scenario, she was determined to save herself.

"I didn't know you were on my side," she said. "But now I do. What can I give you to prove I'm all in for our partnership? The island? Is that what you mean by what was stolen?"

"We wanted that. But now?" Carl leaned his chair back, crossing his arms over his chest. "We'll take nothing less than everything."

"Come on, that's not how allies work." She forced a chuckle.

"You are no ally. All you've done is complicate and delay our plan. Your little stunt in the lake. We could have teamed up then. But you ran off. You left the hospital while Steve was getting me. You chose your side." Carl narrowed his gaze. "And we've made our decision. It's better for everyone if you are out of the way."

A mechanical whirring saved her.

"What's that?" Steve hissed.

"Sounds like the rolling door," Carl said, sighing. "Slip the gun into your waistband, and go check it out."

"What about?" Steve tipped his head. "Her."

His voice cracked. At least some part of Steve's heart remained.

Carl opened a drawer in his desk. "I've got her." He approached and slapped a pair of handcuffs, tethering her right wrist to the chair. "Listen. The door malfunctions. A lot.

That's not your rescue. You make noise while we're gone? We'll shoot you when we get back. Yes?"

Ice poured through her veins, chattering her teeth. She studied Steve.

He gulped but made no other move to stop his father and indicate the threat was idle.

"Yes," she murmured, meeting Carl's glare. She'd reached the end. With no leverage, she couldn't buy her safety.

Steve opened the door.

Carl strode out, all pomposity and ego, shutting the door behind him.

"Steve," she hissed as soon as the door shut. "Don't do this. You're better than him. You're not a criminal, and you're not a murderer." She gulped.

A muscle twitched in his cheek. Steve locked eyes on her and glanced away.

In the second of meeting her gaze, she spotted a dangerous desperation. His father's approval drove his actions. Only Carl's opinion mattered. Steve would take her life as directed.

"I don't have a choice," Steve murmured.

"Yes, you do. You are your own person. Don't let him bully you."

"Without my dad, I'm nothing," Steve said.

The words punched her in the gut. She understood better than anyone else. If not for the restraints holding her in place, she would have doubled over. She struggled growing up with only one, overbearing parent. But she had a clear advantage over Steve.

Her dad loved her. Her heart broke that she hadn't said goodbye and mended their rift. But she never questioned that his hard-headedness about her choices was driven by his unconditional love and worry for her. Steve couldn't say the same. Carl was all about control.

"Listen to me," she said, her chin trembling and teeth

chattering. "You are a whole lot of something. He doesn't deserve your loyalty. I know all about how lonesome it is standing up to a parent. You won't be alone. You'll have me and the support of everyone in town."

"Steve," Carl barked through the open doorway.

"I'm sorry, Ashley." Steve hung his head and walked away. He didn't quite shut the door, the panel swinging slightly ajar.

Could she wheel herself out of the deathtrap? She frowned at the wheels under her rolling chair. The front wheel was cracked. She probably couldn't roll an inch. She strained for any sound of rescue.

"Hey, Carl? You here?" Zach Jenkins called.

She widened her gaze. Wasn't he supposed to be behind bars? Her chest rose and fell. Christopher hadn't given up on her. He'd realized she was missing. Her rescue was close.

"Zach?" Carl yelled. "What's all the commotion? I heard sirens."

"Is Steve with you?" Zach replied. "I'd hate for him to get swept up with Inn nonsense. Some sort of fire or something over there. You know they'd love to pin this on any of us as arson."

"I'm here," Steve shouted.

Heavy footsteps clanged against the decking, seemingly from all directions.

"HANDS UP, HANDS UP, HANDS UP," someone shouted.

"You're both under arrest for the attempted murder and kidnapping of Ashley Hale Lewis," Sheriff Hanks said. "You have the right to remain silent..."

The rest of the Miranda rights became background noise.

Ashley screamed and wheeled herself to the door, forcing the cracked plastic to turn.

The door opened, slamming against the wall.

Wide-eyed and with hair standing on end, Christopher filled the doorway.

She collapsed against the seat. "Oh, thank goodness."

He dropped to his knees, pulling her into his arms.

"Ouch, ouch, stop tugging," she squeaked. "I'm hand-cuffed to the chair."

He pulled back to frown at her arm. "Deputy. Keys for handcuffs," he yelled over his shoulder.

A youngish man appeared, fumbling with the keys as he knelt behind the chair and twisted the lock.

She exhaled the heaviest breath of her life as the cuffs released. "Thank you."

The deputy nodded and rose.

Crossing her arms in front of her body, she hugged herself. She didn't feel any tears in her shirt or bleeding from her adventure through the forest. She circled her aching wrists. She hadn't been secured for very long, but all of the manhandling on the journey to her supposed demise, followed by the total release of all her adrenaline, left her shaky.

Christopher held out a hand.

For once, she didn't argue as he played the hero. She was too lucky to discount his actions as showboat behavior. She placed her fingers in his.

He tugged her to her feet and didn't let go, wrapping her tight. "I thought you were..."

His voice was so low, muttered into her hair, she felt the words in the soles of her feet, the deep vibrations wracking through her. "Dead?" She shuddered. "You thought I was dead?"

He nodded.

"Almost," she sniggered, her gallows humor resurfacing. "You got here just in time. Saving me again. Just another punchline in the ongoing joke that is my life."

She hadn't meant to sound so bitter. Her resolve to make

amends in the present crumbled. She was raw, and she couldn't help herself. She couldn't shield behind a smile anymore. She'd been locked to a chair. At her most vulnerable, she understood how utterly useless and totally hapless she'd always been.

"What are you saying?" Christopher asked softly, pulling away.

"I'm a joke to you." She sniffed.

"You've never been a joke. You make me laugh. You astonish me with your off-the-wall way of looking at something. But never you." He tipped up her chin, tenderly holding her face in both hands. Like she was something fragile and precious. "You matter to me. You mattered to him. You were all he thought about, and he knew what I was doing. I never meant to deceive you."

Her chin quivered. "I guess I'm no saint. I did leave."

"Come back? Let's figure this out together?"

She nodded.

He pressed his lips to hers, kissing her with every ounce of promise and vulnerability. Their past and the future unshakably tied to the present. And in every moment, each other. Two halves reunited to make something better. To become whole.

* * *

Christopher tightened his grip on Ashley. He was too aware of their surroundings and the crowd hovering only a few steps outside. The office was hardly a sanctuary. His eyes and nose itched from the dust bunnies kicked up on his entrance. The room smelled like mold and mildew and fish. But he couldn't let her go. Not again.

His fingers dug into her waist, clutching as much as touching. With his mouth, he laid claim to her just as she gripped his heart in her hands. The world faded away as he shut his eyes and focused solely on kissing her, his heartbeat thundering in his ears. The soft press of her body against his lured him to seek more, to cling to her.

She broke away. Pulling her head back and sliding his hands off her waist. She interlaced their fingers and squeezed.

He took in a shuddering breath and searched her smiling face. She was safe. That was what mattered. The Prims hadn't succeeded in their dastardly plan. Lonnie and Zach hadn't been part of a conspiracy to kill his wife.

As the facts shook loose from the fiction in his mind, he kept circling the main point. She was safe. She was alive. He wouldn't waste another moment. He couldn't wait to get her out of here.

A throat cleared, the loud guttural sound breaking through his peace.

He turned and frowned.

Zach stood nearby.

Close enough, Christopher could see every tiny tell that the man was scared. From his quickly darting gaze to his constant weight shifting from foot to foot, nerves radiated off Zach.

"Ashley, I'm so sorry," Zach said in halting spurts as he tiptoed into the space.

Christopher might have growled. He felt his upper lip curl in a sneer. And she squeezed his hand again, hard. He'd made a truce with Zach while the other man was behind bars. Now freed, he'd helped Ashley and upheld his end of the deal. Christopher had to accept the treaty.

"Did you know what the Prims were up to?" she asked, tipping her head to the side.

Her voice was far steadier than Christopher's. He was glad to let her take the lead.

"No, I swear, I didn't. They were unhappy with the Inn.

They contributed to some of our informal meetings when we discussed our frustrations. But I had no idea how deep the animosity went. I would never wish anyone harm." Zach turned to Christopher. "Even you."

Christopher fought an eye roll and a snigger. "Can you admit that while you weren't involved in radicalizing the men, your constant bombardment of negative and false information stoked a raging wildfire?"

"Yes," Zach said. "I am truly, deeply sorry for how my words twisted them."

"I accept your apology," Ashley said. "Because I think we all need to heal and move on. I trust your sincerity and that you didn't want everything to get so far out of hand. But we have to come together as a community. At the end of the day, we—" she motioned a finger between the three of them "—have shared history, and that accounts for a whole lot more than petty disagreements. We have to do better. Everyone else will follow. It's finally our time. Our generation is in charge, and instead of tearing each other down, we should build each other up. Let's leave the discord and strife behind us."

Zach extended a hand.

Christopher stared at it hard.

"Please?" Ashley elbowed him in the ribs.

He sucked in a sharp breath, rubbing his side. Her bony elbows were the only thing he hadn't missed. In the morning, when he would have inevitably woken up with one of her sharp points poking into his back, he'd have remembered. He stepped forward and shook Zach's hand.

"I suppose I'd better get back to the officers and let them take me back to jail," Zach said heavily.

Christopher crossed his arms over his chest and narrowed his gaze. But he didn't move away from his wife. And she poked him again.

He sucked in a breath and rubbed his ribs. He was going

to have a bruise. Meeting her gaze, he frowned, scowling with every ounce of rage and frustration he possessed.

She met his gaze with a hard stare of her own.

She was determined to be the bigger person. He'd forgotten how magnanimous she could be. He held his grudges tight to his chest like a lifejacket when, in reality, the petty grievances were only links on a chain dragging him down. "I'll drop the charges," Christopher bit out. "We have to give statements anyway. Did the Prims say how they managed the hauntings? The fire?"

Ashley's lower lip trembled.

Christopher's stomach dropped to the floor. The ghost was real? "Sorry, I didn't mean to pry. We'll go talk to the officers and straighten out the details. Let's get home. We can talk about the rest in privacy."

"What will happen to the tour business?" Zach asked. "It's in everyone's best interest that it keeps running."

"I'm sure we can work out something with the Prims' lawyer," Christopher narrowed his gaze. He hadn't stepped foot inside the boat house in years. "Or maybe I should talk to their bank. Looks like they are on the verge of foreclosure. I haven't been inside this building in years. I haven't been on one of their boats either." He stroked his chin.

"They hadn't started operations for the summer yet," Zach said.

Christopher nodded. "I wonder if they had plans to open at all."

"I heard—"

"Enough shop talk." Ashley stood in between the pair, holding up both hands. "Maybe I like you two better as enemies instead of co-captains of industry."

"You're right," Zach said. He bowed and left the room first. "We can discuss business later. I'm sorry again. For everything."

"Thank you," she whispered.

Her voice sounded heavy and weary. Christopher had so much to question. In a night, he had been tossed from his peaceful perch into chaos. He had a feeling he would never be the solitary head of his little kingdom ever again. Wasn't he lucky?

He scrubbed a hand over his face. "You're right. Let's give our statements and get sorted and head home."

She reached for his hand and squeezed.

He hadn't been *home* in almost a decade. Home wasn't a place but a person. Finally on the same page, he could return. She was right. Shared history erased many minor sins. They could build something strong as a community. They could step up as leaders. A team.

He tugged her close.

She slammed into his chest, hitting her head on his chin and widening her eyes.

She chuckled, her laugh low and heavy and shaking straight through him. "Don't you want to get out of here?"

He embraced her, wrapping his arms around her as tight as he could, gripping his opposite elbows. "In a second," he murmured, lowering his lips to hers.

Stronger together than they'd ever been apart, he was eager for a new partnership with her and the entire business community. *Was this why Dad included the odd terms in his will? Had he seen what could be, if only Christopher and I got out of our own way? Had he pulled some strings to ensure we reunited?*

Maybe Xavier was the ghost. Christopher hoped so. He wasn't taking any chances. He'd hold on to her for the rest of his life.

In the days following the rescue, Christopher would have given her anything.

With no more secrets between either them or the town, he had never felt more secure. He'd worked so hard his whole life to find home. He hadn't realized until almost too late that he'd tied his soul to a person, not a place.

He would have thrown her another wedding to symbolize their fresh start. He would have taken her on their long overdue honeymoon. Hotel Lavande would be a wonderful vacation. He would have agreed to a complete renovation of their home in the old stables.

Instead, she asked for the one thing he really didn't want to do.

"You ready?" she asked.

He lifted his head and glanced to his left, folding the latest issue of Seth Boyd's local newspaper. "I guess."

On a warm day, a week after the excitement with the Prims, they stood outside the cemetery gate with an unimpeded view of the resort and lake below. She insisted on running the gauntlet.

"Anything interesting in the special edition?" she neared, tugging the paper from under his arm.

He liked how they'd slipped back into reaching for each other, touching each other like they had every right. Because they did. He hadn't understood the extent to which she was the other half of his soul until he'd almost lost her for good.

She unfolded the paper and scanned the first sheet. "Greed? Or ghost?" She read the headline out loud.

He crossed his arms over his chest and shook his head. "As you might expect, Zach has the byline for that one."

She met Christopher's gaze. "And you don't mind?"

"No, I don't. We found the dangerous culprits. I'm okay with a benevolent spirit floating around."

She chuckled and turned her attention back to the paper.

He truly wasn't bugged about her continued belief in a paranormal being. And in the days that followed the Prims' capture, he believed in it too. The lighthouse haunt had spared the life of the dearest person in the world to him during the explosion. He couldn't help but wonder if it was the specter of a man who was, in his death, unable to abandon her the way he had in life. Xavier and Ashley could never mend their relationship in this world. But Christopher had hope for them reuniting in the next. He was glad for his second chance.

"Another Soupy sighting," she said, shaking her head. "Seth is really working the paranormal angle. He's tying my ghost into the myth."

"Are you disappointed he isn't going the children's book route?"

"No," she sighed heavily. "I understand he wants to reach a different audience. He isn't looking to entertain but to educate. He's determined to get national recognition for Soupy. I can respect that."

Christopher chuckled, the laugh low and deep, coming from the inside out. "No one could relate more than you."

"What do you think? Isn't this the sort of nonsense you've tried to steer away from?" She arched a brow in mock reproach.

"As long as we don't get treasure hunters again, we'll be fine. Besides, we have enough to worry about for next year's quasquicentennial celebration. In ten months, we have to be fully up and running, including the tour boat business."

The Prims had fallen into bankruptcy, alerting no one to their changed circumstances. No sooner had they been hauled to a more secure facility while awaiting arraignment than the news broke. A representative from the bank in Ashland emptied the building of anything they could sell—mostly computers and technology, the boats deemed worthless and not worth scrap—and boarded up the business.

Following the Prims' arrest and the full exoneration of Zach and Lonnie, Ashley brokered the start of peace talks between Christopher and the business owners. He agreed to step down from some of his more stringent requirements. They promised to work together for the good of all.

He needed their support.

Loon Lake thrived thanks to its symbiotic relationships. Once word reached town about the Prims' business, Zach knocked on the door of the Inn for a discussion about next steps.

No one in the chamber of commerce wanted to shoulder the burden of another full-time business, especially not one in such dire straits. Christopher had a potential lead, a peer who had vacationed at the Inn in childhood and since struck it rich with a tech start-up. The man was interested. With any luck, the man would visit in the next few weeks to assess the business. Christopher hoped the community would embrace the not-so-newcomer for the success of all.

Ashley still pushed the dinner cruise idea hard.

Christopher would not attach any strings to the new

owner's purchase. He wanted peace and prosperity. But he had learned the hard way: he couldn't control everything. He was the master of his own responses. That was it.

"Maybe you should invest in Seth's submarine idea," she said. "With a clear view of the bottom of the lake, you'd cast doubt on discovering treasure."

"Unfortunately, our offshoot of the lake is the murkiest body of freshwater in the nation. The submarine will only fuel more speculation about what can't be seen. I'm sticking with a full redesign of the lighthouse and island. Rebuilt with plenty of room for observation though. I've given up on the private suite. I want a lot of people to visit so no one will think treasure is buried anywhere on the tiny patch of land." He turned to her and smiled.

"What's that look for?"

"It's just..." He took a full breath. His limbs were loose and light. He had no worries for the first time in ten years. "We're really partners now."

"I know. I love it." Her eyes twinkled, and the corners of her mouth lifted in her lopsided grin. "Are you stretched and ready?" She crossed one arm in front of the other before stretching both arms over her head and twisting side to side.

Eyeing her, he wondered if she was ready for their morning excursion. It had been her suggestion. She was overdressed under the already warm sun and in the unusually humid air. Wearing a sweatshirt and capri leggings, she'd overheat the minute she reached the bottom of the hill.

He didn't point that out. He was a gentleman. But not so much of a chivalrous one that he wouldn't take advantage of a situation to win.

"Are you sure you want to do this?"

"Run the gauntlet?" She shrugged her shoulders and swung her arms like a helicopter, twisting from one side to the other. "I never back down from a challenge. I'm surprised Zach agreed to let you inside."

"Barely," Christopher mumbled. "But this is probably our last chance before the race is rebranded the Soupy Fun Run for next year's celebrations."

"As long as I beat you, I'll still be the undisputed and forever winner."

"In your dreams."

She winked.

"On your marks," Mr. Willie called.

Christopher positioned himself a few inches from his wife, hoping to distract her with the scent of the aftershave she loved. A couple seconds head start wasn't much, but he'd take every advantage he could against his spry spouse. He forgot to factor in his reaction to her nearness.

From the corner of her gaze, he studied the flutter at the base of her throat, her long lashes on her heavy lids. Her scent perfumed the air with a mixture of sun-warmed cotton and sugar from their lazy breakfast in bed. He wouldn't mind skipping the race. He opened his mouth.

"Get set, GO." Mr. Willie blew a whistle.

Christopher jerked and raced down the hill, full tilt.

But she was agile and fast, blurring past him at top speed. He gave her a head start. If he remembered correctly, she needed a lactose pill before downing the milkshake. She'd forgotten to take one. Or, if she had, she'd kept her actions secret.

He'd let her have a few mysteries. He was coming around to the idea of living his life and letting others run theirs. He hadn't even asked the potential new owner of the old sawmill for a five-year plan. News of the passing of the owner of the old sawmill had hit him harder than he'd imagined.

After losing Xavier, death was no longer an abstract concept to Christopher or Ashley. He hoped the heir had had a chance for a decent farewell. He glanced at the bench as he ran past, almost imagining, for a second, he spotted his father-in-law sitting and smiling at him.

He gave his head a shake. She wouldn't believe his sincerity if he told her. But the sighting warmed him from the inside out. And that was progress. Along with accepting her idea for murder mystery weekends.

He studied the island as he neared the bottom of the hill. The lighthouse folly would be rebuilt to aid the Soupy story. Everyone should have a piece of Loon Lake. Everyone should be as happy as he was.

As long as the ghosts—and treasure—remained hidden.

About the Author

Rachelle Paige Campbell writes contemporary romance novels filled with heart and hope. She believes love and laughter can change lives, and every story needs a happily ever after. Learn more at her website https://rachellepaigecampbell.com/

About the Publisher

Harbor Lane Books, LLC is a US-based independent digital publisher of commercial fiction, non-fiction, and poetry.

Connect with Harbor Lane Books on their website www.harborlanebooks.com, TikTok, Instagram, Facebook, Twitter, and Pinterest @harborlanebooks.

A. L. HATCHER

"I cannot recommend this book enough if you are fans of crime thrillers. This author did a fantastic job with this book!"—Ginger, Goodreads review

"This was such a roller coaster ride of a read! …. I'm so hooked and can't wait for book 2!" — Angelica K., Goodreads review